# Mists
# Of
# Menorca

# Mists
# Of
# Menorca

K. PEARSON BRADLEY

Lawson Press, LLC

ISBN: 9798985915167 (paperback)
ISBN: 9798985915174 (hardcover)
ISBN: 9798985915181 (ebook)

"In darkness God gives you strength; in light you have your own."

*Menorcan Proverb*

# ACKNOWLEDGMENTS

Writing a book is hard work. In the middle of writing this one, my sister was diagnosed with a large meningioma wrapped around her brain stem. After surviving a sixteen-hour surgery to remove it, which included drilling her skull, cracking it open, extracting the tumor, and putting everything back in its place, she adopted the mantra "we can do hard things." She printed the motto on t-shirts emblazoned with the ancient Egyptian symbol of life ♀ and circulated them to family and friends. I often wore my "we can do hard things" t-shirt while writing this book. Thanks, Ginger!

My other sister is an intuitive energy practitioner and transformational life coach. The process of writing this book involved excavating old thoughtforms, patterns, suppressed emotions, and painful experiences; Seba is always struggling to escape from one form of slavery or another (!) My sister helped me process those trapped emotions so I could get them on the page. Thanks, Natalie!

Other family members who lovingly contributed to this book are my daughter, Kate, who traveled to Menorca with me for research; my daughter, Jane, who helped me suss out the heroes and villains; my nephew, Emory, who educated me on the myriad reasons why characters might switch allegiances; and my husband, Dave, who always says yes when I need a sounding board.

Special thanks to the amazing indie author community I joined when I began writing this series. You inspire me! Especially Laura Akers, Collings MacCrae, and Megan Elder Evans, who craft compelling stories and share their hard-won insights to help other authors succeed. They are wonderful writers and generous souls. Go read their books!

A grateful shoutout to cover artist DejaVu, who always creates beautiful designs, knows what I'm thinking before I do, and meets a deadline even when she's thirty-nine weeks pregnant with her second child. And finally, a huge thanks to my developmental editor, Emily Tamayo Maher, who embodies a rare blend of enthusiasm, patience, wisdom, and love. I am thankful for her guidance and support throughout the writing process.

# 1 WOMAN OVERBOARD

*August 1, 1767*
*Balearic Sea, 300 nautical miles north of Menorca*
*Late morning*

Sebastian Krizomatis struggled to keep his balance as he held his mother's shoulders under a torrent of rain. A tangled mess of raven curls had slipped from her red headscarf, slithering wildly over her forehead like a nest of angry adders. Sebastian's fingers dug into his mother's brown wool cloak as she vomited over the railing of the *New Fortuna*.

He yelled over the bellowing wind, "I told you this was a bad idea! Why couldn't you use a bucket like everyone else?"

Agnete Krizomatis was too busy regurgitating half-digested rusks to respond. The bone-dry crackers were known as "hardtack" to the English sailors recruited by Dr.

Turnbull. Seba (as Sebastian was known to everyone but his mother) found this an apt name for the flinty, flavorless biscuits; he had broken a tooth on one several weeks back. As he strained to keep his mother from tumbling overboard, his thoughts came unbidden in the voice of a disgusted and wry observer: *Her rusk came up faster than it went down.*

The *tramontana* winds roared at a pitch so deafening that it obscured the sound of Agnete's retching, a minuscule scrap of comfort in the midst of the tempest. Seba's own belly was empty, twisted upon itself like a hungry ouroboros. When he lost his bicuspid to a stony piece of hardtack, Seba had simply given up eating them, and there wasn't much else left to eat in the ship's pantry. Now, in the roughest part of the Balearic Sea, Seba was grateful for his dry and shriveled stomach.

The crew had promised Agnete would eventually find her sea legs, but it had been nearly a year and there was no sign of them yet. Luckily, the crew had thick skins; Seba knew all too well that Agnete's deadly glower could cause a flower in full bloom to drop its petals, and she often trained her gaze on them, a reminder of their broken promise.

He felt sorry for her suffering, tossing up her chyme each day like a sacrificial gift to Poseidon, but Seba's experience on the sea had been much different from his mother's. For him, the voyage from Chios to Menorca had been exhilarating. He had spent his youth in forced labor for the Ottomans, cultivating the sandy soil of the skinos terraces as his mother's family had done for centuries, coaxing the valuable jewel-like resin—the fabled "Tears of Chios," reputed to have healing properties—from the gnarled trees of the island's *mastichochoria*. But the riches of this harvest went not to the people of Chios, as in the days of Seba's distant ancestors, but instead to Sultan Mustafa III, whose Ottoman Empire laid claim to the island.

Seba's father, Kostas Krizomatis, was not a mastiha farmer but a shipbuilder and engineer of great renown. Seba had only rarely had the opportunity to visit the shipyard of Sessera, their hometown, before his father was kidnapped by agents of the sultan and put to work in Constantinople. But those experiences had ignited a spark in Seba that refused to be put out. It was the sea of his father, not the land of his mother, that beckoned him into the unknown.

It didn't help that the mastiha growers on Chios were slaves, tethered to the ground by governmental obligations and oppressive rules designed to make a select group of people rich upon the backs of others' suffering. He loved the smell and taste of mastiha, and was proud of his mother's heritage, but could not abide being penned into his walled village at night like a husbanded animal.

Freedom and adventure called from the edge of the horizon, challenging Seba in ways he never expected. He often climbed onto the bowsprit during clear days to watch the dolphins racing the ship, jumping in and out of the waves at lightning speed. *I wonder if this is how Odysseus felt, sailing home to Greece after the Trojan War.*

There was no part of sailing that Seba didn't like, but his favorite part was riding the powerful rollers as the cool, salty spray misted his face. Not even the more disgusting aspects of maritime life dampened his enjoyment. He happily swabbed the decks with salt water, using his fingernails to scrape out any fungus that skulked between the deck boards; he held his breath as he carried the captain's chamber pot to the stern and tossed its reeking contents into the sea. Such unpleasantness was a small price to pay for a life free from captivity. When the stink of the ship's crew threatened to overwhelm them, one or more of the Anemoi, the spirits of the four cardinal winds, blithely answered the call. A gentle eastern puff from Euros, a warm southern breath from Notos, a lively western whiff from Zephyros, or even a blustery northern squall from Boreas was enough to refresh their skin and spirits.

The *New Fortuna* was sleek and swift, its wooden keel parting the blue waves in fair weather like a knife scoring bread dough. Seba didn't spend much time below deck, which smelled of urine, livestock, sweat, and anxiety; he preferred the open deck, and to his mother's chagrin, volunteered daily to serve as lookout in the tiny crow's nest.

Today, however, was not a day for the crow's nest. The *New Fortuna* had sailed straight into a raging storm in the northern Balearic Sea, so rough that all but the crew were hunkering below deck in their hammocks, the only place where they could avoid being tossed to and fro like Poseidon's playthings.

Seba's father had tried to convince Agnete to stay below deck and use the wooden bucket designated for seasickness, but she lashed out at him, her brown eyes flashing with anger. Everyone on the ship knew how she had acquired the nickname "five feet of fury," and they kept their heads down as she snapped at her husband; but her small stature belied the force of her temper. "Don't you dare tell me what to do, Kostas Krizomatis!" she had snarled, clutching the post that secured one side of her husband's hammock. "If I had known what awaited me that day in the shipyard, I would have tied you up to Matilde's cart and dragged you inside the village walls myself rather than step one foot on this wooden deathtrap!"

She had a point. When Seba had returned from Smyrna with the news that his lost father was waiting for her on a ship in Sessera's shipyard, nothing could stop her from reaching her husband. She assumed Kostas would be returning with her to the village, to be safe within its stone walls. Upon their reunion, Agnete's eyes had grown wide at the sight of her husband's drawn features, and she tried to convince him to come home so she could nurse him back to health. But Kostas, now a fugitive slave of the Ottoman Empire, could never go home. And Seba, who had helped him escape from Smyrna, was in the same boat. Literally and figuratively.

So Agnete left the land of her ancestors and boarded the *New Fortuna* as it loosed its sails and set a course for Menorca. The early days of the voyage had been a joyous family reunion: Seba's mother and father often seen in a tight embrace after six years apart, the two of them fawning like lovebirds nestled in the branches of flowering myrtle. The trip to Menorca was supposed to last four weeks; and although Agnete preferred the stability of land, she told her son that she could manage a short sea voyage with her husband and her only son at her side. "Saint Paul sailed the Mediterranean Sea to share the news of our Lord Jesus Christ," she had said. "I suppose I can do the same for a short time."

By the second month, however, Agnete had made it plain that she was no St. Paul; while he may have borne his suffering with a glad heart, she had no intention of following his example. She turned her fiery temper on anyone who dared to offer a kind word. Heavy seas and *meltemi* winds drove the ship far off course, adding weeks and months to the journey. When they were almost captured by Barbary pirates off the coast of Malta, Mama had been so incensed that she ran to the quarterdeck and shouted at the barbarians to repent their sins. Seba ran after her and pushed her to the deck as the corsairs' bullets flew over her head. Fortunately, Captain Alexiano's quick thinking and expert maneuvering allowed them to escape, but their hope of replenishing supplies in Malta was dashed.

They were now in the thirteenth month of sailing, in the most difficult weather they had yet encountered. Seba felt responsible for bringing his mother on this adventure; and rather than force her to use the sour-smelling bucket, he donned his wool coat and felt sailor's cap, and followed her onto the deck where he could keep an eye on her.

Agnete gripped the railing so tightly that her knuckles were white. Seba had fastened a rope around her waist and around his own, then lashed it to the railing. The sea was almost black, but for the frothy white waves that crashed against the ship's hull. The brigantine bobbed up and down between walls of water that rose almost as high as the foremast. It was only late afternoon but the sky was dark gray, merely a shade or two lighter than the color of the water below. Dark storm clouds hung overhead, dumping rain like a bucket brigade.

Seba knew his mother must be terrified because she wasn't screaming at him. Under normal circumstances, she would have been keening at him, demanding that he go below and save himself before she sent him to God herself. Her angry tone had intimidated him as a child; but now that he was sixteen years old and had faced death several times, her temper didn't have the same effect.

Agnete lifted her hand from the railing to cross herself. Seba had seen her do it thousands of times—before each meal, in church, whenever anyone mentioned Jesus, Mary, or the Holy Spirit, and especially when she was upset or angry. This time, however, it was a deadly mistake. An enormous icy wave crashed on the starboard side of the bow and washed over the deck, taking Agnete over the ship's larboard side.

Seba screamed, "Mama!" The ship rolled sideways and he found himself staring into a terrifying black abyss; the roiling water sprayed salty jets upward with the force of a geyser. The rope around his mother's waist pulled taut and yanked Seba toward the railing, the force of the frigid wave so powerful that it slammed him into the side of the ship. His head banged against the railing; stars flashed behind his eyelids. He felt a warm trickle past his eye and knew it must be blood.

He watched helplessly as Agnete ricocheted off the side of the hull with the movement of the ship in the mountainous murky waves swirling below. Seba froze. He couldn't pull her back onto the ship without letting go of the railing; but if he released his grip, he would be swept over the rails with her. It would take at least three crewmen to bring them in, and there was no guarantee that any of them would survive the attempt.

"Hold tight to the rope, Mama!" he cried. With one arm wrapped tightly around the railing, Seba waited for the ship to dip into the lowest part of the wave. He was almost upside down, staring straight into the caliginous cavern of curling water. When the ship smacked the bottom of the wave, he seized his moment, yanking with his free hand, using his shoulder to pull the rope toward himself. Desperation gave him strength. His mother came a fraction closer.

As the ship crested each wave, then dove down into the trough between ferocious walls of water, Seba dragged Agnete inch by inch back toward the railing. He could almost touch her hands now, which were bleeding where the rope had ripped the skin from her palms. However, he was afraid to let go of the rope and reach for her. Looking over the side of the ship, he could see the whites of his mother's eyes, full of terror. "One more wave, Mama," he called. "Only one more, and then I'll have you!"

"Don't let me go, Sebastian!"

As the *New Fortuna* fell between two obsidian waves, Seba gritted his teeth and yanked the rope closer still. "Hold tight," he cried. "You're almost here!"

But then the ship rolled sideways. Seba's mother disappeared under the water, pulling him so hard that his feet left the deck; he was turned topsy-turvy, tethered to the ship only by one arm coiled around the railing. The ship righted itself as it climbed the next roller, and Seba felt his body flip, his feet striking the deck with a wet thud. He peered into the blackness to see his mother reappear above the surface, spluttering and gasping for breath.

"Mama, I need your help! Can you use your feet to climb?"

Seba couldn't tell if his mother heard him, but she kicked her legs in a frenzy. As the ship dove into the deepest part of the wave, Seba yelled, "On three! One. Two. Three!" He pulled with all his might, and his mother scrambled up a few inches until she was close enough for Seba to grab her hand. Agnete's fingers raked the skin on his wrist, and the weight of her water-drenched skirts pulled on Seba's back and shoulders until he thought his muscles would snap. He took a deep breath, leaned back, and with one arm still gripping the railing, used his other arm to throw his mother over his head and onto the deck boards behind him.

Agnete lay there grimacing, with her eyes pinched shut and her chest heaving. Seba knelt beside her. "We're not out of the storm yet," he said, raising his voice over the roar of the wind and waves. "We have to get you below where you'll be safe, and the doctor can see if you're injured. Don't try to stand up. I'm going to pull you to the ladder. Do you understand?"

Agnete did not open her eyes, but she nodded. Seba tossed the rope that still connected them around the block securing the ship's wheel and slowly pulled the two of them toward the center of the ship. A wave hit the ship broadside, rolling them back to where they had started. Seba's arm was under his mother's waist and his knees pressed into the wooden deck as he crawled hand over hand toward the hatch, using the rope for leverage. The ship lurched from bow to stern, then side to side as they struggled against the storm. Seba unlatched and raised the hatch as another wave crashed over the deck, sending a flood of water below decks. A cacophony of indignant shouts rose up from below.

"Shut it, shut it!"

"I'm soaked through!"

"I stayed below to stay dry, you dungbie!"

Seba yelled back, "Call Doctor Turnbull! My mother needs him—now!"

Out of the din came the voice of Seba's best friend, Paolo Partella. "What happened?" he asked, muscling his way through the crowd toward the ladder. Paolo never let Seba forget that he was two years older, nearly two inches taller, and (according to himself, at least) ten times stronger.

"My mother was washed overboard," Seba said breathlessly. "Her hands are bleeding, and she might have other injuries. We need to get her to Doctor Turnbull right away."

Paolo's curly mop of nut-brown hair popped up through the hatch and fell into his eyes, as it always did when he was animated. His eyes grew wide as he looked at Agnete, but he vaulted into action, hopping up through the hatch and onto the deck and scooping her up to sling her over his shoulder like a sack of wheat. Paolo might be every bit as strong as he boasted, Seba thought, and this once he was glad of it.

Seba held the hatch open as Paolo maneuvered slowly down the ladder, supporting Agnete with one arm and using his other for balance. Seba felt the rope around his waist pull taut. "Wait!" he called "I forgot—we're bound together. Let me untie it before it tangles you up."

Paolo looked at him with concern. "You weren't tossed into the sea as well, were you?"

"Almost, but I managed to cling to the railing. It took an eternity to pull her up, the waves were so rough, and I'm not sure if she broke any b—"

The ship suddenly listed to one side and Paolo's wet hands lost their grip on the ladder. He and Agnete went plunging down toward the deck below. He managed to roll in midair, pulling her atop him and landing hard on his back. Paolo's head banged the wooden planks; Agnete landed in a heap on his chest and pulled Seba down with her, the rope still looped around his waist. Seba caught the third rung of the ladder and barely avoided crushing his mother in the process. The hatch slammed shut above them with a bang.

Paolo scrambled to a seated position with Seba's mother in his arms. "Mrs. Krizomatis, I'm so sorry!" He shook her shoulders. "Mrs. Krizomatis?"

Agnete opened her eyes and touched her bloody palm to Paolo's face. Her face was pale.

Seba untangled himself from the rope around his waist. "Can you help me carry her? We need to get her to Doctor

Turnbull's surgery. Watch her hands, they're bleeding."

Paolo nodded, rose to his feet, shook off the water like a wet dog, and lifted Seba's mother under her armpits. The ship swayed from left to right and Paolo stumbled toward the nearest bulkhead, but never lost his grip on Agnete.

Seba reached out to pick up his mother's legs, but stopped when the hatch opened again. Captain Alexiano's face appeared. "Seba, Paolo, are you down there?" he called. "We need you right away!"

Paolo threw Agnete over his shoulder again and nodded to Seba to go ahead. "Go! It must be important if the captain's asking for us. I'll carry her to Doctor Turnbull."

Seba took a step toward the ladder, then looked back. His mother hung from Paolo's shoulder like a rag doll, and his father, crippled now by the Ottomans' cruel mistreatment, lay helpless in his hammock. Kostas Krizomatis's face was drawn and the wrinkles on his forehead were deep. Seba knew exactly what his father was thinking, because he was thinking the same thing.

They both wanted to help everyone at the same time—their family, the captain, the crew—but it was physically impossible. Kostas's hip could no longer reliably hold him, which meant that he was stuck in that hammock, no good to anyone; and Seba couldn't be in Dr. Turnbull's surgery with his mother, on deck with Captain Alexiano, and by his father's side at the same time. Seba cringed at the sadness in his father's gray-green eyes. *He needs me.*

Seba felt paralyzed. His father looked so helpless and frail, and he didn't know if his mother was dead or alive. The captain was calling for him, the ship was listing, and everyone on board was terrified, praying for salvation from the storm. Or failing that, safe passage to heaven.

Seba was racked with indecision, but when he locked

eyes with his father, he understood. Kostas set his jaw, made a fist above his head, and nodded. No words were necessary for Seba to catch his meaning: *You can't help me, your mother, or anyone else if the ship plunges into the abyss. Go, and give us a chance to live!*

# 2 ST. PETER'S CROSS

*August 1, 1767*
*Balearic Sea, 300 nautical miles north of Menorca*
*Early afternoon*

Seba clambered up the ladder and threw open the hatch. The rain pelted his head and shoulders; the sable-colored curls that stuck out from beneath his cap were dripping water like a leaky bucket. He ignored the shivering cold as Captain Alexiano gestured frantically toward the crow's nest. Seba looked skyward and felt a bolt like lightning course through his body; suspended below the crow's nest, with the primary topstay twisted around his ankle, was Peter, one of the bravest and most capable members of the crew. Only a few years older than Seba, Peter had sailed with Captain Alexiano since he was a young boy, and moved about the ship as if he were an extension of the sea itself. Now, in the dark torrent, Peter dangled precariously from the rigging like an insect caught between strands of spider silk.

Seba gasped. "How?"

Captain Alexiano, his knuckles white from gripping the ship's wheel, shook his head. "The topsail came loose and jammed up the rigging. He secured the sail and cleared the rigging, but now he's tied up like a trussed bird! I need you to scale the shrouds and get him down." The captain was shouting to be heard over the roar of the waves. His red captain's hat was plastered to his head, his salt-and-pepper beard shooting water out like a fountain. "Where's Paolo?"

"He's in the surgery, tending to my mother," Seba said. "She went over the side! I managed to pull her back, but she may have hit her head on the hull."

Captain Alexiano's mouth gaped for a moment, until rain began pouring into it and he spluttered it out before snapping his cold blue lips together. "Then you'll have to go alone. I can't spare another man; they're all at their stations, trying like the devil to keep us from sinking. Are you able?"

Before Seba could answer, a wave flooded over the starboard deckrail, dousing them both. The captain maintained his grasp on the spokes of the wheel and pulled himself to standing; Seba lost his footing and careened to larboard, only righting himself when a second wave hit the ship from the opposite direction. Captain Alexiano fought to keep the wheel steady, the corded muscles in his neck threatening to pop out of his skin. The wind swirled around the brigantine and a funnel of water spurted up from the sea.

Seba looked upward again. The storm batted Peter about like a ball on a snarled tether. His body slammed against the mainmast, and even above the storm's roar Seba could hear him cry out in pain.

The captain pressed his knife into Seba's hand. "Cut the

lines if you must, but only as a last resort. I believe the other stays will hold, but nothing is certain in this gale." He raised a fist into the air. "I haven't lost any crew members on this voyage, and I'm not losing anyone today. Godspeed!"

Seba clenched the knife between his teeth, grabbed the ladder-like shrouds, and began to climb. He wasn't as broad as Paolo, and his beard was thinner, but Seba was strong. He was lean and ropy, with the physicality of a swimmer. More importantly, thus far in his sixteen years of life, he had never given up. He wouldn't give up now. Paolo's brute strength and Seba's tenacity made them a formidable team.

But this task was Seba's alone. He scampered up the shrouds, his boots gripping the horizontal ratlines as if his life depended on it. The ship listed so violently that at times he was completely horizontal to the surface of the sea, looking down at the black water churning against the ship's hull. As the ship crested a powerful wave, the shrouds and ratlines twisted, flipping Seba backward so his face addressed the ominous clouds of stinging rain. The shrouds groaned under the strain of the wind-whipped mast as the ship bobbed like a cork in a turbulent tub of water. *Help me, Poseidon.*

Seba's muscles screamed as he pulled himself just above Peter's position. Peter hung from the stays below the crow's nest, at least six feet away. Too far for him to reach the shrouds on his own. Seba would have to wedge his legs between the ratlines and lean over to reach him. Peter's tangled ankle dripped blood and salt water; the rope had torn jagged gouges in his skin. His eyes were closed and his jaw was clamped tight, but the rest of his body was exposed to the tempest's rage.

Seba called out around the knife still clenched in his teeth. "Can you use your good arm?"

Peter tried to pull himself up to grasp the rope knotted around his leg, but he winced and fell back down. "I can't reach!"

"Wrap your other leg around the halyard!" Seba didn't need to elaborate; they both knew that if he couldn't secure himself, Peter was not likely to survive the fifty-foot fall.

It was excruciatingly slow, or so it seemed to Seba, who had wrapped both of his legs around the closest ratlines. Peter shifted himself inch by inch toward the halyard, kicking out until his foot caught. He twisted, looping his left foot and lower leg into the line, anchoring himself such that he'd not fall if the rope around his other leg was cut. With his legs stretched above him and his arms extended out on either side, he reminded Seba bizarrely of Saint Peter being martyred on an upside-down cross. He shook the vision away. *Not today.*

Seba yelled, "Ready?"

Peter grimaced and lowered his chin to his chest in a vain attempt to keep the rain from sloshing into his nose.

Seba loaded his legs like a spring and leaped out toward Peter as a flash of lightning split the sky.

The lightning hit the starboard yardarm above them, which exploded, sending a shower of wooden slivers down on them like Trojan archers' fiery arrows. One red-hot shard embedded itself in Seba's right forearm; he bit down on the knife, fighting the impulse to draw his arm to his chest, and the coppery taste of blood covered his tongue. With his right arm still on fire, he reached for the topstay and curled his fingers around it. With his legs wrapped around the ratlines and his hands on the topstay, Seba was slung as if in a hammock high above the undulating deck.

Using his legs for leverage, Seba leaned, pushed, pulled, jabbed, and tugged at the rope with all his might, but it was snarled so tightly around Peter's ankle that any movement seemed to cinch it tighter. Seba's arms and legs were burning, the ship pitching, and the water made everything slick. He didn't have time to keep trying to untie the knot; he had to cut the topstay. Seba willed the other ropes to do their jobs and keep the mast and arms upright. *Please hold, please hold.*

Seba called through his teeth, "Cutting the rope now." Seba had to let go of the rope with one hand in order to remove the knife from his mouth. Being left-handed, that meant he had to grip the rope with his right arm, the one with a burning piece of the yardarm protruding from it. He took a deep breath and prayed in succession to Jesus, who performed miracles; Archangel Michael, who protected; and Hephaestus, who forged with fire. When he squeezed the rope with his right hand, he felt a jolt of lightning from his fingers to the top of his head. He ignored the searing pain in his arm and plucked the knife from his mouth.

Peter's foot, above the knotted rope, was a corpselike white. Seba shuddered, wondering if Peter would have to lose his foot. Seba had seen an amputation during his time in Smyrna; he would never forget the smell of burning flesh as the wound was cauterized. His boot slipped on the ratlines as he considered, and he nearly dropped the knife. *Focus! You can worry later about Peter keeping his limbs.*

Seba held the rope above Peter's ankle with his right arm, which was literally on fire, and sawed the knife back and forth with his left. The rain, the cold, the agony, even Peter disappeared; it was him against the knot, which seemed as solidly unyielding as an ancient oak.

As he drew the blade across the rope, he thought of Alexander the Great. Seba's grandfather, whom he called Papouli, had told him the story of the emperor. Alexander had studied at the feet of the renowned philosopher, Aristotle; he had become a great king not only because of his military prowess, but because he was a creative thinker. Papouli always said it was better to think, rather than punch, your way out of a problem.

In one legend, Alexander and his army paused in their eastward march at the city of Gordion. At the heart of the city lay an oxcart that had centuries before been tethered to a post by the ancient King Gordias, founder of the city. A prophecy said that anyone who could untie the jumbled mass of elaborate knots that secured the cart would become the ruler of the land. Over the centuries, many had tried and failed. Alexander was always game for a challenge, and he, like all the others before him, grappled with the tightly woven mass of ropes with no success.

After a time, however, Alexander drew his knife from his belt and held it high in the air, saying, "It matters not how the knots are loosed." With one stroke of his blade, Alexander unraveled the Gordian knot and fulfilled the oracle's prophecy.

Seba stopped sawing as the story of Alexander the Great sunk in.

Channeling the great leader, Seba reared back and with one mighty chop, severed the topstay. *Thanks, Papouli, wherever you are.*

Peter shook his sickly-white foot and the bottom portion of the rope fell to the deck. Seba used the upper part of the topstay, still attached to the mast, to swing back to the ratlines. Peter dangled upside down, held by his one good leg wrapped around the closest halyard, his arms still outstretched like St. Peter's cross.

"Can you pull yourself up and work your way over here?"

Peter nodded. He swung his other leg over the halyard and was about to curl up to wrap his good arm around the ropes when the ship keeled sideways, sending him flying toward Seba. They crashed together, the impact knocking the fiery splinter from Seba's forearm. Peter caught the shrouds with his good arm and they retreated down the lines faster than either of them had ever done on a fine day, terrified that another wave might toss them into the roiling sea.

Captain Alexiano, soaked to the skin but grinning like a parrotfish, was waiting for them, waving his cap in the air. "Seba, that was amazing work. And Peter, you descended those shrouds with half your limbs better than most with all four. Zeus himself threw a thunderbolt at you! I wouldn't have believed it if I hadn't seen it with my own eyes." Regaining his composure, the captain returned his cap to his head. "Get yourselves to the surgery. I want a full report of everyone's injuries, including your mother's, Seba." He wrinkled his brow. "I'd be sick if something happened to Agnete after all this time at sea."

# 3 IN THE SURGERY

*August 1, 1767*
*Balearic Sea, 300 nautical miles north of Menorca*
*Late afternoon*

Below deck, the scent of mildew and tar mingled with a faint medicinal odor. Seba and Peter limped toward Dr. Turnbull's surgery, located on the berth deck, the merchant brigantine's lowest inhabitable space. Peter's weight made Seba's shoulders burn, although the rest of him shivered from the cold and damp. The air was stifling in the shadowy underdeck; even the shape of the place suggested a coffin. When the voyage began, the passengers and crew had slept here, but as the months passed without reaching their destination, Seba and the others had surreptitiously moved their berths up to the cargo deck, seeking a scrap of natural light and relief from the stench of bilge water. Captain Alexiano, though generally insistent upon sailing protocol, allowed the offense, but only because they'd been sailing for over a year on a crossing that should have taken three months. Now the cargo deck, which already doubled as the gun deck for the *New Fortuna*'s ten cannons, was filled with hammocks, and the old berth deck was simply "the surgery." This arrangement left Dr. Turnbull in relative isolation, but the jolly physician said he didn't mind the deck's gloomy atmosphere; it reminded him, he said, of wintertime in his native Scotland.

The space was partitioned off with oilcloth and a few spare sails, a crude but necessary boundary for the doctor's work. A wooden slab bolted to the deck and covered with old linens served as the surgical table; a simple writing desk with several drawers stood in the corner. The only light came from a brass oil lamp suspended from the ceiling and a few candles in glass jars that had been secured to the desk with wax. Beside the desk was a doctor's case, mahogany with brass-cornered edges and a curved wooden handle worn smooth from use.

Shelves lined the walls and netting hung from the beams overhead, holding surgical instruments, glass jars of laudanum, vinegar, Caribbean rum, turpentine, linen bandages rolled tightly and tied with string, wax-sealed containers of poultices, and a small cracked mirror. Stashed under the surgical table was a bucket of brine for soaking instruments. Next to the bucket, in a honey-brown Windsor chair, sat Agnete, a cool cotton cloth folded across her forehead and thin strips of linen wrapped around her hands.

Dr. Turnbull sat opposite her in a matching chair. The Scottish physician was a portly man, bacon-faced with a bulbous nose. His weak chin was sandwiched between a thick set of jowls that were always moving; in Seba's experience, the Scotsman was either talking or chewing. Despite his large size, his fingers were long and slender, well-suited to writing and surgical procedures.

The gentleman physician maintained a luxurious wardrobe of silks and velvets for public occasions, and though he gave the impression of being somewhat of a dandy, Seba couldn't deny that he took his vocation seriously. Today he wore a plain linen shirt and red cotton breeches under a stained, stiff apron of leather.

Seba stared at the two of them: Dr. Turnbull regaling Seba's mother with one of his many stories about his travels in the Levant, and his mother's face radiant, like a schoolgirl's. Seba blinked several times. *Is she actually smiling?*

Seba cleared his throat. "Doctor Turnbull, can you help Peter?" he said. "His leg got caught up in the rigging. I had to cut him down from the crow's nest."

Dr. Turnbull sprang from his chair to help Seba hoist Peter onto the surgical table. "Good heavens, my boy," he said, looking at Peter's injured leg. "What were you thinking?"

Agnete stood and made the sign of the cross with her gauze-wrapped hand. "God help Peter. Doctor, what can I do to help?"

Seba stepped between her and Dr. Turnbull. "Mama, your hands are still bleeding! *And* you almost drowned. Perhaps you should sit down."

Agnete's eyes flashed for a moment, and Seba immediately regretted his words. He could almost hear her angry voice, as he had so many times: *How dare you address your mother that way?* But though he braced himself to receive her five feet of fury, she surprised him: her face softened and she hugged him close with her forearms.

"Sebastian, you saved my life today." Then she stepped back and held up her bloody mitts. "And that is the only reason why I'm not slapping you with these."

There was a loud, convulsive gasp from the table. Seba spun around. "Peter, what is it?"

Peter sputtered and wheezed, and only then did Seba recognize the uproar as laughter. "Your mother's a hearty treasure, she is," said Peter, tears of hilarity in his eyes.

Dr. Turnbull concurred with a broad smile. "Quite right, my good friend. I couldn't agree more. Agnete, the fire of your Greek ancestors burns bright in you." His eyes fell to the candles on his desk, as if in a trance. "It makes me miss my beloved Maria Gracia more than ever. You and she were cut from the same cloth, and if I might add, it is one more valuable than gold."

Agnete blushed and bowed to Dr. Turnbull. "You are a kind man. You were not born a Greek, but at least you had the sense to marry one."

Turnbull chortled with such force that his apron shook, its stiff folds swishing. Peter guffawed from the surgery table, Seba and Agnete joined in, and the room became lighter. Dr. Turnbull produced a white linen handkerchief, the initials *A.T.* neatly stitched in the corner, and dabbed his eyes. "Agnete, you have lightened this journey for me in many ways. Zounds, you are so like my wife! I confess she's said the same to me about my Scottish heritage on many occasions. Oh, I long to see my beloved Maria Gracia. But, alas for me, she is safe in London, caring for our children."

Seba sighed. He had never met Dr. Turnbull's wife, but aside from food, she had been the physician's favorite topic of conversation during their year at sea. Seba felt as if she was a member of the family; she was also the reason why Dr. Turnbull's attention frequently veered off course. "Er,

Doctor Turnbull," he said. "What about Peter?"

Dr. Turnbull wiped his cheeks and neck and tucked the handkerchief into his pocket. "Oh, yes! Well, he's laughing, which is encouraging. *Laughter and a merry heart are the best medicines.* Proverbs 17:22." His leather apron scraped against the floor as he bowed to Agnete. "I'm certain your mother will correct me if my biblical memory fails."

Seba's mother was positively radiant. "*Polý kalá*, your memory serves you well. Proverbs 17:22 is my father's favorite verse. He is something of a comedian. The two of you would get along like lemons and olives."

"I daresay he sounds like a man after my own heart." Dr. Turnbull rubbed his hands together. "Now tell me, Peter, why does your foot resemble a large rat that's been strangled to death?"

Peter exhaled noisily. "Could we avoid using the word 'death,' Doctor?" he said. "If you don't mind, that is. I can't feel my foot, but I hope it's not, you know. . . ."

"A fine point, my brave friend." Dr. Turnbull reached into his case, its red velvet interior releasing the faint scent of camphor, clove oil, and tobacco. "Speaking of fine points, I'd like to do a little test. This technique was shown to me by one of my colleagues in the Levant Company." He pulled out a folded cloth, which he opened to reveal a row of needles and scalpels. "He was a marvel, which is likely why the Royal Navy gave him a commission. It's a shame he's a military doctor now; I would have liked to have learned more from him." Dr. Turnbull selected a long needle whose point gleamed in the lamplight. "Let's determine whether we can get your blood flowing in that d—er, in that foot of yours, hm?"

After several minutes of poking Peter's foot with the sharp needle, Dr. Turnbull lifted it between his hands. The physician vigorously rubbed and pounded, as if he were threshing wheat, yet Peter never reacted. It was a most disconcerting scene: Dr. Turnbull's face red with exertion, and Peter looking as if the doctor were treating someone else's foot.

Undeterred, Dr. Turnbull continued his aggression on Peter's foot; at last, after several minutes that felt like an eternity, Peter's face grew red and his forehead began to furrow. He lifted himself up to sitting with one hand and tried to pull his foot away. "Ow, have some compassion, Doctor!"

Dr. Turnbull again drew his handkerchief and wiped his neck and head, which were shining with sweat. He patted Peter's ankle and Peter jumped. "You can feel it now, eh? Then you're not going to lose it."

Agnete exclaimed, "Thanks be to God!"

Dr. Turnbull knitted his brows at Peter. "Now let me have a look at that arm of yours. I see you've all but ignored my advice, haven't you?"

"Don't be too hard on Peter, sir," said Seba rather hotly. "He's a hero. The topsail came loose and the running rigging was snarled in the blocks. Peter was the only one who could have furled the topsail and untangled the rigging in that tempest. He finished the job, but before he could retreat, he was twisted up as well. The storm pounded him into the mainmast like a carpenter hammering a nail."

"Duly noted," Dr. Turnbull said. He moved toward Peter's shoulder, held his arm, and gently pulled it away from Peter's body at a ninety-degree angle. "My apologies for my hasty words, Peter, and for the discomfort you're about to feel."

Peter nodded, took a deep breath and closed his eyes. In

a single lightning-quick motion, Dr. Turnbull deftly popped Peter's arm back under his shoulder blade.

Peter was on the verge of releasing a cascade of expletives until Seba jumped up and motioned toward his mother. Peter exhaled loudly. "Ahhhhhh. Much obliged, Doctor."

Dr. Turnbull tapped the front of Peter's shoulder just above his armpit. "Isn't this the hundredth time I've righted this dislocated shoulder of yours, Peter?"

Peter squinted, as if considering the thought. "Naw, it couldn't be. Could it?"

Dr. Turnbull folded his arms across his chest. "You may recall that I told you about joints, young man. Once they get a taste of coming loose, they'll keep at it unless you strengthen the muscles around them."

Peter rolled his eyes. "I'm too busy for that nonsense, Doc. We've got a ship to run." As he spoke, they all felt the *New Fortuna* give a lurch. "Or I hope we'll still have a ship to run, if we survive this storm."

"Raging tempests aside, if you desire to keep this arm in its socket, you can surely spare a few moments each day to strengthen the muscles. Wasn't it your ancient Greek ancestors who invented *kallistheneia*? You'd do yourself a world of good to follow in their footsteps." Dr. Turnbull patted his ample midsection. "Perhaps I might join you. I could do with a dose of calisthenics myself, or so my beloved Maria Gracia often reminds me."

Peter sat up on the table and flexed both biceps, although one side was noticeably weaker. "I feel like new. I'll wager that right now I could run from Marathon to Athens, and do it with a barrel of *tsipouro* on my back!"

Seba chuckled, then stopped; Peter was staring at him strangely. "What is it?"

"There's blood dripping from under your cap. Oh, and your arm as well. Perhaps Doctor Turnbull should examine you."

Seba raised his hand to his temple for the first time since he had smashed it on the deck railing. The skin next to his eyebrow felt gelatinous.

Dr. Turnbull stepped in smoothly. "Peter, massage your foot while I examine Seba's cuts," he said quite calmly. "The next time you see Captain Alexiano, tell him I've put you on a daily regimen of *kallistheneia*, and you are forbidden from climbing the rigging until we reach Menorca." He peered closely at Seba's temple. "My heavens, boy! You've got a nasty gash. It's fortunate that your cap helped to stanch the bleeding." He deftly removed Seba's cap, revealing a ragged cut running at least three inches, from the tip of his ear to his eyebrow.

Agnete peered over Dr. Turnbull's shoulder, simultaneously crossing herself. "Sebastian, why didn't you tell me you were injured?" Her eyes bored into Dr. Turnbull. "Has my boy suffered a grievous wound?"

Dr. Turnbull led Agnete back to her chair. "Of course not, my dear woman. Don't worry yourself another moment. Sit down here and give me a jot of room. I'll have Sebastian's head stitched up in a jiffy."

After encouraging Seba to toss back a shot of rum from his medical case to dull the pain, Dr. Turnbull cleaned the wound and sewed twelve stitches, then wrapped a clean cotton cloth around Seba's head before attending to the cut on his arm. "Nice bit of embroidery, if I do say so myself," Dr. Turnbull said when he had finished. He winked at Agnete. "Twelve stitches on the head, just like the twelve apostles, and three on the arm for the Holy Trinity. I like to infuse my stitches with drops of prayer."

Agnete traced the sign of the cross over Seba's temple with her gauze-wrapped hand. "May the Lord bless Sebastian's recovery."

Seba pulled the cap over his bandaged head, woozy from rum, blood loss, and fading adrenaline. "Thank you, Doctor Turnbull. I don't know what my family would do without you. We all owe you our lives. After the way you rescued my father in Constantinople, and dressed my mother's wounds, and now—"

The doctor raised his palm. "Hush, my boy. I've told you a hundred times, it was pure serendipity that your father was allowed to leave the Ottoman shipyard in Constantinople for a demonstration of the *New Fortuna*'s craftsmanship. The credit goes to Captain Alexiano and the good Lord. Although Kostas was a slave, he was still the Ottoman Empire's best engineer. The captain convinced the overseer that if Kostas were permitted to observe the *New Fortuna*'s maneuverability by sailing with us for just an hour, Kostas could apply the design to the sultan's fleet."

Dr. Turnbull patted Peter's ankle again, causing Peter to wince. "How were we to know that a rogue wave was surging toward Constantinople at that very moment? Had we not been sailing around the Sea of Marmara when the wave made landfall, we'd all be dead. As I said, pure serendipity."

"God was with all of you that day," Agnete said. "Especially my husband. I need to go to him. My dear Kostas must be worried sick." She held out her arm. "Sebastian, escort your mother to the cargo deck."

Dr. Turnbull bowed very low, almost hitting his head on the arm of Agnete's chair. "Quite right, my good woman, as always. God was with us then and now. Go to your husband; I've seen the improvement in him since the two of you were reunited. He has a long recovery ahead, but with your care and the healing breezes of Menorca, he'll be a plump currant in no time."

Agnete happily curled her arm around Seba's elbow and bowed. "From your mouth to God's ears, Doctor Turnbull."

Seba guided his mother up the ladder to the new berth deck, and climbed up behind her. The ship's violent rocking had subsided to a mere aggressive swaying, and Dr. Turnbull's poultice had numbed the discomfort in Agnete's hands. Seba's father lay in his hammock like a corpse, his gray cotton shirt and loose woolen trousers matching his gray skin. His salt-and-pepper hair was matted around his head, his whole being devoid of color but for a faded blue sash around his waist.

Agnete cupped Kostas's cheeks with her gauzy mitts, shaking with emotion. "*Kardia mou*," she whispered.

Kostas's eyes brimmed as he struggled to keep his composure. "My prayers are answered. You're alive." Kostas's voice broke. "Let the tempest rage, *agape mou*. We are together and nothing else matters."

Agnete petted Kostas's cheek and kissed his forehead. "*Kardia mou*, you may be content with me on this floating stack of timber, but I will not be satisfied until we are on dry land." She looked upward, as if conversing directly with God. "The sooner the better."

Kostas chuckled. "Seba, I hope you find someone to love as much as I love your mother."

Seba squirmed. His parents had always behaved like this, and he admired their relationship, but sometimes it was more than his sixteen-year-old sensibilities could withstand. "I have to report to the captain," he said. "If you need anything, send someone to find me."

"Oh, I do need something," said Agnete fiercely. "To

reach our destination as soon as possible! You tell that captain I am not pleased with our current state of affairs, and I expect him to do something about it!"

Seba sighed. His mother had harangued the captain for most of this seemingly endless voyage across the Mediterranean—more than two thousand nautical miles all told—and he knew that Captain Alexiano had much more on his mind than bowing to his mother's demands. *Still, if nothing else, it's obvious she's feeling better.*

# 4 STORYTELLING


*August 1, 1767*
*Balearic Sea, 300 nautical miles north of Menorca*
*Early evening*


Seba left his parents and found Captain Alexiano on the quarterdeck. The rain was moving east, bucketing down in thick, dark sheets a hundred yards to larboard. *Did I really climb to the crow's nest in that wall of water? What was I thinking?*

The captain leaned his elbow against the ship's wheel, opening and closing his hands as if trying to regain feeling in his fingers. "It appears the *New Fortuna* has weathered the storm with no lasting damage," he said. "Paolo tells me that Doctor Turnbull produced a healing poultice for your mother's hands, and she is recovering well. Now tell me, how fares Peter?"

"Doctor Turnbull saved Peter's foot and mended his shoulder, but he says Peter must stay off the lines until we reach Menorca."

The captain clapped his wet hands together, sending droplets of water into the air. "*Opa*! Between you and Paolo, I think we can manage without Peter until we reach Port Mahón." The captain, his curly gray hair escaping from his vermilion cap, waggled his bushy eyebrows up and down playfully. "Lucky for him we'll be there in less than three days' time."

Seba smiled weakly. Now that the journey was almost at a close, it was good to see the captain show some levity. Captain Alexiano was an optimistic man, but this voyage had taken its toll. "I hope that's soon enough to satisfy my mother," he said lightly. "She said to tell you that she wants her feet on dry land by tomorrow, and she seems quite sure that's within your power."

The captain took off his cap and slapped it on the ship's wheel, bellowing with laughter. "Thank God for your mother! Her strength is one of the reasons I've survived this aeonian voyage with my wits intact." He pulled his cap over his wiry hair. "She reminds me of my grandmother; stubborn like a donkey. Still, it's good to have standards."

He pulled a brass compass from his jacket. "This is one of the most important guides for a sea captain, Seba, but not the only one. Throughout our long journey, driven off course again and again, I needed only a few words with your mother to find my north star. She is a force of nature, as strong as the wind and tide. Not to mention, I appreciate her humor."

"Er, I don't think she meant it as a joke, sir."

That made the captain laugh even louder. "Oh, I thank God for that woman every day! I'll go below and report our location to her myself. She might not put her feet on solid ground by tomorrow, but she will be able to spot dry land.

I'll offer her my spyglass. Who knows, she might even climb to the crow's nest to set her eyes on Menorca's coast."

Seba doubted that, particularly with her abraded hands; but he knew from experience that if he told his mother she couldn't or shouldn't do something, that was a near-guarantee that she would try.

Paolo climbed up the stairs to the quarterdeck, carrying a basket full of wriggling mackerel and sardines and grinning from ear to ear. "We'll eat well tonight, thanks to the tempest!"

Seba said, "All those fish washed onto the deck?"

"They sure did. They heard my stomach rumbling and volunteered to remedy the problem. There's enough here to fill all our bellies. Seba, do you want to help me carry these to the cook?"

The captain chuckled. "Just a moment, Paolo. That was very resourceful of you, and the crew will be ravenous after fighting the storm all night and day." His voice took a more serious tone. "Before you go, I want to ask both of you a question. I've been impressed with the speed at which you boys have learned the jobs aboard the *New Fortuna*, from the rigging and the sails to the night watch and the ship's maintenance. I've seen many good prospects fall victim to the boredom and beer, but both of you have managed to avoid those traps, which is remarkable given that this is the longest voyage across the Mediterranean I've ever navigated."

Seba and Paolo stood a little taller at that. "As you know, after we deposit Doctor Turnbull's recruits at Port Mahón, we'll be traveling on," the captain continued. "Corsica, the Greek islands, and the port towns of Anatolia. We're to gather more volunteers for the doctor's business venture in East Florida. I'll need hands I can trust. Would you like to join my crew? As true mariners, wages and all?"

Seba and Paolo exchanged glances. They had been best friends since their chance encounter the prior year, and most of their conversations revolved around their dream to become sailors.

Paolo was about to accept enthusiastically on behalf of them both, but Seba interrupted him.

"That's a great honor, sir, and a big decision. Could we have a day or two to think it over?"

The captain waved his hand generously. "Of course. We'll likely reach Menorca in two days, and we'll have to resupply the ship there. Give me your answers when we reach port." He pointed to the rain, which was moving away quickly. "Deliver your fish to the galley and then we'll hoist the sails. The sea air will dry us out in no time."

After taking the fish to the cook, who was surprised and delighted not to be serving hardtack for supper, Seba and Paolo were back on the weatherdeck in less than fifteen minutes, positioned at the foresail lines.

Paolo couldn't contain his excitement. "Seba, this is perfect! Why did you ask the captain for more time? If we accept his offer, we won't be sitting around on that island waiting for Doctor Turnbull to come back with more recruits; we'll be doing the recruiting!"

Seba shook his head. "My mother almost died today, and my father looks like a ghost. I want to see that my parents are safe before I sail back across the Mediterranean without them."

Paolo blew air through his teeth. "Oh, they'll be fine. Doctor Turnbull said there's an entire Greek community in Port Mahón. They even have a Greek church. Your mother will be thrilled."

Seba took his exasperation out on the rigging, which

thudded aggressively against the foremast. "Paolo, my father can barely walk. I've finally reunited my family, and I don't want to abandon my parents in a foreign land."

"Setting them up in a nice home where Doctor Turnbull pays for everything is not abandoning them," Paolo scoffed. "Ugh! I can't imagine being stuck on an island for months until Doctor Turnbull returns. I'll die of boredom. My muscles will become weak. I'll forget how to fire the cannons. The only storms I'll see will be old women arguing in the market. The horizon will be blocked by fences. I'll get so soft I'll start writing poems about donkeys. Donkeys, Seba!"

Seba laughed; but he couldn't stop thinking about his father and his injured hip. *I can't leave him when he needs me.*

At last, the sails were raised, the storm was behind them, and the *New Fortuna* was back to making good time toward Menorca. Seba and Paolo were exhausted, wet, and tired, looking forward to their bountiful fish supper and their familiar berths. They descended the creaking ladder to the deck below, where the gunports were shuttered tightly against the chill and shadows danced along the curved ceiling beams.

When their feet touched the cargo deck, they heard Agnete's voice, warm and clear. She sat cross-legged on a barrel, her hair tied up in a new headscarf to replace the one she'd lost. Sailors with weather-beaten faces leaned forward, elbows on knees, spellbound. The Greek and Italian passengers they'd picked up along the way sat wrapped in threadbare shawls or coats, wide-eyed, clutching tin cups or each other's hands. Others, like Peter and Kostas, listened from their hammocks, eyes closed as if lulled by a childhood bedtime story. Even the grizzled cook stood still in the hatchway, a ladle forgotten in his hand. The storm had subsided, the sun had set, and Seba's mother was the evening's entertainment.

He and Paolo stood near one of the far posts, beyond the range of the oil lamps' light. No one paid them any mind; everyone's attention was on Agnete, who was gesticulating energetically with her gauze-wrapped hands. For an instant, Seba was happy to see his mother in high spirits, but as he tuned into her words, his stomach flipped.

"As God is my witness, I was dangling over the side of this miserable ship, which was perched on the crest of a wave the size of Mount Provateio. The only thing separating me from that ferocious sea was the rope that my courageous Sebastian had tied around my waist. I told him I didn't need it; I was simply going to heave the contents of my stomach over the railing and return to my hammock. Of course, Sebastian was right all along. How could I have doubted him? My son is a hero, the greatest voyager to sail the Seven Seas!"

Seba slunk backward toward the ladder, mortified. His mother must have been training with Dr. Turnbull in the art of exaggeration. His skin tingled as a rash of embarrassment broke out on his arms and neck.

He resisted the urge to run up on deck and douse himself with a cold bucket of salt water. He must have actually made a move toward the ladder, because Paolo put a firm hand on his shoulder, and hissed, "You're not going anywhere, Odysseus." Paolo grinned in the low light. "Or should I call you Perseus? It sounds like you battled a sea monster, after all!" He was enjoying Seba's embarrassment a little too much. "As long as she doesn't liken you to Heracles. That's *my* moniker."

Seba now had two reasons for embarrassment, but he remained silent.

Agnete continued, "I know my son must have inherited my penchant for obstinance, because no matter how I argued with him to leave me, he insisted on tying the rope around my waist and then to himself. As the ship plunged down that mountainous wall of water, I found myself so far below the surface that I opened my eyes under water and saw the ship's keel above me. I've never felt so much fear in my life. I prayed for Jesus to save me from this tempest, just as he calmed the waters on the Sea of Galilee. The ship ran up the next wall of water, and again, I was dangling from the ship's railing, my brave son tethered to my body like an umbilicus. I gave him life, and he saved my life."

Agnete stopped to take a breath and one of the passengers brought her a ladle of water, which she dramatically slurped before continuing. *And I thought Papouli was our family's storyteller.*

"If not for Sebastian, I would be at the bottom of the sea. When the ship ran up the next wave, Sebastian hoisted me back onto the deck in that raging torrent of water. My fearless son never once thought of himself. His only concern was for me. I tell you that selfless and unflinching bravery has not been seen since the apostles of Jesus walked the earth."

The group could see that Agnete was tiring from her long account, but storytelling was one of the best ways to pass the time on a ship. Agnete seemed to have inherited some of her father's gift for loquaciousness, so it was with minimal encouragement that she kept the story going.

"Did you swallow seawater?" asked a young boy.

"A barrelful, at least," Agnete nodded. "I've been coughing it up the last few hours."

"Could you feel the hand of God?" asked a young mother.

"I never lost faith in my Creator."

"You must have seen Davy Jones himself down there," grinned an old deckhand.

Agnete put her hands on her hips and frowned. "Who is this Davy Jones you sailors go on about day and night? If he lives in the sea then I have no use for him. In any case, he's no match for my brilliant son. As you may have learned on this voyage, I am not a swimmer. I prefer dry land, the drier the better."

Several in the audience murmured their agreement. For many of them, a year under sail had created a deep yearning for terra firma.

"However, my heroic son swam the Strait of Chios. It's eight miles wide, with the deadliest and most frigid current in the Aegean Sea, you know. Sebastian taught me his secret to surviving the murderous waters. I heard his reassuring voice in my head, telling me to count slowly, and the moment my head broke above the water's surface, to inhale as if I were sucking the entire sky into my lungs." She took a big belly breath and held it; Seba noticed that everyone around her did the same.

"As I held my breath and counted, I prayed for God to deliver me from this tempest. How did the Creator answer my prayers? Not with a whale. Not a dove. Not even a host of angels. No, it was *my* son." Agnete tapped her heart with the tips of her bandaged fingers.

Paolo began a chant of "Seba! Seba! Seba!"

Seba shot his friend a glare with such force that, had it been a dagger, it would have split Paolo's large head in two. But Paolo was impervious to the dagger stare, and anyway it was too late: everyone had picked up the chant. Paolo lifted Seba bodily and raised him over his shoulder, causing Seba's stitched-up head to bump against the low ceiling.

"Put me down! Just because you're bigger than me doesn't mean you can throw me around," Seba cried. "*Ouch!* Watch the ceiling, you ox! My skull's not a wine cask!"

The crowd clapped and joined in the chant, including Agnete from her perch on the barrel and Kostas from his hammock.

Seba pounded on Paolo's shoulder with his fist. "I mean it, Paolo! You'll knock out what's left of my wits."

At last, Paolo dropped Seba, who landed on his backside with a thud. "Sorry, Seba," he said sheepishly. "I got caught up in the emotions. You can't deny that was the worst storm we've encountered in a year, and we all survived. Not to mention that you were a Greek hero today, like Odysseus fighting the Scylla and Charybdis. And you saved your mother's life!" He pointed at Agnete. "Look at her!"

Seba slowly got to his feet and stared at his mother. Her face was shining like the saints painted in gold at Nea Moni, Chios's 400-year-old Byzantine monastery.

"Today she was as good as dead, and now she's alive again," Paolo said. "Because her only son saved her life. Don't take her celebration away from her."

Against his will, or perhaps despite it, Seba walked slowly toward his mother and gave her a hug. "You were very brave, Mama. I wasn't the one suspended from a rope over the edge of a three hundred-ton ship in the middle of a storm. And you're barely five feet tall." Seba pointed to the ship's walls and the sea beyond. "The bluefin tuna swimming out there are bigger than you."

Agnete took Seba's hands in hers. He felt her fiery heat radiating through the gauze. *No wonder she's five feet of fury. She feels like she's made of fire.*

In that moment, it was as if Seba truly knew his mother

for the first time, as if he were gazing into her soul, and what he saw shamed him. She had never asked for her husband to be kidnapped, and when she found herself alone with a child who didn't understand her, she must have felt like Cassandra in the Thymbraean temple. There was a reason why she called Kostas her heart. She and her ancestors had coaxed the mastic tears from the skinos trees for centuries, and that was the reason why she encouraged Seba to accept life as an Ottoman mastic slave; her family's legacy was all she knew. And now she was on a ship over a thousand miles from the only home she'd known, like a goat adrift in a flood.

Seba shook his head, willing the emotion welling in him to stay hidden. *What have I done?* His family was reunited, but his father had a difficult road to regain his full health, and they were going to an island where people spoke a different language and followed different customs.

In that moment, Seba vowed to give his parents a future that was brighter than they ever imagined. Agnete renewed the praise for her only child, but Seba had stopped listening. *I will make it better, Mama. I'll take care of you and Papa. I promise.*

# 5 QUARANTINE ISLAND

*August 3, 1767*
*Quarantine Island, Menorca*
*Early afternoon*

The captain made good on his promise to Seba's mother: near sunset on the day following the storm, he invited her to peer through his spyglass. When she spotted land, she squealed with delight and made the sign of the cross. The captain caught the spyglass before it dropped into the sea.

"God bless you, Alexander Alexiano!"

The captain said, "That is the island of Menorca, and we'll be there within a day."

Agnete patted his arm. "I never doubted you for a moment."

The port of Mahón, into which they sailed the next day, was approximately three miles long and more than half a mile wide, the largest natural harbor in the Mediterranean. The *New Fortuna* entered the protected harbor and sailed past several miniature islands jutting out from the channel's center. They were headed for one such island almost two miles from the mouth of the harbor, *Illa de la Quarantena*. Quarantine Island.

The island was no more than ten acres in size, and shaped like a gourd with the widest part aimed toward the harbor's mouth. The *New Fortuna* moored on the northeast side, facing a series of military wharfs on the harbor's northern shores. On the harbor's southwest shore, separated from Quarantine Island by a narrow channel only a hundred yards wide, stood the steep cliffs that rose a hundred feet straight up from the water's edge, on top of which sat the busy center of commerce known as Port Mahón.

They could just glimpse the town's stone walls atop the cliffs, and roofs of varying heights and angles, anchored by the steeple of a church pointing heavenward behind them. Serins trilled bright songs as barn swallows raced across the sky, their forked tails dancing acrobatically above the sparkling waves. Small wooden warehouses lined the water's edge below, most stacked to the ceiling with barrels of wine, oil, wool, and grain. A dozen packet boats bobbed at the wharfs, waiting for the dockworkers to load them with crates of olives, cheese, and oranges.

The *New Fortuna*'s wooden gangplank smacked the ground with a loud wooden thump and the passengers lined up to disembark after a year at sea. Anticipation sparked like static electricity. Agnete was first in line when the captain called "All ashore!" She ran down the gangplank as if Jesus himself was waiting for her on Quarantine Island.

Seba looked on mortified as his mother flung herself to the earth and kissed the rocky ground. Between sobs, she crossed herself and exclaimed praise and thanks to the Virgin Mary, Jesus, the Holy Spirit, God, and every saint she knew. *Pull yourself together, Mama.*

Seba took a step toward the ship's railing. He stopped when he felt a familiar, yet feeble, grip on his shoulder. "Papa, let me go!" he said. "Everyone will think she's *trelós.*"

Kostas leaned heavily on a cane made of burl oak with the handle carved into an eagle's head. It had been a gift from Dr. Turnbull, made by an artisan in his Scottish hometown. "Where is your heart today, Seba?" he said with a note of sadness. "The woman who brought you into this world had never so much as stepped one toe off the land of her ancestors. She's spent the last year sailing rough seas, battling seasickness, homesickness, and pirates. Have you forgotten Malta? And only days ago she almost perished. Have some compassion and grant her this moment."

But Seba's only thought was to put an end to the spectacle his mother was making. He extricated himself from his father's grasp and took three steps down the gangplank toward her before his legs failed. He teetered and tottered, swaying right and left like a drunkard.

Despite his best efforts, Seba stumbled face first onto the lower end of the gangplank, unable to regain his balance or break his fall. His head exploded with pain. He scrambled to dry land and plopped down next to a large rock, holding his head. His mother's voice still reverberated off Port Mahón's ochre cliffs.

Paolo called down from the ship's deck, "Seba, that was spectacular! I couldn't have disembarked any better if I tried." He easily ran down the gangplank. "Welcome to Menorca, my friend!"

Seba felt around his temple for signs of blood. "Can you

stop my mother's wailing?"

Paolo looked over his shoulder at Agnete and shrugged. "Why? She's happy to be on land, just like all of us."

"It's embarrassing."

Paolo laughed. "You must be joking. She's expressing her happiness. What's embarrassing about that?"

Seba shook his head. "You don't understand."

"Perhaps I don't," Paolo snorted. "But if my mother were alive and I had the good fortune to share one of the happiest moments of her life, I'd be grateful." He stretched out his hand and pulled Seba up to standing. "Anyway, don't focus on your mother. Look around! Isn't it magnificent?"

High in the eastern sky, the sun dripped gold onto the serpentine harbor, which stretched deep inland, flanked by snuff-colored cliffs and green slopes stippled with wild fennel and tamarisk. Ships of every size—corsairs, merchant brigs, jennies, snows, and British cutters—bobbed on the shimmering water. Toward the mouth of the harbor, the British naval fort loomed in its hulking, sun-scorched glory. Paolo was right, it *was* magnificent.

"I suppose quarantining on this rock will be an improvement over my smelly hammock," Paolo said. "But I don't understand why we have to wait *ten* days."

Seba looked down the beach at their temporary dwellings on Quarantine Island, situated between the boulders strewn about tiny isle. Small and dun-colored, with shutterless windows and flat thatched roofs, the huts were rudimentary, though no more so than their berths on the brigantine. "I don't know either," he said, lifting his chin to catch the air. "But this breeze feels good."

Paolo clapped his hand on Seba's back. "Can you smell the fruit?" he moaned. Paolo sounded like Seba's childhood donkey, Matilde, who *ee-orred* at Seba whenever he dawdled with her dinner.

Seba filled his lungs with air; the aroma of figs and ripe melon was overwhelming. His stomach gurgled and his mother's cries faded into the distance. "How could I miss it? It smells like heaven. It's making my mouth water."

Paolo squeezed his stomach with his fingers. "And the crew ate all those fish I gathered off the deck. I'll be a ghost by tomorrow if these Menorcans don't bring us some food."

Seba smiled at his friend's reference to ghosts. On the day Seba met Paolo, a little over a year earlier, Paolo had mistaken Seba for a ghost. Granted, Seba had swum the Strait of Chios's dangerous currents and survived an earthquake after climbing out of the freezing water on to the Anatolian shores, so he probably looked more ghostly than human to Paolo at the time. Seba had been delirious with exhaustion and a broken wrist, lying in the scrub brush with the clucking nightjars, imagining his grandfather and Aristotle there with him, trying to convince him that the nesting birds were evil goatsuckers. He was on the brink of death and didn't care. Another few hours out there alone and he *would* have been a ghost.

Paolo, on the road to Smyrna, had heard Seba's delirious raving and pulled him from the bushes. After a few dried dates and a hunk of hard cheese (an epic feast to a starving boy), they had traveled together to the bustling port city of Smyrna. Paolo had done most of the talking on their journey, and his obsession with ghosts, spirits, angels, and demons dominated the conversation.

Seba, who could still feel the sting of Paolo's handprint on his back, said, "I'm sure Doctor Turnbull will arrange for food for us while we're in quarantine. He's not one to take chances when it comes to food."

Paolo nodded. "I'll say. Lord knows that man never

misses a meal."

Seba stared at the wooden crates lined up on the docks. "What if one of those crates accidentally fell in the water? I'd swim this channel for a box of fresh figs."

Paolo whistled. "Oh, like you swam the Strait of Chios? Perhaps you should tell that tale again; I've only heard it about a hundred times. *Gennaíos. Allá poly anóntos.* You're brave, but also very stupid."

Seba grinned. "You said it was heroic."

"It *was* impressive. Eight miles in cold water against a powerful current."

"And sharp rocks."

Paolo held up a finger. "What you forget, is that you would have given up the ghost if I hadn't found you."

It was Seba's turn to slap Paolo on the back as hard as he could. "Yes, Paolo, and I've thanked you a thousand times since then. I also saved you from a lifetime in prison, where you'd be now if you had killed Nasir Beyzade Paşa during that brawl in the Aigókeros. You're lucky I stopped you before you went too far."

Paolo made a fist and smacked it into the open palm of his opposite hand. "You would have done the same if that little man had donkey-kicked *you* in the head."

Seba sighed. He *wouldn't* have done the same. That was the difference between them, but he thought it better to change the subject. "I said I'd swim the channel for fresh figs. What would you swim for?"

"Persimmons," said Paolo. "When they're ripe they taste like honey from the comb. You'd be floundering in my wake."

Seba smirked. "I doubt it. Remember that time I swam the Strait of Chios?"

Paolo laughed heartily. "Perhaps we'll have a swimming

competition someday." He was bigger and stronger than Seba, but he couldn't deny Seba's doggedness.

"I can't wait."

Their banter was interrupted by Dr. Turnbull, who disembarked the *New Fortuna* with a flourish. In contrast to his attire during the journey, Dr. Turnbull now wore the full regalia of a British gentleman. His clothes were of a tightly woven cotton, brightly colored in indigo and vermilion, his ruffled shirtsleeves peeking out from his jacket. His waistcoat featured a geometric pattern of red and fern-colored blocks with intersecting lines of gold and blue. Dr. Turnbull called it his tartan, a nod to his Scottish heritage. His boots were coal-black leather decorated with gleaming brass buckles, reflecting the sun like pointy-toed lamps. His waistcoat and bright blue overcoat were adorned with brass buttons. As was his custom in public, he had donned his gray periwig made of horsehair curled around heated clay pipes.

"Hello, my young gentlemen. Discussing Mahón's delightful viands? A splendid subject, one I know well." He patted his belly, which protruded from under his plaid waistcoat and hung over his dark trousers. How he managed to remain so plump after a year at sea was a mystery to Seba. "My dear wife, Maria Gracia du Robin, says I have rather a sweet tooth, although I often remind her that I do not discriminate when it comes to the subject of banqueting. Savory, sweet, spicy, seared, saccharine, or sauteed—they all garner high marks from me."

While fluent in Greek, Dr. Turnbull had taken it upon himself to teach Seba and Paolo English over the course of their year-long voyage, noting that English would serve the boys well in the New World. As such, Seba and Paolo knew all of Dr. Turnbull's ways to describe food: *first-rate, splendid, marvelous, capital,* and *tip-top,* to name a few. Not surprisingly, their English vocabulary was heavy on foods and their descriptors.

"Trust me, my dear boys, you haven't eaten until you've enjoyed a Menorcan feast." He clapped his hands together enthusiastically. "Mahón cheese is the best in the world! And the island's *pudin de requeson,* my friends, is a delight." He held his hands to his heart as if recalling a cherished friend. "Delicate whey cheese combined with eggs, flour, sugar, and butter, flavored with lemon zest, cinnamon, and nutmeg, and baked to perfection. A creamy cloud of heavenly bliss! My favorite version comes from the twin sister of our illustrious ship's captain. Theodora Alexiano lives right here in Port Mahón, and in addition to being the locality's lead councilwoman, she is a superb baker. *Ensaïmadas, formatjades, polvorones,* and the list goes on; there is nothing she can't conjure from sugar and flour. Theodora tops her pudin de requeson with raisins, pine nuts, and fig jam. The flavor is pure ambrosia."

Paolo threw his hands in the air. "Doctor, stop! I can't bear this torture when we have nothing to eat."

Dr. Turnbull pushed his arms out in front of him, his white-gloved palms facing toward Paolo. "Ah, my dear boy. There's that Greek passion that I've come to adore, just like my beloved Maria Gracia." A great accommodating smile spread across his face. "Never fear, Captain Alexiano has already sent word for the port captain to dispatch supplies to us. Unfortunately, it's a somewhat laborious process, given the fear of infection."

"What infection?"

"They're very cautious here in Port Mahón, Seba, and with good reason. In the last several years, ships from all over the world have arrived with passengers and crew carrying yellow fever, typhus, and other such maladies. The local population was devastated. Hence, the establishment of Quarantine Island. But don't you worry your handsome Greek heads one iota, my friends. They'll shepherd us into the island's rather modest dwellings to await the delivery of our victuals. You're welcome to stay on the ship with the crew if you prefer." He extended his arms to simultaneously pat them both on their backs. "In any case, we'll have food in our bellies before you can say *galaktoboureko*."

Dr. Turnbull was true to his word, and those in quarantine enjoyed a feast that evening. The scent reached them before the platters did, filling their noses with rosemary, grilled fish, and the honeyed warmth of fresh figs. By the time the food was laid across the long wooden tables, the sun had dipped low and a cool breeze floated through the huts' open windows.

Olive oil glistened atop slices of Mahón cheese and rounds of crusty *pa de xeixa*. Oval plates of octopus stewed in wine were nestled beside bowls of chickpeas dressed in lemon and mint. There were fire-roasted aubergines stuffed with spiced meat, tomato, garlic, and chard. For dessert, sweet ensaïmades were coiled like seashells in a basket with figs and sugared yeast breads. The centerpiece, as Dr. Turnbull promised, was Theodora Alexiano's famous dessert: pudin de requeson.

Agnete asked them all to join hands around the table. "Lord, we are grateful for your mercies, made new with the rising of each day's sun. Bless the sacrifices that brought this bounty to our table. You are our sanctuary, now and forever and to the ages of ages. Amen."

Paolo added his own enthusiastic "God bless Menorcan cows!" as he tore a piece of *pa de xeixa* roughly the size of his forearm and slathered it with creamy yellow *mantega*.

Seba's favorite dish was an aromatic soup called *oliaigu*, a bright-red concoction served in a wide-lipped vessel decorated with blood orange stripes. The soup was steaming, and the glorious scent of tomatoes, onions, green peppers, garlic, and warm spices made Seba's mouth water. He filled his crock twice, drinking in the familiar scent of olives, smoked paprika, and spicy *ros de Mallorca* peppers.

Agnete, an excellent cook herself, took a liking to the rolls topped with anise seeds. She said with approval, "*Polý kalá*," as she handed a roll to her husband.

Kostas took a bite. "Very good indeed," he agreed.

Seba looked up between spoonsful of soup to see Paolo piling a fig-topped toast with a tower of cheese, sausages, and an entire stuffed pepper. Smashing it down with his hand, Paolo managed to force the assembly into his mouth, grinning at Seba as he worked to chew and swallow his masterpiece.

Seba understood the grin. After so many weeks at sea, often feeling nauseated from the huge ocean swells and the overpowering stench of too many humans in close quarters, he felt as if he had reached the promised land, flowing with milk and honey. He chose a straw mattress near his parents', where he could monitor his mother's convalescence and his father's hip. Paolo took a mattress nearby; but it wasn't more than ten minutes before he jumped up, complaining that he hadn't yet gotten his land legs back. He grabbed his boots and returned to his berth on the ship. Many of the crew did the same, preferring their familiar swaying hammocks to the hard ground.

As he lay on the straw mattress next to his parents, Seba dreamed of goats frolicking in the pasture and bees drinking the nectar of late summer blooms.

# 6 HIT AND RUN


*August 4, 1767*
*Port Mahón Harbor, Menorca*
*Morning*


KA-BOOM!

The ground below Seba's improvised mattress shook, rousing him out of his paradisaical dreams. A panicked thought ran through his mind: *Earthquake!*

He was up in a flash, tugging on his boots and running to his parents. "Mama! I'll get Papa! Run before these walls fall in on us."

Kostas lifted himself up from his straw pallet. "Seba, no."

Seba reached for his father's shoulders and tried to drag him to standing. "Hurry, before the roof collapses! We must get out now."

Kostas said much too calmly, "It's not an earthquake. We are safer inside."

Seba knew that his father's slavery in the shipyards of

Constantinople had left him with a dislocated hip, but he wondered now if there were other effects, such as the addling of his brains. "What else could it be?"

Before his father could reply, Seba heard a familiar ear-splitting sound.

CRACK-CRACK-CRACK-CRACK-CRACK!

Realization dawned: it was the sound of the *New Fortuna*'s cannons. The ship must be under attack.

"I have to help the captain!" Seba cried, racing toward the hut's doorway.

His mother, who was huddled against Kostas, called after him, "Sebastian, no! Stay here! It's too dangerous." But Seba ignored her, running east toward the dock. The thick, acrid smoke choked him as he squinted into the darkness. He heard Captain Alexiano's voice, roaring orders to the crew. *This must be why the crew sleeps on the ship.*

Seba raced to the ship, stumbling and coughing in the sooty smoke. Two seamen were already pulling up the gangway. Seba called out to them, but they seemed not to hear; the plank was now at least six feet away from the dock. Seba leaped as high and far as he could, barely catching the edge of the plank as the sailors pulled it onto the main deck. He scrambled aboard.

Smoke poured from the starboard side's open cannon doors as the crew maneuvered the ship out of its berth. The *New Fortuna* was preparing to fire her larboard cannons.

Seba bounded down the ladder to the gun deck. The merchant ship carried only ten cannons, five on each side. Captain Alexiano said ten cannons were just right; the *New Fortuna* was built for speed, to carry as much cargo as possible, and was better equipped to outrun any predators than to stand and fight. In all the time that Seba had traveled on the *New Fortuna*, the ship had returned cannon fire only twice, when the captain found it absolutely necessary. Both times it had been to keep pirates at bay and give the *New Fortuna* time to get away. Paolo recounted the details of these incidents weekly, praising the captain, the crew, the cannons, and even the cannonballs for their performance.

Each cannon required at least five crew members to operate it, and the *New Fortuna*'s crew totaled no more than twenty-five. Paolo was stationed at the first cannon on the larboard side; spotting Seba, he shouted for him to give Peter a hand with the fifth cannon, the last in the row.

Seba loaded the cannon with shot from a neatly-stacked pyramid inside a rectangular box nailed to the deck boards. The *New Fortuna* turned to face the north side of Mahón's harbor, and the crew called from pillar to post as they prepared to fight:

"Blasted Frenchies! What are they doing here?"

"Two miles inland from the mouth of the harbor? Those scoundrels are bold!"

"How'd they get past the guns at Saint Philip's?"

"Snuck in under cover of darkness, those slippery eels!"

"Filthy poltroons are going for a hit-and-run!"

"When we're finished with 'em, they'll suffer a hit-and-sink!"

Smoke from the cannon fire poured in through the gunports, and the ship rocked from side to side as the harbor waters churned, whipped up by cannonballs smacking the surface like flaming meteors.

From what Seba could piece together from the shouts of the crew, a French privateer had stolen into the port of Mahón's navy warehouses with the intent to plunder not from another ship, as they often did, but from the British navy itself. It *was* a bold move to attack the military side of the harbor rather than the merchant side. The crew seemed equally angry and impressed by the privateer's tactics.

As he tried to keep his balance and pack the cannon with powder, Seba asked, "Are you sure they're French?" They had been attacked by Barbary pirates near Malta and had been chased by several vessels in the Tyrrhenian Sea, but the Mediterranean was full of pirates flying all manner of flags. Seba remembered the flag of every pirate and privateer they encountered, but he had never seen this one before.

An old crew member laughed derisively, showing a snaggling row of teeth beneath his grizzled mustache. He pointed out the gun door. "See? Frenchies put those lily flowers atop their pirate skulls. That's how we know they got the froggy king's backing. Just like those Johnny Crappos to slap a lily on a dead man's head!"

Another crew member gasped. "It's a red flag, by God."

Seba had never seen a red death's-head flag, but it was clear from the crew's reaction that this was a bad omen. Before he could ask, they heard an explosion above them and the hiss of water turning to steam as the fiery cannon shot hit the water's surface away to starboard.

The old sailor looked at him. "A red field on the pirate flag means 'dead men tell no tales.'"

Paolo looked at Seba questioningly, and Seba knew why. Paolo believed that dead men told plenty of tales, if only you stopped to pay attention.

"I can see the name on her prow," called the gunner's mate. "It's the *Hasard*!"

"Infamous vessel," grumbled the old sailor. "Her captain is equal parts cunning and ruthless. He'll give no mercy."

Seba set his jaw. He wasn't inclined to ask for mercy anyway. He hadn't traveled the Mediterranean Sea for an entire year only to be sunk in the harbor the day after their arrival.

The *New Fortuna* turned toward the northside warehouse pier, which Seba could barely make out through the open gunports. The sky was turning from deep inky purple to pale indigo, chalked by white smoke; many of the naval storehouses had been set on fire.

Seba squinted, bringing his head almost even with the opening. What he saw made him shudder. A small, two-masted schooner, no more than 150 yards away, was sailing directly toward them. It sat low in the water, occasioned by its guns. The *Hasard* carried twice the number of cannons as the *New Fortuna,* all pointed directly at Seba. The other sight that struck fear into Seba's heart was the aforementioned red flag, bearing three bone-white skulls with black French fleur-de-lis emblazoned on their foreheads, and two curved sabers intersecting beneath them, the points violently stabbing upward through the flag's scarlet field.

A crewman jabbed him in the chest with a packing rod, rousing him. "Get ready to take fire!"

Time slowed down. The crew seemed to be caught up in a dance, their words dreamy and garbled as they prepared to fire the cannons in rapid succession. Seba, Paolo, and Peter followed the lead of the other gunners, waiting for the order to fire. Their hearts pounded in their throats.

Before the order came, the floor below them exploded, sending up pieces of the hull mixed with shredded decking boards, shattered casks, and other debris. Seba was thrown into a nearby post as the master's mate shouted, "Fire all guns!"

Sparks flew as the cannons were lit. Then came the thunder of the guns. The cannons kicked back; Paolo was knocked off his feet, where he landed beside Seba, who was bleeding profusely. The suture on his forehead, all of Dr.

Turnbull's neat handiwork, had split wide open. There was a hole in the decking, and water flooded in through the gaps in the larboard side. The ship was now listing heavily.

Paolo's face was red-hot with anger. Seba had seen that look before, in the middle of a tavern brawl in the Greek quarter of Smyrna. Paolo had almost killed Nasir Beyzade Paşa that time; his rage this morning was even more ferocious.

"I'll kill those corsairs!" Paolo shouted, leaping to his feet. He raced to the ladder above deck. Seba stood and Peter gestured with his head for Seba to reload the cannon for the next run. Peter's arm was hanging from his shoulder, limp as a dead ferret. He yelled, "Seba, bring me a shot! That explosion! My shoulder!"

Seba couldn't see through the blood pouring into his eyes, but he managed to feel around the box containing the eight-pound round shots. Peter used his right arm to pack the cannon with gunpowder and Seba loaded the shot into the gun. They rolled the cannon through the gunport and waited for the other cannons to fire, as they were the fifth in the row of five. As Seba looked through the opening again, his stomach dropped. The pirate ship was less than thirty yards away, preparing to fire at them a third time.

Seba wiped his head with the sleeve of his shirt, but he couldn't stanch the blood that poured from his torn stitches or the new gash that had joined them. He looked around to find some scrap of cloth he could tie around his temple; but the gun deck was in complete chaos, the smell of smoke mixing with sweat, blood, and gunpowder. He envisioned a cannonball from the privateer coming directly through the gunport and splitting him in two, the upper and lower halves of his body shooting off in opposite directions.

Seba's head was swimming, and the gundeck swirled

around him. He fell to the ground, not able to think clearly or move.

KA-BOOM! Seba couldn't string any coherent thoughts together; his mind was mush. He simply stared out the gunport in a daze, not sure of what he was seeing. The privateer was still there, sitting even lower in the water; but beyond the red flag there was another flag, this one belonging to the Royal Navy.

The British naval ship was monstrous. She towered above the French schooner, and her hull appeared to be made of cannons. As the naval ship turned her stern to position for another series of cannon fire, Seba caught the bright gold letters that identified her, and recognized a word that Dr. Turnbull had taught him several weeks before: *Authority*.

The sight of the naval gunship threw the *New Fortuna*'s crew into a frenzy of jubilation. They shouted and danced, cheering on the British ship. The guns of the *Authority* were situated much higher in the water, owing to her sheer size. Her cannons were angled downward toward the waterline, poised to obliterate the *Hasard*, which seemed a mere fishing boat by comparison.

The cannon fire was deafening, like thunder but a thousand times more powerful. It felt as if the sky was being ripped apart, and Seba, still dizzy and half-blinded by the blood in his eyes, looked up into the morning sky to make sure it was still there. A single ball from the *Authority* took out both of the *Hasard*'s masts, and the topsails fell into the water as the fore and aft masts broke in two. At this distance, it was obvious that the cannons from the *Authority* were at least three times the size of those on either the *New Fortuna* or the *Hasard*.

The *Hasard* foundered a few yards away, her long

bowsprit pointing directly at the *New Fortuna*. Her rudder had been blown to pieces, and, unable to navigate, she was listing dangerously close to the *New Fortuna*, still taking relentless cannon fire from the *Authority*. The remainder of the French privateering crew had leaped overboard to escape the fire caused by the Royal Navy's cannons.

The *Hasard's* bowsprit was so close that Seba could almost touch it through the gunport. And then the *New Fortuna's* cannons fired again, exploding into the hull of the *Hasard*, and the force diverted the ship a half-second before impact. The gun crew grabbed for their pistols and blades, and ran up the ladder to the main deck. They'd retrieve the *Hasard's* stolen booty before she sank. The corsairs had gambled that they could sail away with King George's oil, fish, and gin, as well as the Royal Navy's tools, wood, and weapons. However, they'd gambled and lost.

Seba could not savor the victory. He saw to his horror that the survivors of the privateer crew were now swimming toward Quarantine Island, no doubt with murder on their minds. His parents would be helpless; his father could barely walk, much less run, and the red flag meant they took no prisoners.

Seba stumbled toward the ladder up to the main deck, but Paolo stopped him. "Seba, your head is streaming blood," he said. "We need to get you to the surgery now."

Seba shook off Paolo's hand, and the movement made him feel sick. "No!" he slurred. "Pirates. Swimming. Red flag. Papa. Mama."

He knew he wasn't making sense, but Paolo seemed to understand. The older boy threw Seba over his back and climbed up to the main deck, leaving spatters of blood on each ladder rung. "Don't worry, Seba," Paolo rumbled. "Those stinking pirates will never make it to Quarantine

Island." Seba tried to respond, but his brain was so fogged that no words escaped.

They alighted on the main deck and Paolo ran to the quarterdeck, Seba still slung over his shoulder like a sack of barley. "Pirates are swimming to Quarantine Island! We have to save Seba's parents!"

"It's well in hand," called a crewman, "Look."

Seba watched upside down through the haze as the *Authority* maneuvered closer to the swimming pirates and trained its cannons on them. Paolo lowered his feet to the deck; Peter had emerged from below decks, and together he and Paolo held Seba up as the *Authority* took its final position.

The sound of ten cannons fired in succession split the air with a series of thunderous booms. The water turned red; when the smoke ascended off the water, not a single pirate was left alive.

A cheer went up from the *New Fortuna*'s crew.

"I never seen the like," shouted a crewman.

"Bit excessive, wouldn't you say?"

"Maybe so, but I reckon that's how the *Authority* earned her name!"

"Yep, that big ol' behemoth showed them froggies."

Leaning on Paolo and Peter, Seba saw the *Hasard*, which was now split into two halves. The half that held the bow could barely be seen above the surface of the water, its descent quickened by the anchors that hung on each ship's side. The other half was taking on water, the stern jutting up above as the contents of the hold poured into the harbor. The *Hasard* would be in the depths of the channel before day's end.

The last thing Seba heard before he lost consciousness was Paolo saying, "I believe I'm going to like it here."

# 7 RECOVERY



*August 10, 1767*
*Port Mahón Harbor, Menorca*
*Midday*

One fortuitous consequence of the *Hasard*'s attack was that Port Mahón lifted the *New Fortuna*'s quarantine. Everyone was released to the town except Seba. Dr. Turnbull had re-sewn the gash in Seba's head, adding ten more stitches to the original twelve, and ordered his young patient to remain under the physician's care for at least a week.

In addition to monitoring Seba's recovery, Dr. Turnbull remained on the ship to settle his accounts, review his business plans, order more supplies, and write letters to his investors, William Duncan and George Grenville. They'd each been granted 20,000 acres in East Florida, and Dr. Turnbull was sailing the Mediterranean on behalf of the partnership, gathering volunteers to populate their land.

The plan was to farm indigo, cotton, silk, and other crops of economic importance, which in a few years would make them all absurdly rich.

Dr. Turnbull assured Seba and Paolo that if he and other English merchants could source indigo dye from the New World rather than the Far East, everyone involved would stand to make a fortune. Indigo's hue, vibrant blue kissed with dark violet, seemed as exotic as the process of producing it. Europeans couldn't get enough of the "blue gold" for their textiles, pottery, and paints; on his East Florida plantation, which he intended to name New Smyrna (after his beloved Maria Gracia's Aegean birthplace), he'd create an indigo empire to benefit him and his Greek volunteers.

Paolo often visited Seba onboard, bringing stories of the food and the welcoming people. And of how he, as Seba's older and more experienced friend, was keeping watch over Seba's parents. Seba felt fine; he didn't need Dr. Turnbull as his nursemaid. But by his second day "under observation," Seba understood the true reason why he was being held back. Dr. Turnbull wanted a captive audience for his stories, someone to pass the time with.

It could have been worse. Dr. Turnbull invited Seba to convalesce in the Scotsman's own luxurious quarters for the week, helping him string his hammock from two strong hooks in the corner. The doctor's rooms occupied the broad stern of the *New Fortuna*, where the light spilled in through a row of paned windows on either side, burnishing the polished wood with a warm golden sheen in morning and evening. A crimson velvet settee was ensconced beneath the windows, its walnut legs carved with swirls of acanthus leaves. A writing desk, tidy but well-used, stood against one wall, with a map of East Florida, an inkstand, and scattered stacks of folded correspondence. A mahogany dining table anchored the room, flanked by four tall-backed chairs with chartreuse tufted cushions.

The scent of tobacco and old paper permeated the space, undercut faintly by lemon oil and the medicinal tang of camphor. Dr. Turnbull's narrow bed, draped in linen and a woolen coverlet, was tucked against the inner bulkhead, and Seba's cat, Artemis, often curled up for a nap on the doctor's pillow. The crew had christened Artemis their North Star on account of her silver fur that shined like moonlight and her bright emerald eyes that glowed like a summer woodland glade. She'd become somewhat of a celebrity during the voyage, often appearing on the main deck, her latest catch wriggling between her teeth. She showed off for the sailors by tossing the rats by their tails and swatting them left and right like balls of twine. In appreciation, the crew convinced Captain Alexiano to offer her a sailing contract, which he did with great ceremony.

One morning, several days into Seba's recovery, Artemis strolled through the window of Dr. Turnbull's quarters seeking food or a saucer of milk, which the doctor had taken to leaving out for her on his sideboard. Seba dozed under a light blanket as Dr. Turnbull droned on about mulberry trees, indigo, grapevines, and gold. After lapping her dish of milk, Artemis coiled herself on Seba's chest, purring so loudly that Seba could feel the vibrations through his ribcage. Dr. Turnbull was seated on a green-cushioned chair, enjoying a simple breakfast of ripe quince, figs, and aged Mahón cheese; the process of eating this meal didn't hinder one whit his ability to prattle on. Neither did the black tea in his favorite gold-trimmed porcelain cup, which had gone cold with his storytelling.

"I've enjoyed our time together, Seba. It eases the ache of

distance from my beloved Maria Gracia."

Seba opened his eyes and wriggled up in the hammock. "Thank you for sharing your quarters. It's a far cry from the cargo deck."

Dr. Turnbull raised his teacup to point at Seba's head. "Yes, a serene location for your bloody coxcomb to heal."

"I've heard you mention this 'bloody coxcomb' several times, but I don't know what it is."

"Have I not shared with you the genius of William Shakespeare? Marvelous wordsmith. He could only be improved if he'd been a Scotsman." Dr. Turnbull pointed to Seba's bandaged head. "I hadn't thought of him for ages, but your head injury put me in mind of one of his plays, *Twelfth Night*. Fortunately, I procured a bound copy of the First Folio from a highly esteemed bookseller in Glasgow. I always travel with it."

Seba cocked his head. "First Folio?"

"Naturally, you are unfamiliar. Shakespeare's works are stage plays. In fact, I've had the honor of seeing *Twelfth Night* in person no less than seven times. I believe it was three years ago that I attended a performance of *The Comedy of Errors*." Dr. Turnbull snorted. "They'd snipped it to pieces, of course. These days, any theatrical impresario who can sober up long enough to hold a crow-quill feels himself qualified to improve upon the words on the page. Why, when I was at university . . ."

Seba knew Dr. Turnbull was about to spend the next hour recounting every theater performance he'd ever attended, including the ticket price, what he'd worn, the decorations in the venue, and every statement that beloved Maria Gracia had made during the play. *He needs to focus.* Smiling politely, he broke in: "So the First Folio has a bloody coxcomb?"

Dr. Turnbull cleared his throat and raised one eyebrow. "You were born in late December, weren't you, Sebastian? Yes, I recall your mother mentioning it. I could have guessed, my young friend; you have the determined focus of the Aigókeros, or Capricorn, as they say here in Mahón. You'll be a boon to our project in East Florida, keeping me on task, I have no doubt. Now our friend, Paolo, on the other hand, has the heart of a lion, a Leo through and through. Born in the dog days of summer, so he tells me. Two capable and courageous young volunteers, exactly what my indigo plantation needs."

Seba fought back a sigh of exasperation; his head began to throb and he strove to keep his expression neutral. *What is he talking about?*

The corner of Dr. Turnbull's mouth turned up toward his raised eyebrow. "But let me return to my point, my adamantine Aigókeros. Back to the 'bloody coxcomb.' In *Twelfth Night*, the revelrous Sir Andrew and Sir Toby find themselves in an altercation with the twin brother of a girl named Viola. Now, this Viola was disguised as a boy named Cesario, but Sirs Andrew and Toby didn't know that. The twin brother, Sebastian, who had been thought drowned in a shipwreck, was very much alive."

Seba sat up straighter in his hammock. "I'm kindred to *Twelfth Night*'s Sebastian?"

Dr. Turnbull chuckled. "No, no, no, my boy, although it's very perceptive of you to make the connection. But no. When Sir Toby and Sir Andrew encounter Sebastian in the street, they attack him, thinking him to be Cesario, whom they perceived—incorrectly, I might add—to be Sir Andrew's rival for the love of Sir Toby's niece, Olivia. Sebastian, who survived the shipwreck and is an apt fighter to boot, defends himself with unexpected aggression. He beats them both around the head and Sir Toby and Sir Andrew flee to the doctor, complaining that Cesario has given them both 'a bloody coxcomb.'"

Seba pressed a finger to his wound. "Oh, it's the name for a head injury? Now I see."

Dr. Turnbull stood and clapped his hands together gleefully. "Yes, my boy, but it's so much more! A coxcomb is also the name for a fool's hat, a bright-colored, three-pointed cap adorned with bells and other foppery. A rooster's crest is also a coxcomb. And the immortal red flower of ancient Greece is a coxcomb, with petals like blood fountaining up from the stem." His paunch jiggled mirthfully.

"Er, is that funny?"

Dr. Turnbull hopped from one foot to the other in unbridled gaiety. "Don't you see, Seba? Shakespeare used words to describe Sir Toby's and Sir Andrew's physical injuries while simultaneously conveying that Sebastian had made immortal fools of his attackers, sending them away crying and crowing like roosters. It's genius, pure genius!"

Sebastian frowned. *This whole conversation is making my bloody coxcomb hurt.*

Artemis must have felt the same way; she leaped from Seba's chest to the sideboard and bounded out the open window onto the quarterdeck.

"Don't be alarmed, Sebastian. You'll catch on to the humor in due time. Your English vocabulary is growing by leaps and bounds, and you've a solid foundation of Greek wisdom from your school days on Chios. William Shakespeare is not unlike the ancient Greek comedian, Aristophanes, who played with words while contemplating the absurdity of man's existence. See for yourself." He reached into his wooden trunk and handed Seba a small book bound in red leather with gold markings. The brown calfskin cover was warm in Seba's hands.

"Go on, look inside." Dr. Turnbull's eyes were twinkling as if he had given Seba a hoard of silver coins. Seba opened the book to the middle and gasped. In the language of his childhood were written the words *ΑΡΙΣΤΟΦΑ'ΝΟΥΣ, ΤΑ ΝΕΦΕ'ΛΑΙ*. "Aristophanes, *The Clouds*." This was identical to the book he'd seen in the classroom of his teacher, Brother Timotheos, years before.

"It's one of my prized possessions, a collection of the great works of Aristophanes, printed in Venice over two hundred and fifty years ago. It was a gift given to me by the father of my beloved Maria Gracia on our wedding day. Despite our distance, I feel close to my dear wife whenever I read from this book."

Seba held the book as if it were a fragile bird. "What if the pirates had stolen it?"

"Yes, well, there is always a risk when sailing, especially these days, with corsairs and privateers skulking beyond every horizon. And yet, what is life without risk?"

Seba ran his fingers over the fine calfskin cover. *I would have left this treasure behind with beloved Maria Gracia.*

His thoughts were interrupted by his mother's excited voice. "Sebastian! Doctor Turnbull! I have good news!"

Agnete raced across the threshold of Dr. Turnbull's quarters, ran to Seba, and squeezed him so hard that he almost toppled out of the hammock. Next came Paolo, along with a girl Seba did not recognize. She was almost as tall as Paolo and had the most remarkable hair; rather than being long and braided like every other woman Seba had met, her locks were short, falling in waves that skimmed the tops of her shoulders. Even more dramatic was the color: an oxblood hue like that of a fire smoldering in the hearth on a winter evening. Her amber eyes danced with curiosity as she surveyed Dr. Turnbull's luxurious quarters.

She was dressed in a long camel-colored skirt with a pale blue overskirt that reached to a pair of brown ankle-high boots held together by iron buckles. Atop her skirt, she wore a coal-black blouse with a white lace shawl fastened at the throat with an ebony bow. She was smiling broadly, her white teeth gleaming against her copper skin.

Agnete reached for the girl's arm and gently pulled her into the center of the room, exclaiming, "Sebastian, I would like to introduce you to Fernanda Rementeria Arandia. We've been invited to live with this beautiful soul! Her residence is more lovely than I could have imagined. Oh, your father is happier than I've seen him since the day you were born." She held up the basket that Fernanda carried, which was filled to overflowing with persimmons, quince, small loaves of bread, cured sausages, and golden Mahón cheese. "Look at this bounty! It's all from Fernanda's garden."

Agnete noticed the book in Seba's hands and halted abruptly. Her eyes bore into Dr. Turnbull like flaming arrows. "What is that?"

Seba could see her mind racing behind her eyes. She had told him a million times that the only book worth reading was the Bible. In her mind, Aristophanes and the other ancient playwrights and philosophers, although part of her heritage, were a waste of time. She did not approve of any talk of gods, goddesses, battles, or mythical creatures. This mystified Seba, especially given that most of the ancient stories he'd learned had come from her own father, Seba's Papouli. Indeed, Papouli often said there were just as many gods, goddesses, battles, and otherworldly creatures in the Bible, if we took the time to look.

Agnete's eyes darted from the book to Seba's bandaged head and her expression softened. "Is it a medical text? Doctor Turnbull offered to take you on as an apprentice?" Agnete clasped her hands in front of her heart.

Dr. Turnbull deftly removed the book from Seba's hands, making sure to keep the title well hidden. He quickly returned it to his trunk and closed the lid. "Agnete, your son would make an excellent surgeon. He's very determined."

Paolo wiggled his eyebrows at his friend. "Doctor Krizomatis. I like it. If I or one of the crew gets in a scrape, you can patch us up."

"*Mister* Krizomatis, if you please," said Dr. Turnbull. "The title of doctor is reserved for we few who attain the degree of *Medicinae Doctor*. But there's nothing preventing Seba from apprenticing as a surgeon's mate. Paolo is quite right, after all. I can't be everywhere at once, can I? It would be a capital idea to take on an apprentice. Seba's disciplined and not easily distracted. Born in late December, if memory serves." He tipped Seba a wink.

Agnete ushered the young woman forward. "Fernanda Rementeria Arandia, I would like you to meet my son, Sebastian Krizomatis." She squeezed Fernanda's arm as if to say, *That's my son. You'd like to marry him, wouldn't you?* "And his mentor, the illustrious Doctor Andrew Turnbull."

The physician bowed deeply. "It is my honor to make your acquaintance, Miss Rementeria Arandia." Turning to Agnete, he said, "What's this of a new home? You know, I've asked Mahón's lead councilwoman, Madam Jurada Theodora Alexiano, to assist me in finding acceptable lodgings for your family and my other Greek volunteers. Your living expenses shall be covered by myself and my investors."

Agnete dismissed him with a wave of her hand. "No, no,

no. I've made arrangements with Fernanda and her family myself. She lives with her sister, Camila, and her brother, Ignasi. They have a gorgeous estate west of town."

Dr. Turnbull raised his eyebrows. "You never cease to astound me. Seba must inherit his determination from the maternal line."

Agnete curtsied demurely. "Meeting this Menorcan family was divine providence. Every day I prayed for deliverance from this infernal ship, and my prayers have been answered."

It was Fernanda's turn to curtsy, after which she strode toward Seba's berth, her leather boots clicking resolutely on the wooden floor. She offered Seba a very firm handshake. "It's a pleasure to make your acquaintance, Sebastian. Your mother and Paolo told me of your injuries." Her voice was smooth and self-assured. "I am sorry that your first day in Mahón resulted in harm, but it is also the reason I met your mother."

Fernanda turned to Agnete and flashed her a smile. "When we learned of the attack, we ran to the wharf to offer our assistance. That's where we encountered your parents, who had just arrived from Quarantine Island. God brought them to us, and we are honored to share our home with you. I trust you are recovering well." She spoke slowly and her Greek was heavily accented, but Seba understood her perfectly.

Dr. Turnbull said, "Your Greek is quite good. Are you related to the Alexiano family?"

Fernanda turned and took Dr. Turnbull's hand into both of hers, shaking it with such vigor that Dr. Turnbull wagged his eyebrows at Seba. "My family is Menorcan, but my sister and I are childhood friends of Nicolas Alexiano, nephew to Alexander Alexiano and his twin sister, Theodora. My sister

Camila is engaged to Nicolas." A momentary frown crossed her face. "Perhaps I should say she *was* engaged to him. In any case, he has tutored us in Greek since we were children."

"Nicolas, eh?" Dr. Turnbull snapped his fingers as if remembering something important. "Ah yes, now I recall! Theodora has mentioned him. He's the youngest son of her older brother, also named Nicolas. Formidable Greek stock, like my beloved Maria Gracia du Robin."

Fernanda's gaze flitted across to Dr. Turnbull's trunk. "Nicolas advised that if I continue my studies, one day I may be able to read the great Greek playwright, Aristophanes, in his native language." She smiled sweetly at Dr. Turnbull and winked at Sebastian.

Seba felt his face get hot, and Dr. Turnbull pulled a face at him. Seba knew he and the doctor were thinking the same thing: *She's sharp.*

Fernanda turned toward Agnete and said, "We are glad to have you as our guests in Mahón for as long as you wish. I believe my sister and brother will benefit greatly from your nurturing presence."

"You must keep track of your expenses," Dr. Turnbull said. "You will be properly compensated for your contribution to our cause. I've not met Theodora's nephew Nicolas, but I expect that I shall someday have the chance."

Fernanda said, "Thank you, Doctor Turnbull. This island has been my family's home for many generations, and we will be here long after you and your novitiates are gone. No compensation is necessary. We are proud to show our new Greek friends the hospitality of the Menorcans."

Seba expected Dr. Turnbull to insist upon paying, but instead he smiled warmly. "Your munificence is unsurpassed, Miss Fernanda. My investors and I are deeply indebted to you. If there is any favor whatsoever I can bestow on you or your magnanimous family, please do not hesitate to make your needs known to me."

Agnete kissed Seba on the forehead. "*Antío*, my darling boy. Doctor Turnbull says you'll be well enough to join us in Mahón tomorrow. We'll have everything ready for you when you arrive. There's a friend of Fernanda's coming to row you to port. He's a charming boy; Kristobal is his name."

# 8 NICOLAS

*August 10, 1767*
*Port Mahón Harbor, Menorca*
*Evening*

Seba packed his meager belongings in preparation for the next day, excited that his week-long stint on the ship as Dr. Turnbull's captive audience was coming to a close. Dr. Turnbull had accepted an invitation to dine with Captain Alexiano in his quarters, and offered to bring Seba along, but Seba declined, pleased to have the physician's spacious rooms to himself for the evening.

He was surprised to see Paolo for a second time that day. His friend returned to the *New Fortuna* that evening with a young wine merchant he'd met at the wharf. "Seba, this is Nicolas Alexiano. He's the captain's nephew, the one Fernanda told us about this morning."

Nicolas resembled Captain Alexiano in size and shape,

with dark tight curls around his head, a sharp chin, and thick eyebrows. The primary difference was that Nicolas's beard was tidy and well-groomed while his uncle's was wild and wiry. Nicolas wore a loose cream-colored linen shirt with voluminous sleeves gathered at the wrist and dark wool trousers that stopped above his soft leather boots. A wide silk sash in deep burgundy was wrapped around his waist, and atop his head sat a black wool, flat-crowned cap with a small visor and a decorative maroon braid around the circumference. He looked every bit the successful merchant who dressed for the practicalities of maritime life. He held out his hand to Seba.

"Nicolas Alexiano, at your service. I've been visiting with my uncle before I leave for Corsica tomorrow morning. He and Doctor Turnbull speak highly of you."

Sebastian introduced himself. "Would you like something to eat? Doctor Turnbull is dining with your uncle, but they told the cook to deliver the same meal to me here. I've plenty to share." Seba pointed to the mahogany dining table, on which the cook had earlier placed dishes of cured olives, hard-boiled quail eggs, anchovies, slices of fresh melon, and grilled sea bream with charred tomatoes and a dish of thick, creamy sauce that the cook said was a Menorcan favorite.

"I had a bite with my uncle and the doctor, but when you're sailing, you never know when you'll eat. I appreciate the invitation. Particularly when the fish sauce is *La Mahonesa*."

Noticing his companions' puzzled expressions, Nicolas pointed to the pale yellow condiment. "It's simple, really, but nothing compares to the flavor. Egg yolks, Menorcan salt, a few drops of vinegar, and a good quantity of olive oil. Beat them together until a sweat forms on your brow, and you've created a Menorcan masterpiece named for our great city of Mahón."

Paolo's face lit up with a curious smile. "A Menorcan food I haven't yet tried? Don't mind if I do." He seated himself in a green-cushioned chair and cut several discs from a length of cured sobrassada before loading his plate with a large portion from each dish, liberally slathering everything with the mahonesa. "Nicolas, what are you waiting for?" he said. "Take a seat and fill your plate. Seba hasn't seen the town yet, and it's his last night under doctor's orders. Tomorrow he'll be free to explore the bounty of Menorca. We need to celebrate."

Nicolas pulled a pouch from his sash and tossed it in the air, easily catching it in his palm. "Congratulations, Seba. You're going to love Mahón. In light of our celebration, I will donate these rosemary-spiced candied almonds that I won from a trader in Malaga. He and his friends thought they could best me in a game of Crown and Anchor, but the dice were on my side. These sweet treats were all they had left after I'd won their silver."

Seba tilted his head to the side. "Crown and Anchor? I've never heard of it."

Nicolas laughed and took the seat opposite Paolo. "Today is your lucky day. I'm happy to teach you. I'm not too proud to say you'll be learning from the best."

Paolo stopped short, his hand holding an anchovy sandwiched between two slices of melon. "We should eat first, then you can teach him your games. Seba has a head injury, so it's probably best he fills his belly before you go filling his noggin."

Seba said wryly, "What would I do without you, Paolo? You always have my best interests at heart."

"Yes, I do. To that end, we, er—I mean you—need a

portion of potables to wash down your meal." Paolo's eyes scouted the room, landing on a nondescript walnut cabinet tucked away against a bulkhead.

"Paolo, no. The liquor cabinet is locked, and Doctor Turnbull keeps the key on his person."

Paolo pouted like a child. "We need libations to properly celebrate your release."

Seba grabbed a bottle from Dr. Turnbull's writing desk. "This, however, was given to Doctor Turnbull by the captain, and Doctor Turnbull gifted it to me. He said it was made by a Greek family from Corsica."

Nicolas laughed. "Ha! That's one of mine. I gave it to my uncle yesterday. It's an excellent wine, and the doctor is correct. It's from one of the best winemaking families in Corsica, who happen to be Greek like us."

Seba retrieved three small-stemmed glasses from the sideboard. "It must be divine providence, as my mother always says." He poured wine into their glasses and they held them in the air. *"Stin ygeía mas!"*

When the three young men had filled their stomachs and shared their favorite ancient Greek deities and demigods (Hephaestus for Seba, Heracles for Paolo, and Dionysus for Nicolas), Nicolas said, "Are you ready to gamble?"

Paolo wagged his finger at Nicolas. "You're not taking my silver, what little I have."

"Not to worry, Paolo. We'll make bets with my candied almonds in place of silver. I brought them to share, so the victor eats the winnings. What do you say?"

Paolo relaxed. "That's all I needed to hear. Edible winnings are better than silver, as far as I'm concerned."

Artemis must have decided that the boys would provide her a better meal than the rats on the orlop deck, because she appeared on the windowsill of Dr. Turnbull's quarters at that very moment. Seba placed a few discs of sobrassada and a dollop of mahonesa on a small plate for her under Dr. Turnbull's writing desk, and she tucked in as if she were as hungry as Paolo.

Nicolas spread the worn oilcloth board across the table, with six symbols, slightly faded, at the edges: heart, diamond, spade, club, crown, and anchor.

"It's simple," said Nicolas, shaking the dice in a wooden cup. "Pick a symbol and place your wager. If your symbol comes up on one die, you win even money. Two dice, double. All three? Triple your stake."

Seba eyed the anchor skeptically. "And if it doesn't show?"

"Then you lose." Nicolas grinned. "The mathematical probabilities indicate you'll love the crown but get stuck with the club. That's what the game's banker anticipates."

Nicolas generously taught them his secrets for reading other people's reactions and making bets with the best odds, as Artemis looked on with detached indifference. It was easy to see why Nicolas was a successful wine merchant: he had an amusing personal anecdote for any subject, a boisterous laugh, and a generous disposition. As the night wore on, Seba couldn't help but think that Nicolas might be descended directly from Dionysus, the Greek god of wine and theater.

"Did I tell you about the time I accidentally sold communion wine to a brothel?"

Seba and Paolo said in unison, "How?"

"My wagon was stacked five feet high with wine barrels that day, two barrels designated as sacramental wine, each crafted under the bishop's strict regulations. I delivered the first barrel of communion wine to the church in the morning and went about my deliveries for the day. By late afternoon,

I had two barrels left over, and the brothel's proprietress offered to pay me double for them. I was so thrilled by the sale and distracted by the goings on at her establishment, I forgot about the last stop on my route. As I made my way back to the harbor, an altar boy flagged me down, saying I'd skipped my last delivery, a small chapel in the fields above the village. It was then that I realized that my last sale, quite without the bishop's involvement, would likely sanctify half the town."

Paolo raised his glass of Corsican vermentino. "Here's to salvation—"

Seba clinked Paolo's glass. "—from unexpected sources."

They laughed until their faces ached as Nicolas told stories about his time in Corsica, Malaga, Leghorn, and Sardinia. Nicolas also knew everyone in and everything about Port Mahón. "The place is prospering since the British have returned. They regained control of the island four years ago, and they're trying to create another maritime stronghold like Gibraltar. Good for trade. And even better for King George's naval superiority."

Seba thought of his home island of Chios, conquered first by the Genoese and then by the Ottomans. "And the people of Menorca?" he said. "How do they feel about it?"

Nicolas shrugged. "If we must serve one or the other of the great powers, we could do worse than the British. They've taken a heavy hand with some of the Menorcan people, it's true, but there are bound to be growing pains under a new regime."

"Your aunt sits on the local council, is that right?"

Nicolas nodded, swallowing the last of his wine. "And if you think my Uncle Alexander is a sturdy character, wait until you meet my Aunt Theodora. She's as flinty as iron, although you'd never guess it at first glance."

"A politician *and* a baker?" Paolo said in a wondering tone.

Nicolas leaned in. "That she is. An exceptional politician, but I believe she prefers the baking." He worked the hair of his well-trimmed beard with his thumb and continued, "I dare say my aunt has her hands full trying to keep the peace between the Royal Navy and the locals."

Paolo said, "What is everyone fighting about? I'd think they'd all work together against the pirates."

"Pirates are not the only cause of conflict," Nicolas said. "Everyone wants something different on this island, everything from security and resources to recognition and influence. It's my Aunt Theodora's job to keep everyone happy."

Seba said, "If she's anything like the captain, then Port Mahón is lucky to have her. I'm eager to see the town. And our new home."

"It's a grand estate, the Rementeria residence," Paolo said. "It brings to mind those merchant homes that dot the hills above Smyrna, with the walled gardens and outbuildings. Remember Doctor Robin's home, Seba? Fernanda's farm is similar. A Menorcan paradise."

Nicolas's shoulders dropped. "Yes, it's a wonderful farmstead. I've known Fernanda and Camila since we were children. Ignasi is a few years younger." But for the first time all evening, there was no enthusiasm in his voice.

Seba frowned. "Nicolas, what is it? You don't find them acceptable? Should we look for lodgings elsewhere?"

Nicolas tried, and failed, to recover his companionable manner. "It's nothing. They're a wonderful family. Kind and generous. And their home is as beautiful as you say, Paolo."

Paolo leaned in. "Stop ducking the subject and tell us what's on your mind."

Seba added, "Yes, perhaps we can help you."

Nicolas thrust his hands out. "I'm not here to burden you with my troubles. Let's talk of something else."

Paolo tapped the table. "Nicolas, we're all Greek, for goodness' sake. If we're not here to carry each other's burdens, then what's the point of our heritage?"

"You'll feel better if you tell us," Seba added. "We've faced many dangers; we can handle whatever it is."

"Fine," Nicolas sighed. "But I warn you, it's a sad tale." He took a deep breath and squared his shoulders. "I became engaged to Camila several months ago. I've been waiting most of my life to marry her. I've loved her since we were five years old. She accidentally dropped a basket of apples on my head as we helped our parents in the orchards, and I knew in that moment that we were meant for each other."

Paolo was enraptured. "What happened? She left you for another? I know how that feels."

Nicolas shrugged. "A few weeks ago, she called off the engagement. She wouldn't tell me why. Fernanda tells me Camila is not herself. She claims she is no longer fit to be a wife." He clenched his fists helplessly. "I want to help her, to comfort her. Anything that may have happened to her cannot change my feelings. But she won't listen to me. She won't even speak to me. How am I going to marry my love when she won't confide her troubles to me?"

Seba stood and put his arm on Nicolas's shoulder. "Don't worry, Nicolas. My mother is the most tenacious Greek woman to walk this earth, and if we're going to be living with Camila, my mother will sort it out. She'll have you married before you can say 'Crown and Anchor.'"

Nicolas smiled, but it was half-hearted. "I don't know,

Seba. I pray your prediction comes true. I'm thankful that God brought us together, my new friends. You've given me hope when I thought there was none. If you and your family are able to reunite me with the woman I love, I will be forever indebted to you." Nicolas returned the oilcloth and dice to their canvas pouch and pulled a brass pocket watch from his sash. "It's long past midnight, and my ship leaves for Corsica in a few hours. I'd best be on my way."

He shook Paolo's hand, then Seba's, and turned to leave. He immediately reconsidered and ran back to draw them both into a bear hug. "God bless you, my friends. And welcome to Menorca."

#

After Nicolas left, Paolo and Seba considered what they'd learned. Seba said, "I like Nicolas. He reminds me of my Papouli. I want to help him."

Paolo nodded. "He's a good man, a successful merchant, and barrels of fun. He's got more seafaring stories than Doctor Turnbull *and* he knows how to stick to the subject at hand." He looked thoughtful. "Fernanda says Nicolas travels quite extensively, and his return home is always cause for celebration."

"Did Fernanda say anything about Camila's change of heart?"

Paolo shook his head. "I'm guessing there was some bad business with the British. No one will say it outright, but they drop hints. Not only did Camila call off the wedding, but their brother Ignasi was arrested just before we arrived."

"Will my parents be safe there? Is the family an enemy of the government?"

Paolo flicked his wrist, as if brushing away a fly. "It's nothing like that, I don't think. Nicolas told me that unruly locals are always being arrested for one thing or another. Even the soldiers are publicly flogged if they break the rules. The government gives them all a few lashes in the town square, then sends them along their way."

That didn't quite add up for Seba, but as always, Paolo seemed sure of himself. "In any case, I believe your mother has taken it upon herself to convince Camila that if she loves Nicolas and he loves her, nothing should keep them apart. Now that Camila's engagement will be your mother's primary focus, she'll be too busy to try to manage your life for you. You'll never have to worry about her embarrassing you again." He swiped his hands together as if brushing off dust. "Everyone wins."

"And what about my father? Their home sounds a far distance from any physician. He needs care."

"Fernanda cares for their horses," Paolo said. "Great gorgeous black beauties called Menorquín. I've never seen anything like them, and they're very important to the island. Fernanda knows so much about these horses' muscles and organs that she's practically a physician herself. Your father's already taken to her in the short time they've known each other, asking her a thousand questions about the stables, what the horses eat, how Fernanda cares for them, and how she and Camila train them. Last night, your father and Fernanda talked for hours about how to mend broken bones. Their jabbering put me right to sleep. You've nothing to worry about."

Seba leaned back in Dr. Turnbull's high-backed chair. *From your mouth to God's ears.*

# 9 COUSINS



*August 11, 1767*
*Mahón, Menorca*
*Morning*

The next day, Fernanda arrived on a small skiff that pulled alongside the *New Fortuna* to retrieve Seba; she was accompanied by another young woman, whom Seba knew instantly must be her sister. The resemblance was unmistakable, though Fernanda was taller. The petite girl's hair was tawny rather than red, but she too wore it short, falling in waves to her collarbones. She seemed a smaller, gentler version of her confident sister. *That must be Camila.*

Both women were dressed modestly, with long caramel-colored skirts topped with coral-tinted overskirts open at the front. They wore identical long-sleeved shirts, a dark chestnut color that Seba imagined must be hot to wear in the midday sun, and their shoulders were draped with sheer white lace shawls. Both wore richly embroidered head scarves, Fernanda's a coppery color scrolled with viridian vines and Camila's a pale pink dotted with bright red poppies. Camila carried a woven basket with a long curved handle, from which a twisted loaf of bread and several golden apples peeked out. The skiff bobbed in the water as wake from passing ships lapped against its shallow hull, but Camila remained implacable on the thwart, never looking up from the basket.

A boy whom Seba guessed must be the Kristobal of whom his mother had spoken, steered the skiff through the choppy water. The boat was eighteen feet long and Kristobal looked to be younger than twelve, but he operated the skiff like a seasoned sailor. There was an extra set of oars for a strong-armed passenger to assist him in rowing to port when his boat was overloaded with cargo and travelers.

On this trip, however, Kristobal had only three passengers. Aside from Fernanda and Camila, there was a large, furry dog, nearly as big as a donkey, sitting straight and tall on the bow like a captain surveying the tide. Then it ran to the stern and howled at a nearby fishing boat. The beast sounded like an oversized chanticleer heralding the dawn.

As Seba and Kristobal secured the mooring lines, Seba laughed aloud to see the enormous dog stretched out across the thwarts between the sisters as if he were a king and they, his imperial litter bearers. His head lolled on Camila's lap next to the basket of bread, and his tail slapped a happy rhythm on Fernanda's leg. Camila gripped the dog's neck as if it were a lifeline.

Fernanda shoved the enormous dog from his perch. "*Kaliméra*, Seba! I've brought my sister, Camila, to escort you to our new home." She introduced the skiff's pilot: "This is Kristobal, the unofficial mayor of Mahón." The dog crowed; Fernanda rolled her eyes and added, "*And* his big baby, Gall."

Seba waved to them, then turned back and nodded his thanks to the *New Fortuna*, his floating home for the past year. *I'll get my parents settled, and I'll be back on board before you can say galaktoboureko.*

Seba climbed into Kristobal's small boat. "It's a pleasure to make your acquaintance, Camila and Kristobal. Thank you for coming back for me. I wish I could have helped my family move into your home, Camila. I will do what I can to repay your generosity."

Camila's ears turned maroon, and she lowered her eyes to the floorboards.

"Bah!" Fernanda spoke quickly to fill the awkward silence. "We are practically cousins now, Seba. Your parents found several Greek relatives in common with my sister's fiancé, Nicolas. There is no obligation to repay the kindness of family, is there?"

"That's what my Papouli always tells me," Seba said. "But I *am* grateful. I don't know what to say."

"That's for the best," Fernanda snorted. "The men in this town do too much talking anyway. And don't worry, we'll find plenty of jobs on the farm for you if you want to work. Won't we, Camila?"

Camila spoke shyly, but her Greek was as good as, if not better than, Fernanda's. "Seba is our guest. Be kind, sister." Her eyes welled and her voice trembled. "And please, stop mentioning Nicolas. He is *not* my fiancé."

Fernanda looked exasperated. "Not *that* again! Of course he is, and Seba is his cousin, so we're all a happy family. That includes Nicolas, who was smitten the day you dropped that ridiculous basket of apples on his head."

Camila winced, but remained silent, her grip on Gall as

tight as a vise. Gall licked her face and his howl pierced the air. "Aahhrrooooo!"

Kristobal spoke up at last, and his accent was markedly better than either Camila or Fernanda's. "Pleased to meet you, Seba. I apologize for Gall's boisterous howling. He can't help himself; that's why we named him 'Gall'. It's Menorquín for 'rooster.'" Kristobal may have looked like a street urchin, but his manner was that of a man of the world. He sounded like the old Greek sailors on the *New Fortuna's* crew. He looked like them, as well, with his scruffy face, unkempt dark hair that stuck out in all directions, fingernails so dirty they looked like the black claws of a bear, and scrawny arms and legs that poked out from a shirt and trousers two sizes too big.

Twenty minutes later, during which time Kristobal did most of the talking, they disembarked at Port Mahón's wharf. Fernanda gave Kristobal a few coins, an apple from Camila's basket, and a kiss on each cheek. He bowed graciously and busied himself securing the oars before heading off to assist a fisherman mooring at the pier's opposite end.

Seba followed Fernanda and Camila up the steep steps carved into the cliff. At the top, the town of Mahón opened before them like a cormorant spreading its wings. Fernanda said, "Before we tour the town, turn around and prepare to be dazzled. This bird's eye view is my favorite."

Seba turned and gasped. The sun sparkled over Mahón's harbor, tiny diamonds winking and hopping across the tongue of bright blue water that stretched out toward the east. White sails puffed and billowed below, pushing various vessels along the inlet as the anglers, traders, and local salt merchants brought their catches and caches to the people of Mahón. The breeze carried a hint of coolness off the ocean, signaling that autumn would soon be shortening the days and sending Menorca's inhabitants indoors for the winter. But for now, the sky was a glorious blue dabbed with cottony clouds of white, lavender, and pink, beneath which the gulls and pelicans soared, searching for their next meals.

The port-based midshipmen were hard at work, hammering, sawing, and expanding the Royal Navy's new pier. The job had been halted by the privateer attack, and now took on new urgency. The port was alive with the energy of renewal, and the island appeared to welcome the attention.

"You should see it at sunset," Fernanda said. "The sky catches fire and reflects over the water so the whole harbor glows like the forges of Vulcan."

Camila smiled wryly at that. Fernanda explained, "When our mother was alive, she didn't like it when we spoke about the old gods of our culture; she said we were blaspheming the Lord. We tried to tell her that to us, they are as present as Santa Maria, Marta, Jesús, and the saints."

"You've just painted a perfect portrait of my own mother," Seba said. "She used to chase me with a wooden spoon if I asked my grandfather about the deities of Olympus. If she caught me talking about them, she made me recite Bible verses all afternoon." He smiled. "I won't tell if you won't."

Fernanda giggled; even Camila's mouth turned upward in the faintest hint of a smile. She said, "Perhaps you are a harbinger of better things to come."

The cobbled streets climbed and curved between rows of painted buildings with wooden shutters flung wide. Laundry flapped happily from iron balconies and the familiar clack of donkey hooves on stone echoed down the narrow lanes, its subtle rhythm low and comforting beneath the chatter of townsfolk about their daily chores.

Market stalls spilled out from every lane, the aromas mixing and mingling in the salt-tinged air. Fresh figs were piled beside stacks of grilled fish, barrels overflowed with cured olives, and wedges of cheese peeked out from folded fig leaves. The smell was warm and ripe: sea brine, crushed herbs, and the ever-present trace of manure. A boy skipped past with a basket of fresh-baked bread, and in the distance a fiddler played a tune that reminded Seba of his grandfather's favorite dance, the *tripatos*.

To Seba, who was accustomed to the broad boulevards of Smyrna and the hushed skinos groves of Chios, Mahón felt both crowded and expansive. Spanish, British, and Menorcan voices crisscrossed like ship's rigging under a headwind, and each brightly painted doorway boasted a new flavor, fresco, or face for Seba to explore.

Camila pointed to the west. "Our home is a short walk from here, not far from the western gates of Mahón."

As they meandered past the market stalls, Seba observed Camila's behavior. She was composed until they approached anyone in a British uniform; at that point, she shrank behind her sister, pulled her scarf tight around her face, and kept her head down.

A young child ran to Camila and threw her arms around Camila's legs. As Camila bent down to greet the little girl, Seba held Fernanda back to ask a question.

"What's wrong with your sister? Every time she sees a uniform, she retreats into her shell like a tortoise."

Fernanda lowered her voice. "I know, Seba. It's awful. She was attacked by a drunken British officer several weeks ago. She wakes up screaming every night. It's horrible."

"Attacked?" Seba's eyes grew wide as Fernanda's

meaning became clear. "I'm so sorry."

"And to make matters worse, Camila was to marry Nicolas, as I said on the ship. She broke off the engagement after she was assaulted, claiming she is no longer a suitable bride for him."

"I met Nicolas last night. It's obvious he loves Camila very much."

"I agree, Seba. Nicolas is a wonderful person. He's made a good name for himself as a wine merchant and he knows everyone in town. Camila thinks if Nicolas marries her, it will ruin his business."

Seba pursed his lips. "I don't think Nicolas agrees."

Fernanda scoffed. "Of course he doesn't. He thinks it's nonsense, as do I. He's loved her since we were young, all attending the convent's school together. Look at her! She loves children; all she ever wanted was to raise a big loving family with Nicolas. Now she's isolated herself, saying she'll mourn the loss of her maidenhood forever."

Camila said goodbye to the little girl; when she looked at Seba and Fernanda, her eyes shone with tears.

Seba recalled a quote that his teacher, Brother Timotheos, had him memorize from the great Greek tragedian, Aeschylus: *God has to all the world ordained, that wisdom shall be gained by pain. And drop by drop into the heart, thus learning comes unbid, unsought.*

At each market stall, Fernanda greeted the owner by name and asked after their families, desperately trying (and failing) to include Camila in her palaver. Seba couldn't understand their conversations, so he drifted away toward the cheesemongers' stalls, drawn by the buttery scent of aged rinds and the soft tang of sea salt.

Under the woven canopies, wheels of Mahón cheese were stacked like huge gold coins, their rinds rubbed with olive oil and paprika until they glowed a rich russet color. Apron-clad vendors cut thick wedges with knives stained orange at the tips, offering samples on curled fig leaves. *"Tierno,"* one said, proffering a soft slice that oozed at the edge. *"Curado,"* said another, tapping a firmer wedge that smelled of almonds and brine. Seba tasted both, savoring the grass and salt air in each bite, the flavor of the very island magically imbued to the cheese.

On the cobbled streetcorner, cured meats, sausages, and smoked bacon were strung across wooden racks under bright canopies, beckoning Seba with the aroma of paprika, fennel, garlic, and black pepper. A girl fanned flies from a coil of sausages with a long rosemary switch, while an old butcher in a wide-brimmed hat shaved fine curls from a cured loin onto a slab of wood. *I'd like to taste one of those.*

Fernanda caught up to Seba and, without a word, purchased a thin sausage from the man in the hat. She broke it into three pieces as Camila rejoined the group. Fernanda offered the sausage to Seba and Camila, Seba wondering if mind-reading was another one of Fernanda's many talents.

She said, "Seba, this is *carnixulla*, a traditional raw sausage of Menorca. It has been prepared here since the time of Christ."

Seba took a bite; the sausage melted in his mouth, a celebration of savor, salt, and spicy black peppercorns. He took a deep breath and smiled, remembering Paolo's words from the prior week. *I believe I'm going to like it here.*

#

Outside the town, verdant hills rose up as the elevation increased, resplendent with bursting orchards, fields of barley, and sylvan pastures. Large brown and white cows leisurely strolled the hills, stopping to graze before congregating under the shade of an oak or wild olive tree.

They followed a dirt path that wound through the hills until they came to a stacked stone wall that marked the Rementerias' home. It stretched on as far as Seba could see in either direction.

A brace of wooden gates were attached to either side of a break in the stone wall. There were seven horizontal bars across, made with wild olivewood limbs at least six feet long on each gate. They were only a few inches around, with three slightly thicker shoots to the right, left, and center, running perpendicular to the seven slats. The top slat was rounded, making the shape of an arch, and there were diagonal supports from the top corner to the bottom where they attached to the stone wall. It was sturdy and beautiful, like a piece of art welcoming visitors to their home.

Seeing Seba's fascinated gaze, Fernanda said, "Oh, do you like the *barrera*? It's made from *ullastre*, the wild olive tree that grows everywhere on Menorca. My father took great care to create the flowing shape."

"It reminds me of the arches in our village church in Sessera."

Fernanda tapped the stone wall. "The dry stone walls keep the cows and sheep inside, and the *barreres* do well to withstand the elements. We can't make fences out of wood here; the *tramontana* winds are so strong that our animals would be halfway to Ciutadella if we didn't have these." She opened the gate. "You'll see. When the tramontana blow, there is no escape."

Camila shuddered as Fernanda closed the gate behind them. Seba could see a large stone farmhouse in the distance, as well as stables, a barn, and lots of sheep, cows, and goats roaming the fields. "Come meet the pride of the family," Fernanda said.

They walked along a dirt path to the stables, and Seba

stopped short. Two shiny black horses, taller than any he'd ever seen, were demurely munching grass in the pasture east of the stables.

Seba had seen camels in the caravans bringing Silk Road goods into Smyrna; they had been as tall as these horses, but slow and plodding. These ebony Menorcan horses were sleek and stately, almost human. *You're stunning.* The horses raised their heads and Seba could have sworn that they nodded at him before returning their attention to the sweet grass beneath their hooves. *Perhaps they're the ones who taught Fernanda to read minds.*

Camila took a small apple from her basket and offered it to one of the horses, who nuzzled her shoulder before gently taking the fruit in her teeth. The other horse snorted and Camila laughed, taking another apple from the basket and extending it in her hand. The second horse stamped its foot before taking two steps toward Camila and snatching the apple from her outstretched palm.

Camila seemed as comfortable with the horses as she had been with the giant dog Gall or with the child in the marketplace. A favorite Bible verse came to Seba's mind: "Let the little children come to me and do not hinder them, for to such belongs the kingdom of heaven." *She's a gentle soul; look how she bonds with God's guileless creatures.* When she smiled at her horse, her face came alive in a way that made Seba think of the midday sun sparkling over the harbor.

Camila said, "This high-spirited fellow is Euros. He and Fernanda are cut from the same cloth, as if you couldn't tell." She reached up to pat the other horse's shoulder. "And this is my darling Zephyr. She is as swift as the west wind for which she's named."

Fernanda asked, "Seba, have you ever ridden a horse?"

"No," he admitted. "But I rode my family's donkey, Matilde, back in my village on Chios."

Fernanda broke into peals of laughter and Seba's face bloomed scarlet. Camila's eyes grew wide and her mouth twitched upward, but she held in her giggles. Camila's kindness caused Seba's face to flush an even deeper shade of red.

"Ba-ha-ha-ha, a donkey!" Fernanda slapped her leg in merriment. Camila shot her sister a stern look, but when their eyes met, her own reserve crumbled. Soon the sisters were tittering at each other like a duo of Balearic warblers. Even the horses joined in the merriment, their heads bobbing up and down as if they'd never heard anything so funny.

This kind of embarrassment would have sent Seba running to the stone roof of his village home when he was a boy, but his Papouli had explained that being humiliated by a girl was a rite of passage for every Greek man. Seba tried to remember exactly what Papouli had said to make him feel better, but he couldn't concentrate with Camila and Fernanda falling all over themselves.

Fernanda finally caught her breath. "Phew! Camila and I haven't laughed that hard for ages. Thanks, Seba." Fernanda used a large rock as a mounting block, twisted her hands around Euros's mane, and pulled herself onto his back. "Euros loves a good joke, don't you, boy? Why don't we show Seba the difference between a donkey and a Menorcan *cavall*?"

Euros and Fernanda trotted over to the dirt path leading to the house, Euros's tail swishing right to left as he basked in the attention. When they reached the hardened path, Euros reared up as if it were the most normal thing in the world for a horse to do, and began walking on his back legs, with Fernanda clutching his mane so as not to slide off his back. After they had walked about twenty yards, they turned around and walked the other direction on the path, Euros finally dropping his front legs and trotting toward Seba, his dark lips pulled back in what appeared to be a satisfied smile.

"That's amazing! How did you train him to do that?"

Fernanda said, "Oh, it's not me training him; it's the two of us communicating with each other. A true partnership in every respect. If your donkey-riding skills are as you say, perhaps Euros might permit you to ride him, as well."

Camila patted the other horse's neck. "Perhaps Zephyr would be a better choice, sister. She's fast, but very gentle." Camila giggled. "And she's not nearly as stubborn as a donkey."

The sisters helped Seba climb onto Zephyr's back. "I'm curious," he said. "Why do your horses have names from the Greek stories?"

It was Camila who answered. "Mahón has a vibrant Greek population, what with the proximity to Corsica, and Greek islanders fleeing Ottoman rule." She led Zephyr slowly around the field as she spoke, Fernanda and Euros walking beside them. "We've grown up with the Greek stories. Fernanda and I have known Nicolas and the Alexiano family since we learned to walk. Our father, before he passed, said he didn't care what we named the horses as long as they could walk on their hind legs for the entire length of *Carrer de Ciutadella*."

"Does your brother ride as well?"

Camila stopped short and Fernanda frowned, sending a shiver up Seba's spine. *I guess I should have kept my mouth shut about their brother.*

Fernanda inhaled long and slow, as if gathering the

courage to speak. "Ignasi does not ride," she said. "Perhaps we can discuss it another time, Seba. Suffice it to say that he's been arrested, despite the fact that he's done nothing wrong."

Camila turned and ran toward the house.

Seba shook his head. "I'm so sorry. I didn't mean to upset her," he said. "It was the first time she seemed happy all day, and I ruined it."

"It's not your fault, Seba. We can't discuss our brother around Camila, because she feels responsible for his arrest, even though neither of them was at fault." Her brown boots stomped the ground, kicking up a cloud of dust. "Oh, I wish these occupiers would leave us alone! We managed quite well for many years without their interference."

Seba had a hundred questions, but Fernanda seemed too upset to talk; indeed, she was on the verge of tears, far from the high-spirited girl he had met yesterday. He would have to wait.

# 10 ON THE FARM



*August 11, 1767*
*Mahón, Menorca*
*Late Afternoon*

Seba and Fernanda returned the horses to the stables and trekked up the hill to the house. The late afternoon light slanted low across the hills, gilding the dry grass and stone walls as Seba followed Fernanda up the path. The farmhouse emerged above the sloping hill, a substantial structure. Its stone façade was sun-bleached and timeworn, with warm umber trim outlining the doors and windows like an old grandmother watching over her brood.

The house showed signs of having grown with the family over the generations: wings added in stone of slightly different hues, lintels patched, and rooflines staggered with varying shades of earth-baked clay. A covered terrace stretched along one side, shaded by weathered wooden beams and a climbing vine boasting effusive blooms of blue jasmine. Chickens scratched in the dust nearby, and the smell of rosemary drifted from an herb garden beside the kitchen door. The muted green paint of the shutters, open to catch the breeze, contrasted with the terra cotta tiles nestled on the roof above. Seba could almost imagine generations of riders returning from festivals, tired horses resting in the stables below, and music drifting up the hills from the town.

As they neared the large oak front door, Seba saw his mother standing beside his father, her arm wrapped around his waist. Kostas leaned on his eagle-handled cane wearing a wide smile. Seba's parents were positively beaming.

Agnete ran to Seba and squeezed him. "My darling Sebastian! Look around. The Lord has answered my prayers and led us to these beautiful angels, Camila and Fernanda! Thanks be to God, I will never set foot on a nauseating sailing ship again!"

"I'm glad you're happy here, Mama," Seba said. "I can tell that Camila and Fernanda have taken good care of you and Papa."

"Yes, they have." Agnete put her hands on the sisters' faces and drew them close to her. "I know your parents in heaven are so proud of you."

After a moment, Kostas said brightly, "Why don't the angels show Seba to his room?"

"Of course," said Fernanda. "Kostas, Agnete, please make yourselves comfortable in the kitchen. Perhaps Seba would like some of that delicious Greek coffee that Nicolas procured for us last week."

The three young people walked to the end of a corridor and Camila opened the door to a spacious room with a large window, a wooden bedframe with a straw mattress covered with a cotton quilt striped in red and gold, a wooden table with a washbasin and pitcher, and a stack of men's work clothes, neatly folded, resting on a chair in the corner next to a set of sturdy leather boots. Seba was incredulous. "This is all for me?"

Fernanda nodded. "We noticed that none of you brought much with you from the ship, so we divided up our father's clothes and gave some to Kostas. The remainder are here, along with Papa's old boots. We hope they'll fit you."

"I'm sure they will be perfect," Seba said, looking around the room. "I've never had this much space to myself in my life. In my village on Chios, I shared a sleeping space next to my grandfather when I wasn't sleeping on the roof, and in Smyrna I slept in the loft over my friend Buğra's animal pen." He laughed. "And I'm certain Nicolas has conveyed how cramped it is on a sailing ship."

Camila said, "We're happy to be able to share our family's home with you."

*Meee-owwww.* All three of them turned as Artemis walked into the room. Fernanda said, "See, your cat has already decided that she likes it here. She's very smart."

Seba was dumbfounded. "Artemis, you were on the ship with us just last night. How did you find your way here?"

"Oh, she knows the way," Fernanda grinned. "She came with your mother the first day, acting as if Kristobal was her personal ferryman. She hopped onto the skiff, batted Gall across the nose as he tried to sniff her, and positioned herself on the foremost part of the gunwale. It was love at first sight for Gall; he all but knocked your mother in the water to reach his new sweetheart!"

Artemis circled Seba, rubbing herself against his ankles. She had saved his skin several times in the three years since she had adopted him as her companion. Seba lifted her up, stroking the silky silver fur that shone like the Greek goddess of the hunt. "It's good to see you, girl. Thanks for helping Mama and Papa get settled here."

With a loud meow and a swish of her tail, Artemis leapfrogged out of Seba's arms, walked in a circle around Fernanda's legs, and strode out of the room.

Fernanda looked suddenly serious. "I believe your father's hip is dislocated. I can tell by his gait, but I didn't want to ask him without discussing it with you. Do you think he would let me examine it? I may be able to help."

Seba nodded, so overcome with gratitude that he could not speak.

They heard Agnete calling from the kitchen, "Pumpkinhead, where have you been?"

Seba and the sisters looked at each other; Paolo must have arrived.

Sure enough, as they walked back down the hallway, they heard his cheerful voice. "Mrs. Krizomatis, must you call me that? It was not so long ago that I rescued you during a pirate attack on Sessera. Don't I deserve a reprieve?"

Agnete laughed heartily. "Ha! I'm sure I don't know the meaning of that word. How about a nice hot meal of homemade *revithada*? When your belly is full you won't care what anyone calls you."

Paolo hugged Agnete, picking her off her feet and swinging her in a circle. He towered over her by a foot, and although she repeatedly smacked his head in mock protest, Seba could tell she secretly loved it.

Agnete had been cooking her favorite Greek meals all day to welcome Seba to their new home. She had picked the spinach, peppers, and tomatoes from the garden and added the onions and garlic that the sisters had stored in their root cellar. She added seasonings from the herb garden behind the kitchen, which overflowed with oregano, marjoram, dill, sage, parsley and thyme. Cuttings of wild mint tied together with twine festooned the kitchen, giving it a cool, earthy smell.

Paolo said, "You're right, Mrs. Krizomatis, you can call me whatever you want if you're serving revithada."

They sat around the sisters' large rectangular wooden table, twice the size of the one in Seba's home in Sessera. Usually Agnete gave the blessing, but today Kostas spoke before the meal. "For six years, I was chained to a bed at night after toiling for the Ottomans, building ships in Constantinople. I dreamed of seeing my family again, of feeling the warmth of their hands in mine, and being lifted by the sight of their smiles. As the cold iron cuffs dug into my ankles, as my body ached from the abuse, I prayed. My conversations with God sometimes lasted all night, and always the message was clear: You will see them again. I didn't understand, but I believed."

Kostas's voice was raw with emotion. "Now I understand. And in addition to bringing my family together, we have been welcomed with a *philoxenia* that is unmatched. It brings to mind the story of Abraham and Sarah, who were visited by three weary strangers at the oaks of Mamre. Abraham and Sarah tended to them personally: washing their feet, offering them rest under the great oaks, and feeding them with milk, bread, and cheese curds. Later did they learn that their visitors were none other than the Lord, Archangel Uriel, and Archangel Raziel, who blessed them in their old age with a son named Isaac. I daresay Abraham and Sarah were no more generous to their strangers than Camila and Fernanda have been to us.

"And so, in grateful praise of our Menorcan guardian angels, Camila and Fernanda, and in thanks for all of the gifts bestowed upon us by God through the bounty of

Mother Earth and all of the plants and animals who thrive in this glorious kingdom, I ask for blessings upon the food we are about to eat. May it be for our highest and best use, under grace and in perfect ways. God is, God is, God is. Amen."

They shared a salad of bright chard, pale green leeks, and slices of juicy white-fleshed melon. Camila squeezed half of a lemon over the salad and passed the wooden serving bowl around the table. Camila had made small loaves of pa de xeixa, one for each person, except Paolo, for whom she'd made two. When they had eaten their fill of the lemon-dressed salad, Agnete brought the cast-iron pot from the hearth to the table and filled each person's wooden bowl with the unctuous revithada. The stew filled the room with the heavenly smell of roasted onions, garlic, tomatoes, and peppers, seasoned with oregano, dill, parsley, and a hefty helping of mint. They slathered soft, unaged Menorcan cheese on the xeixa bread and dipped it in their bowls of revithada.

When everyone was stuffed, including Paolo, Fernanda brought a surprise. "We heard from a little bird that you cannot get enough of the pudin de requeson of Menorca, our most delightful *postre*. Nicolas purloined the recipe from his Aunt Theodora."

Paolo asked, in a voice that perfectly mimicked Dr. Turnbull's, "My dear woman, is that the delicate whey cheese mixed with eggs, flour, sugar, and butter, flavored with lemon zest, cinnamon, and nutmeg, and baked to perfection? The creamy cloud of heavenly cheese-filled bliss smothered in fig jam and topped with raisins and pine nuts?"

Fernanda guffawed so forcefully that the pudin de requeson jiggled and slid across the stone serving dish. Had

Camila not grabbed the end of the platter, the cheese-filled bliss would have ended up on the floor.

Camila said, "Paolo, how do you know the ingredients of this dessert? Nicolas claims he barely escaped with his life while trying to get the recipe!"

Paolo grinned and responded in Dr. Turnbull's most supercilious tone: "Can I help it, my dear woman, if I have an ear for food?"

#

Later that evening, after the dishes had been washed and put away, the family sat around the large pine table drinking coffee from small earthenware cups. Kristobal and Gall had come for a visit, and Gall flopped down beside Camila's chair, his big head resting in her lap.

Kristobal said, "I don't know what it is, but Gall whines and cries if he goes more than two days without seeing you, Camila. He made such a racket that I thought I might get him out of the house by delivering you a few jars of datil pepper jam."

Paolo said, "What is this? Another food I haven't tried?"

Kristobal replied with a grin. "It's a delicacy here, although my father told me it originally hails from an island in the Caribbean. In any case, it's a tiny sunshine-colored pepper, no bigger than the knuckle on my thumb, but with a smoky heat that will knock you down."

Paolo wiggled his eyebrows. "Hand it over, Kristobal."

Though they were stuffed like hogs before market day, they couldn't resist tasting the jam. Agnete cut several large quince into wedges, enough for everyone to eat a whole quince slathered in the sweet and spicy jam.

Paolo said, "Seba, remember the *shakshuka* that Meleia made for us at the Aigókeros?"

Seba would never forget that meal. It was one of the best

foods he'd ever tasted: fire-roasted tomatoes and red peppers, cooked down into a thick sauce with onions, garlic, and spices she claimed were a family secret, into which Meleia had made several indentations for beautiful golden eggs to cook. She had covered the pan with a lid to allow the egg whites to color, and when they were ready, she sprinkled them with parsley, black pepper, and flakes of Aleppo pepper.

The datil-covered quince burned Seba's mouth into temporary silence, but he knew exactly where Paolo was going. After swallowing the fiery snack, he used a wooden dipper to fill his cup with cold cow's milk from the stone amphora and gulped it down.

Seba said, "I think we discovered one of the ingredients from Meleia's secret recipe."

"Exactly! Aleppo peppers are not this hot, but when I asked her what she used to make her shakshuka so spicy, she wouldn't tell me. It's these peppers. I know it!"

Seba agreed with his friend, and he was happy to learn that he had not left those peppers behind in Smyrna; she'd given him a whole pouch full of seeds when they said goodbye. "Kristobal, do you grow these peppers?"

"Oh, yes! They're like weeds if you properly water them, sprouting spicy golden fruits like fireflies at night." Kristobal smiled sheepishly. "Don't handle them with your bare hands, though." Pointing to his eyes, he said, "I learned that lesson the hard way, and now I use a cotton rag to harvest the little devils."

A voice called from the entryway. "Did someone call for a little devil? Here I am, at your service."

Agnete ran to greet Nicolas. "I thought you were off to Corsica this morning! You can't have been there and back already."

Nicolas kissed Agnete on both cheeks. "The ship's carpenter found a small crack in the hull. He's a marvel, that Francesc Pellicer. I doubt anyone else would have noticed the sliver of an opening, but fortunately for us, Francesc has the eyes of an eagle. We thought we'd be shipshape by this afternoon, but when he began the repairs, he found several other issues that needed attention. We'll be in port another two days."

Nicolas shook hands with Seba, Paolo, and Kostas, embraced Fernanda, and stood in front of Camila—or tried to, because Gall was jumping on him, crowing like a rooster and bathing him in dog slobber. "Gall, down! I'm trying to greet my fiancée."

Camila looked up from her chair, but did not rise. "I've told you a thousand times, Nicolas, I am unfit to marry anyone." Her voice shook. "Especially you, who deserves to have a wife who is pure and blameless."

"And I've told *you* a thousand times that nothing could change my feelings for you. Are you not the one who trained Zephyr to walk on her back legs in the Festival of Our Lady of Grace? Are you not the one who mediated the dispute between Juana and Teresa over who was to wear the banner of Santa Maria in the feast day parade? Are you not the one who helped Diana fetch a fair price for her salsas when other vendors tried to undercut her? Were you not the first to arrive on Isla del Rey with warm broth for the sick?"

Camila's eyes welled, but Nicolas went on. He said, "Let me answer for you. Yes, you are that person. The one who made me the happiest man alive when you agreed to marry me. Nothing has changed."

"You are a merchant with beautiful words, Nicolas, but they won't change my mind."

Agnete cupped her hands on Camila's cheeks, her fiery

eyes burning into Camila's grief-stricken face. "Camila, you must have faith in the power of love. As Saint Paul said in his letter to the church at Corinth: 'Love bears all things, believes all things, hopes all things, endures all things.' Not *some* things, but *all* things. This man loves you with all his heart. You must bear, believe, hope, and endure. Not alone, but together."

Something transpired between Agnete and Camila, a kind of message or understanding, although Seba couldn't quite say what it was or how it happened. Tears streamed down Camila's cheeks, and Agnete nodded to Nicolas.

Nicolas spread out his arms wide and spun around. "Here, in front of our family, new and old, I declare that you are my heart, *kardia mou*, from now until the end of time. Your beauty encompasses the virtues of the soul, and neither person, nor government, nor tragedy can mar that beauty. It is your very being."

Nicolas pulled a silver brooch from the pocket of his trousers and nudged Gall out of the way as he fell to one knee before Camila. The brooch bore a device of a cluster of grape leaves that spiraled out from the center, and included emeralds and sapphires that looked like little grapes peeking out from behind the leaves. "You give your heart to everyone in this community, and you give it freely, caring for them as if they were your own children. Please, make me the happiest merchant in Menorca, and allow me to give my heart to you. Camila Rementeria Arandia, will you marry me?"

Gall threw his forelegs onto Camila's lap, as if he were joining in Nicolas's renewed proposal. Camila raised her chin then bowed in a silent agreement, her tears flowing freely now. Nicolas kissed her tears away and pinned the brooch on her shawl.

Rising shakily to her feet, Camila threw her arms around Nicolas, and the room erupted in applause. Gall let out a loud crow, and Paolo, not to be outdone, shouted, "*Opa*! Nicolas, you better have brought some of that Corsican wine. We're celebrating!"

# 11 SEVENTY-FIVE LASHES



*August 21, 1767*
*Port Mahón, Menorca*
*Afternoon*

Ten days later, Seba would finally have his questions answered regarding the girls' brother, Ignasi. They all prayed it would be as Paolo said: merely a few lashes for unruly behavior, and then Ignasi would be sent along his way. According to Nicolas, these public punishments had been the status quo for the last four years, since the British had won Menorca from the French.

Seba didn't have the chance to verify this with Dr. Turnbull, however, because as soon as the *New Fortuna*'s repairs were completed, Dr. Turnbull, Paolo, and the crew were off on a two-week trip to the Italian city of Leghorn to solicit more recruits. Seba reluctantly begged off, feeling the need to stay with his parents and help the sisters around the farm. *It's only two weeks.*

The public *plaça* was the midpoint of Mahón, a large

open space surrounded by the homes of the richest merchants, several governmental buildings, and a hulking stone church. A crowd had formed around the edges of the square, the townsfolk pressing in from the adjacent streets. They closed in on each other, jostling to get a better view.

At the center of the plaça was a wooden platform surrounded by men in military uniforms. A man wearing a coarse linen shirt was tied to a post on the wooden platform. He was large, with muscular shoulders and arms the color of raw umber; Seba could see the whites of his eyes, which showed a mingled visage of terror and rage. Although his face was broader and his features sharper than his sisters', Seba knew this must be Ignasi. He pulled against the ropes that held him; they were so taut that the post seemed to be leaning in Ignasi's direction. A short man in a military uniform faced away from Seba as he addressed the assembled group. He spoke to the crowd that had gathered. Seba guessed the language was Menorquín, which he was slowly learning from Fernanda and Camila. However, Seba hadn't absorbed quite enough to understand what the officer was saying.

Camila stopped abruptly. "No." She turned to Fernanda. "I thought I was prepared, but I can't watch. I feel responsible."

Fernanda snapped, "You are *not* responsible. Ignasi makes his own decisions, and he needs us right now."

"It's too much to bear, and it's all my fault. He would not be in this position if it weren't for me."

Fernanda said, "Ten lashes will be over before we know it, and then he'll be back home."

Seba strained to see over the crowd.

"No! I won't bear witness to this torture." It was the first time Seba had seen Camila angry. She sounded exactly like

Fernanda. Camila spat the words at her sister, who reached for her hand. It was too late; Camila stomped through the crowd with a terse "*Perdon*" to everyone she jostled, until she was out of sight.

When Seba and Fernanda reached the edge of the plaça, Fernanda made a growling sound, like a wild animal. "Brumbaugh."

The short man in uniform turned around. He was dressed in a traditional Royal Navy uniform, complete with brass buttons and a bicorn hat. By the amount of gold trim on his long overcoat, it was obvious he held a high position. The man was not much taller than Camila, but he was muscular; his calves bulged prominently in his white silk stockings. His complexion was ruddy and his brows appeared to be knit into a perpetual frown.

Seba said, "BRUM-baw?"

Fernanda replied, "Captain Elias Brumbaugh, Acting Commander-in-Chief and Post-Captain of the Defense Squadron and Dockyards of Port Mahón, including Saint Philip's Garrison and the Naval Shipyards on the North Shore." She gave another low growl. "He's only been recently appointed to that position, but he announces his title every time he appears in public. He's a tyrant. And a pompous ass."

Fernanda translated as the charges were read out, punctuating it with several Greek curse words that Nicolas must have taught her. Brumbaugh branded their brother, Ignasi Rementeria Arandia, as an enemy of the realm who had brutally assaulted a British officer.

"He's saying Ignasi would have killed the officer with his bare hands if Brumbaugh hadn't intervened," Fernanda hissed. "That's not true—Brumbaugh wasn't even there!"

Brumbaugh said something else and everyone in the

crowd gasped.

Fernanda's hand flew to her mouth. "He wouldn't."

"Fernanda, wouldn't what? What did he say?"

"Seventy-five? For defending my sister's honor? No!"

Seba pulled on Fernanda's shoulder. "Seventy-five what?"

Fernanda whispered, "They've never sentenced anyone to more than fifty lashes, and that was when someone accidentally set fire to the garrison's stores of gin. The soldiers rioted, and we had to stay in our homes for three days until a ship arrived from Gibraltar to replenish the warehouse. The man who accidentally caused the fire was flogged fifty times."

"Did he survive?"

Fernanda nodded. "But he's never been the same since." She put her hands on her head and twisted her fingers into her oxblood hair. "Ignasi was in an altercation with a British soldier, but the soldier was at fault. They always are. Ten lashes is the common punishment for these kinds of fisticuffs. They happen every week." She shook her head in dismay. "Seventy-five lashes might as well be a death sentence."

"Why would they do this to Ignasi?"

"I don't know, but Brumbaugh is lying about the incident. It makes no sense." They watched as a stocky soldier uncoiled a leather whip from his belt. Ignasi strained mightily against the ropes. He was so strong that he almost pulled the post down onto the soldier dealing the blows.

*Crack!* The whip lashed against Ignasi's back, leaving a red arced line across his shoulder blades. The stocky soldier drew back again and again, crisscrossing Ignasi's back with welts that were beginning to bleed through his shirt.

But for the intermittent, explosive sound of the whip,

and the soft crying of a few spectators, the crowd was eerily silent.

Fernanda's eyes bored into her brother, willing him to look at her. To know she was there. Ignasi's back looked like a pulverized piece of meat; the sight made Seba gag. After the thirtieth lash, Ignasi's body may have been in the plaça, but his consciousness was elsewhere.

Seba put his hand on Fernanda's arm. "Can we not stop this somehow?"

"Not unless you want to be next."

Seba tried to understand why a powerful British officer, the new leader of the outpost in Mahón, wanted to publicly torture a Menorcan man who defended his sister's honor. *Dr. Turnbull said his government is charged with protecting the people. What's wrong with this Brumbaugh person?* He cocked his head in confusion, feeling more adrift in this moment than in all his days at sea.

After the seventy-fifth crack of the whip, Brumbaugh motioned for two soldiers on the platform to release Ignasi from the post. This took a few moments, as the soldiers fell to squabbling about who would untie the ropes and who would lower Ignasi to the ground. The rope was the easier job, because of Ignasi's size, and both wanted to do that. Finally, Brumbaugh shouted a terse word that sounded to Seba like "IHNUFF," and the larger soldier acquiesced, using his shoulder to hold Ignasi up until the other soldier, having loosed the rope, could run to assist him. Together, they dropped Ignasi onto his stomach with a thud.

Brumbaugh stepped over Ignasi and addressed the crowd. Seba couldn't understand what he said, but it must have been bad; again he heard Fernanda's low grumbling, like the wild jackals that roamed the mountains of Chios. If Fernanda had her druthers, it was clear that Brumbaugh, and not her brother, would be the one to be flayed alive.

After the incendiary oration, Brumbaugh's bulging calves carried him off the platform. An attendant helped him onto a large ebony horse that looked similar to Euros and Zephyr, save for the black canvas blinders that restricted its vision.

When Brumbaugh and his horse were out of sight, the townspeople ran up to the platform and got to work, loading Ignasi face down onto a litter consisting of an olivewood frame with heavy burlap stretched across. After ensuring that Ignasi was still breathing, Fernanda quickly peeled away the bloody scraps that had been his shirt. "It's best to do it now," she said, as if to herself. "While he can't feel the pain."

Kristobal appeared with Gall attached to a wooden dray. Ignasi's litter was fixed to the cart and Kristobal called out, "*Anem!*" Gall leaped forward, crowing and straining against the leather straps of his harness. Gall was strong, but Ignasi was enormous. Kristobal, Seba, and Fernanda took their places behind the dray and pressed with all their might.

The wheels of the cart squeaked into motion. A group of local townsfolk followed along, snaking their way through the streets of Mahón to the western gate in a bizarre and somber procession. As the road outside of town began to incline toward the hills, friends and neighbors traded places with Fernanda, Kristobal, and Seba behind the dray.

When they reached the Rementeria home, Camila saw them coming and ran through the arched wooden barrera; she stopped short, though, when she noticed her brother's back. She knelt at the cart, her face even with Ignasi's, their heads touching. Camila whispered to her brother.

Fernanda paced up and down the path, giving Camila an

opportunity to share her heart with her brother, right up until a fly landed on one of Ignasi's bloody welts. "Later, sister," she said urgently. "We need to clean and dress these lacerations before they become diseased."

They pushed the cart up to the front door and Agnete came running from the garden, crossing herself as she approached the cart. "Holy Mother of God, what's happened?"

"Ignasi is hurt, and we need to wash and treat his wounds. I have a salve in the root cellar. Please, hurry!"

Kostas hobbled toward them from the stable, moving as quickly as his eagle-headed cane allowed. He took one look at Ignasi and shuffled swiftly toward the kitchen. "We need clean water! Stoke the fire and I'll fill a bucket from the well."

It took several hours, but Agnete, Kostas, and Fernanda tended to Ignasi's wounds, dipping clean cloths into the hot water and washing dirt and debris out of the deep cuts that zigzagged across Ignasi's back. Ignasi remained unconscious, which Fernanda said was a blessing, both for him and for Camila, who sat in a chair in the corner, chewing the cuticles of her thumbs until they bled.

When Ignasi's wounds had been cleaned and dressed, he was made comfortable in his room, prone on his straw mattress with his head turned to the side.

Returning to the kitchen, Kostas gave a weary sigh. "Times like these call for a pot of *avgolemono*," he said. "Camila, would you assist me?"

Camila stared into the fire and didn't respond.

Kostas put his hand on her shoulder. "Men whom I considered brothers were tortured before my eyes when I was enslaved. Let me help you."

Camila looked up into Kostas's eyes and burst into tears.

Kostas allowed her to cry into his shoulder and Agnete embraced her from behind until the three were like one. They stayed that way for a long time. Fernanda and Seba stood in Ignasi's doorway, silently praying, almost afraid to leave him alone.

Later, Agnete slipped past them and pulled a wooden chair beside Ignasi's bed. "Go, you two, rest. You must be exhausted. I'll stay here with him. The Blessed Mother is with us. She understands all too well the pain of a tortured son."

Seba and Fernanda left the room, but Fernanda continued pacing up and down the hall, her brown boots clacking with anger.

"Shouldn't we water the horses?" Seba asked. "We've been gone all day."

Fernanda said nothing, but nodded her assent.

When they got to the stable, Seba again broached the subject, hoping that Fernanda would feel better if she recounted the whole ordeal. He was right. Fernanda seemed relieved to disclose the full story.

"A few weeks ago, Camila was working with Gall to move our flock of sheep to the easternmost pasture, the one closest to the city gates. It was early, barely past dawn, and we expected them to return for the midday meal. She was gone no more than an hour before she ran into the house and locked herself in her room.

"She refused any visitors and threatened to throw herself out her second-floor window if we brought in a physician. When Nicolas tried to console her, she wailed through the door that the marriage was off and she would never lay eyes on him again."

"I'm so sorry."

"At first, we didn't know what happened. Camila never

breathed a word. Several days later, a uniformed officer came to our home. His arm was in a sling and he walked with a limp. He brought a written order for us to surrender our 'murderous dog' to him, to be shot on sight. I told him we didn't have a dog, and he must have gone to the wrong house. The officer was so angry that he grabbed my arm and threatened me. He dragged me through the house, searching for this 'murderous dog.' Ignasi heard the commotion and rushed up the hill from the stables."

Fernanda plopped onto a bale of hay and lowered her head, her oxblood hair hanging in curtains around her face. "It was then that we learned the truth of it, but not before Ignasi and the soldier had a tussle. The morning that Camila and Gall moved the flock, the soldier had been wandering the roads outside of town, still drunk after a night of debauchery. He must have smelled the orchards and came upon Camila in the pasture. He forced himself upon her."

For a moment, Fernanda could not go on. Seba swallowed hard. At last, she found her voice again. "Camila fought back, of course. She screamed for help. Gall was in the far field, chasing down an errant sheep, but when he finally heard her cries, he raced to the pasture, tackled the soldier, and tore a chunk out of the man's leg. And according to the officer, Gall's jaws clamped so hard on his arm that they broke the bone in two."

Seba's eyes grew wide. Gall didn't seem to have an aggressive bone in his furry body; but this incident explained why he was so protective of Camila.

"Ignasi came running to help me, but when it came out what the soldier had done to Camila, he went berserk. The soldier was on his own when he came to the house; I suppose he imagined he'd have no trouble intimidating a woman, who knows? He'd left a handful of his fellows stationed at the gate. When they heard the ruckus, the others ran into the house, pulled Ignasi away, put his wrists in iron cuffs, and took him away. That was over two weeks ago."

"I see why Camila blames herself." Seba slammed the water bucket to the ground. "But that man was at fault."

Fernanda poured the water into a large wooden trough. Euros and Zephyr walked slowly toward them, as if they didn't want to interrupt. "It's that vile drink the British brought with them," she said. "Every travesty that befalls us begins with that poison they call gin. The soldiers stagger about, brawling, shouting profanities, so slack-faced that they attack us for sport." In her frustration, she kicked out at a bale of hay. "Either that, or they're lying drunk in the roads for days on end. And their officers don't lift a finger to address the violence."

She pointed back to the house. "And now they've destroyed the only family I have left. It's not fair."

Seba nodded understandingly. "I lost my father once, for six years," he said. "He was held captive in that Ottoman slave camp. He has marks on his back like the ones on Ignasi's. I think that's why knows how to treat Ignasi's wounds." He rubbed his chin. "What I don't understand is why they ordered seventy-five lashes. Why would the commander mete out such a harsh punishment when it was plainly his own soldier who instigated the whole thing?"

"You saw him, Seba. Brumbaugh's barely taller than Camila. He's the kind of man who cannot abide being embarrassed, made to feel small. And we challenged his authority. We not only refused the garrison's order to turn over Gall, we exposed the treachery of a soldier under his command. When his men run wild, it makes Brumbaugh look weak; he cannot tolerate that. So he covers it up and puts the blame on us."

"What can we do?"

"I won't speak for you, Seba, but I know what I'm going to do," she said. "And that is to stay as far away from Elias Brumbaugh as I can."

#

Later that evening, Seba and Kostas sat by the fire long after everyone had gone to bed. Logs of *carrasca*, the oak tree native to Menorca, popped and crackled in the hearth, and Seba was reminded of his childhood on Sessera, where he would listen as a boy to his father's stories about sailing ships and his ancient Greek ancestors.

It felt good to be here with his father, sipping hot coffee from small earthenware cups, but Seba was uneasy. Trouble seemed to follow them everywhere. After a dangerous voyage, finally in the safe harbor of Port Mahón, they had been attacked by pirates, leaving Seba with a scar on his temple he would bear for the rest of his life. They had found beautiful lodgings with a wonderful family, only to find that the family was now the target of a power-hungry maniac named Elias Brumbaugh.

"Papa, will it ever end? I'm not sure that you and Mama are safe here. Perhaps we should board a ship and go elsewhere. I don't want to be left behind when Doctor Turnbull leaves to solicit more recruits." He sighed. "I can protect myself, but I'm worried for you. What if the soldiers come back? You don't even understand the language yet."

Kostas uncrossed his legs and tried to cross them the other way, but his hip refused to cooperate. He planted both feet on the floor. "Remember when you asked me what sailors do when the *meltemi* winds push them off course?"

"Yes, but we're far west of the meltemi winds. Personally, I think these tramontana winds are even stronger."

Kostas laughed. "Remember the larger lesson. What does a good sailor do when he's driven off course?"

"He adapts to conditions," Seba said. "But I don't see how we can adapt to a tyrant."

Kostas's gray-green eyes, the ones that mirrored Seba's, held the hint of amusement. "You're on the right path, Seba. I suppose I can thank Brother Timotheos for your excellent education. That's exactly the right question. How do you adapt to a tyrant?"

"I don't know! I was asking you!"

Kostas truly chuckled now. "Seba, I couldn't love you any more than I do right now. I am grateful that God reunited us."

Seba didn't know what to say. His head felt as empty as a nutshell, yet his father was praising him. "I'm grateful, too, Papa," he said. "Another man might have lost his wits in that slave camp, but you obviously didn't, because whatever you're thinking, it's beyond my comprehension."

Kostas rubbed his chin; Seba suddenly realized that he made the same gesture when he was thinking. "I believe you'll get there, Seba," he said. "And you'll have a much better understanding if you do it on your own than if I feed it to you with a spoon."

"You're not going to tell me?"

"Not yet. We'll discuss it again when you've given it some thought. Do you realize that in a few months, you're going to be seventeen years old?" Kostas raised his coffee cup to his lips. "Let us revisit this discussion then. We'll see how you've learned to adapt."

# 12 FIDDLE AND DRUM

*August 30, 1767*
*Mahón, Menorca*
*Morning*

Camila and Nicolas chose the Feast Day of Saint Lluis for their wedding. He was the patron saint of marriage, parenthood, and large families. At first, Camila believed it was too soon after Ignasi's ill treatment, but Ignasi would not hear of any delay for his sister's wedding; the sight of her marrying Nicolas, he said, was the healing he craved.

The day of the wedding dawned cool, a welcome blessing in late August. Soon after daybreak, the wedding party walked to the convent of the Sisters of the Virgin Mary for the ceremony. The convent had been built in 1740, dedicated to the nuns of the Blessed Virgin, and was a city unto itself within Mahón's walls. The best part of the compound was the stables; the nuns kept a string of noble black Menorcan steeds who were kin to Euros and Zephyr.

The sisters rarely rode them in the town, preferring to ride Menorca's remote northern hills when they weren't trotting within the convent's extensive grounds. Like Seba's home monastery of Nea Moni, the convent boasted gardens, orchards, kitchens, a large cistern for collecting water, and a welcoming chapel. The convent's atmosphere was cheerful and earnest, like the sisters who lived there.

As they crossed the chapel's threshold, the church bell greeted them, pealing exuberantly across the morning sky. Inside, flickering tapers flanked each pew, their light dancing off the bright whitewashed walls. A young girl lit seven beeswax pillars atop the altar, which was decorated with rosemary and almond blossoms. The scents of honey and almond permeated the nave, rising up to the vaulted ceiling in the cool morning air. Early light streamed through the narrow glass windows, falling on the young couple like a blessing.

Seba took his place on the chancel's stone floor near Nicolas. Family and friends, including many of the Sisters of the Virgin Mary, were clustered together in the wooden pews on either side of the center aisle, murmuring softly in quiet anticipation.

An unseen musician struck up a tune on the harpsichord as Kostas escorted Camila down the aisle. The music was sprightly and precise, the intricate arpeggios evoking a feeling of energy and vivacity. The harpsichord was tucked into a corner of the side chapel. Seba stood on his toes, trying to catch a glimpse of the musician. He nearly lost his balance when he saw it was none other than Kristobal, his dirty fingernails flying over the wooden keys.

Camila kissed Kostas on each cheek, and Kostas took his place beside Agnete, who was already dabbing the corners of her eyes with the lace handkerchief Fernanda had given her.

Camila joined hands with Nicolas. His forehead was beaded with perspiration. Nicolas regularly sailed the Balearic Sea, talked and drank the Mediterranean winemakers under the table, and had a snappy quip for any situation; but not today. His gleaming face and shaky legs betrayed the magnitude of the moment he'd been envisioning since he was five years old. He squeezed Camila's hands and rubbed his thumbs back and forth across her wrists as if he were kneading dough. Camila, by contrast, was a pillar of stability.

The abbess greeted the couple and the celebrants, and commenced the sacrament of marriage. She asked the couple, each in turn, if they were willing to accept the other in holy matrimony.

"*Sí, vull.*" Camila's voice was buoyant.

Nicolas focused on Camila like a ship fixed on a lighthouse. "*Sí, vull.*"

The couple then exchanged their vows, Camila's voice as steady and sweet as a stream of warm honey.

"Today, in the presence of God and our loved ones, I choose you, Nicolas Alexiano, as my husband. I am honored to stand beside you and join my life with yours, trusting that whatever may come, be it boon or blight, we will face it together. I give you my hand and my heart, vowing to love you always."

Nicolas took a breath and rediscovered his confidence.

"Today, in this holy sanctuary, before our families and our Creator, I choose you, Camila Rementeria Arandia, as my wife. Through this bond of true love, I pledge to you my devotion and faithfulness. I thank God every day for your beauty, strength, and wisdom and for your great generosity in choosing me. I vow honesty, patience, and adoring love to you always."

Agnete was now visibly crying. She blew her nose in Fernanda's handkerchief.

The abbess blessed the emerald brooch with holy water and handed it to Nicolas. *"In nomine Patris, et Filii, et Spiritus Sancti."*

Nicolas pinned the brooch on Camila, and they were invited to share the kiss of peace. He pulled Camila into a tight embrace and twirled her around, her tiny feet stretched out behind as her dress flowed around them like a wreath of flowers.

#

Following the ceremony, the wedding party spilled out into the street en route to El Gos for the marriage feast. El Gos was a favorite tavern among the locals of Mahón as the place for music, dancing, and mirth. It stood inside the city's western gate, called the Portal de Sant Roc, named for a French patron saint of dogs revered for his success in healing those afflicted with plague.

Legend held that Sant Roc fell victim to the plague himself and traveled deep into the forest to recover. A miraculous spring emerged and supplied him with fresh water, but there was no food to be found. He would have perished but for a local dog who brought him loaves of bread and licked his wounds, curing his disease. Afterward, they traveled the land together, healing the sick and sharing bread with the poor. Everyone in Mahón knew the story, including the dogs, who lounged around El Gos as if they knew the establishment was named for them.

The merrymakers skipped past the dogs through the bright red door of the tavern, which opened into a cavernous, high-ceilinged space scattered with bright pine tables, benches, and stools. The well-worn flagstone floors led to a long wooden bar with a corner turn, behind which bottles and glasses rested on rustic shelves. After the young couple was introduced, the abbess offered the blessing of the food, and everyone feasted on mussels, squid, spiny lobster, and platters of arroz de la tierra, a traditional Menorcan dish made from cracked wheat, sweet potatoes, tomatoes, and five different kinds of sausages. Pomegranates were piled high in porcelain bowls, symbols of fertility and abundance.

A group of musicians capered through the front door, guitarras, floutas, violes, and timbals at the ready. When everyone was stuffed to the gills, they pushed the tables and benches toward the walls and the band performed lively fiddle music as family and friends kicked up their heels. Camila and Nicolas led a line of dancers through El Gos, and out and around the block, with Fernanda and Gall bringing up the rear. Fernanda held the canine's forepaws as he romped and danced about on his back legs, crowing with delight.

Seba extricated himself from the dancers to fetch a drink, and found the busy barkeep to be none other than Kristobal. His fingernails were relatively clean, and he'd attempted to manage his unruly hair with some kind of oil or pomade, with marginal success. However, his clean chemise and matching vest fit him well, and his fingers were adorned with several gold rings, each bearing an amber gemstone, including a large topaz ring on his thumb.

Kristobal filled a xato with ruby-red wine and handed it to Seba.

"Kristobal, are you a steward, too? You played the harpsichord beautifully this morning, and Fernanda says you tend to the horses in the convent's stables. I know you're employed to ferry passengers from Quarantine

Island to town, and I've seen you helping the fisherfolk with their nets. What don't you do?"

Kristobal grinned, his chocolate-brown eyes twinkling. "I'll never tell. I've been running this town since I was six years old. You'll find there's nothing that goes on in Mahón without my involvement."

Kristobal held up his own xato and clinked it on the side of Seba's. "Cheers to Nicolas and Camila, their marriage, and their Corsican wine!"

As Seba raised the glass to his lips, he heard a familiar voice: "I couldn't agree more, my dear boy! And, if you don't mind my saying, your gilded gemstones are positively dapper. Two glasses of wine, please. One for my dear friend, Madam Jurada Theodora Alexiano, and one for myself."

Seba's head swiveled around so fast that he spilled his entire drink down his white shirt. "Doctor Turnbull! What are you doing here?"

"When have you known me to miss a celebration? It's simply not in my nature, my boy. Particularly when invited by Mahón's highest-ranking councilwoman and her twin brother." Dr. Turnbull grinned widely. "Speaking of which, where is he? The man well-nigh ripped the *New Fortuna*'s sails to shreds to make port in time for the wedding. Damn near dumped poor Peter into the sea, that's how close the crow's nest was to the waterline. I haven't had so much fun since my beloved Maria Gracia and I honeymooned in the Canaries."

Kristobal poured two xatos and handed them to Dr. Turnbull, all the while staring at the well-dressed gentleman with interest. Seba found himself between two of the most influential individuals on the island: one a fifty-year-old Scottish physician and the other an eleven-year-old

Menorcan boy.

Kristobal refilled Seba's xato and handed him a rag. Seba dabbed at his shirt and raised the glass to his lips again. This time he felt a hand clap him on the back, causing him to spill, yet again, the entire contents of his drink down his already soaked shirt.

Paolo said, "Seba! It's good to see you. I wish you'd been with us. We've never sailed so fast in our lives!"

Kristobal laughed heartily and handed Seba another cotton rag, enjoying the unexpected entertainment. Seba gave up on the wine and instead threw his arms around his friend.

Paolo looked down at his shirt, which was now streaked red thanks to Seba, and laughed.

"It was exhilarating! The captain caught Boreas and rode that old north wind faster than I've ever seen. Said he couldn't live with himself if he missed his nephew's wedding."

A woman with glistening chestnut eyes and impeccable posture stood behind Dr. Turnbull, patiently waiting for him to hand her a xato of wine. Her skirts were brick-red, dark and bold, and she wore an intricately-tatted white lace shawl over a hazelnut-brown blouse. Her jewelry was sparse but significant. On one gold chain hung a gold ringed cross encrusted with emeralds, while a second held the scales of justice, wrought in silver and gold with white enameled bowls. She was the spitting image of the captain, with salt-and-pepper hair pulled into a tight bun.

Seba took the xato from Dr. Turnbull and handed it to the woman. "Good afternoon. My name is Sebastian Krizomatis, and you must be Theodora Alexiano. I'm pleased to make your acquaintance."

Dr. Turnbull flushed. "Oh, dear me, where are my

manners?" He swept his arm across his chest and bowed so low that his periwig brushed his kneecaps. "Allow me to introduce my distinguished guest, who is not only a learned judge of civil matters here in Mahón, but also the town's highest ranking councilwoman, a politician of extraordinary talent, and most importantly, aunt of the groom. The one and only Madam Jurada Theodora Alexiano. Theodora, these are my very good Greek friends and future business associates, Sebastian Krizomatis and Paolo Partella."

The woman smiled, her white teeth dazzling in the dappled light of El Gos. Her voice was crisp and inviting. "It is my honor to meet the courageous young men who sail with my brother Alexander. Doctor Turnbull gives me too much credit, I'm afraid. I'm a simple civil servant doing my best for the citizens of Mahón."

Dr. Turnbull said, "Come, now, my dear Theodora, you do yourself a great disservice. As a former diplomat, I understand how difficult it is to bear the slings and arrows of political conflict, and you navigate your position with more skill and grace than anyone in the whole of the Mediterranean."

Seba said, "I didn't know you were a diplomat, Doctor Turnbull."

"British consul at Smyrna, my boy," he said, standing a trifle straighter. "I daresay I was quite good at the job, but my dear Theodora puts us all to shame."

The Madam Jurada held up her hand. "Andrew, enough of this political nonsense. Sebastian, Paolo—tell me about yourselves."

By the time they'd regaled Theodora Alexiano with tales of their adventures across the Mediterranean, including emphatic interruptions by Dr. Turnbull, the councilwoman had dubbed them "Jason and the Argonauts."

By then, Dr. Turnbull was on his third xato of wine. "What do you think of the musicians? A splendid surprise for the wedding feast, wouldn't you agree?"

Seba cocked his head. "You brought the musicians?"

"And the dancers as well. They're our Italian and Corsican recruits from our last voyage. They've more meager lodgings here in town than you have out on the Rementeria Arandia estate, and the Madam Jurada agreed they'd be a welcome addition to the wedding festivities."

Dr. Turnbull drained his glass and held it in the air for Kristobal to refill. "I purchased a few fiddles, flutes, and drums here in town and bestowed them on our new friends, who were quite overjoyed. I'm not one to cry roast meat, but by God, it was a splendid idea! Very talented bunch, and they take pleasure in sharing their musical gifts. In fact, I'm going to join them!"

Dr. Turnbull removed his blue velvet jacket and stepped into the middle of the dancers. They laughed and applauded, their faces red with joy and exertion as they encouraged their jolly patron to step lively. He was happy to oblige them, skipping, leaping, and hopping first on one foot, then the other. Surprisingly agile for his size, Dr. Turnbull fell into lockstep with the other dancers as they cavorted around the tavern. Even the Madam Jurada joined in, allowing Dr. Turnbull to spin her around the dance floor.

They approached Nicolas and Camila, and switched partners, Nicolas laughing with his aunt while Dr. Turnbull twirled the blushing bride in a circle.

Seba said, "That was very generous of Doctor Turnbull, don't you think?"

Paolo's voice took on a cynical tone. "Perhaps. A storm hit the *New Fortuna* only days after these volunteers joined us at Leghorn, and the men were worried about what they'd signed up for. Doctor Turnbull wants to keep them happy."

Seba raised his eyebrows but said nothing.

As the dancers came around again, Dr. Turnbull spun over to the bar and grabbed Seba and Paolo by their shirts. In an instant, they were all dancing in a circle, kicking their legs and leaping in time with the music.

Dr. Turnbull, out of breath yet effervescent, said, "Jolly good time, don't you agree? And to think, our true adventure hasn't yet begun. I'm off again to the Levant to gather more volunteers. Paolo's already agreed to join me. What say you, Sebastian? Don't dawdle in your decision; the *New Fortuna* is in tip-top shape! We leave tomorrow and won't be back for several months."

Seba was aghast. "But you've just arrived. You're leaving tomorrow?"

"Yes, my boy! We only stopped in Mahón to drop our recruits, resupply the ship, and enjoy the wedding revels. I've no time to waste; my land in East Florida isn't going to farm itself, you know."

On the other side of El Gos, Seba spied his father, seated in a chair by the window. Agnete stood behind the chair, her hands caressing his salt-and-pepper head of hair. Seba's heart lurched.

"Thank you, sir. I'm not sure I'm prepared to leave my parents just yet. We were apart for so long, and I know they'll worry about me sailing back into Ottoman territory."

Dr. Turnbull raised his xato and touched it to the one in Seba's hand. "I understand, my boy. Your father has a long recovery ahead of him."

"Fernanda has been working on my father's hip. She says our bones aren't significantly different from those of her horses."

Dr. Turnbull winked. "Sharp woman. I'm sure she's correct. I feel certain that your father will continue to improve under her care."

"Thank you, sir." Tension drained from Seba's body and he felt something stir inside him. *Perhaps I can join Dr. Turnbull after all. Papa will be fine with Fernanda and Camila to care for him; he enjoys spending time with Ignasi. And he'll have his kardia, Mama.*

Dr. Turnbull captivated the crowd with his fancy footwork late into the night, while Paolo tried his best to convince Seba to rejoin the crew. "Your parents are content here. Do you see how your mother has taken to Camila? They're like two petite peas in a pod!"

"Yes, my mother seems very happy here. It's my father I'm worried about."

Paolo slapped his hand on the bar and pointed to Kostas. "You said yourself that he's improving! He bent my ear for an hour over there about farm tools, crossbows, philosophy, and the best combination of food to keep the horses in peak shape for the festivals. Fernanda might even be able to cure his hip! If you're here, you'll only get in the way of his progress."

Seba exhaled audibly, frustration playing across his features. "Thanks, Paolo."

"Of course," said Paolo airily. "That's what I'm here for. You can't be expected to think for yourself. You're fortunate to have me as your mentor."

"Very fortunate."

Paolo was immune to Seba's sarcasm. "Anyway, it's only a few months. You'll see your parents before spring, and then we'll be off to New Smyrna. Would you rather spend the winter cooped up in that house with your parents, or sailing the Aegean Sea?"

Paolo made a good point. Fernanda said the tramontana winds of winter often forced the islanders indoors for days on end.

"I don't know. I wish I had more time to decide."

"Well, you don't. I'll walk back with you to the estate and load a bag with food from the pantry, then turn right around and board the ship lest she leave without me. I encourage you to do the same."

# 13 THE LOFT

*August 31, 1767*
*Mahón, Menorca*
*After midnight*

Later that night, when stars dotted the dark sky like far-off fireflies and the wedding party had long retired to their homes, Seba and Paolo walked through the Portal del Sant Roc toward the Rementeria Arandia home.

Seba breathed deeply, taking in the scent of the surrounding trees. They were cousins of the skinos trees of Seba's village of Sessera, thousands and thousands of them, ripe with dark red, almost black, berries bursting with the glorious aroma of pine, sweet mint, cedar, and crisp herbs. *Mastiha.*

The locals called the trees *arbres de llentiscle*. Their resinous perfume transported Seba back to his childhood on Chios. Menorca's mastic trees didn't drip diamonds from their branches, but instead bore tiny rubies between their leaves. Seba approached a tree, bowed to it, and asked if the tree minded sharing its bounty with an adventurer considering a decision to embark on a new journey. The tree seemed more than pleased to have been asked, and Seba picked five large handfuls of mastic berries, which he dropped into the pockets of his trousers. He popped a few berries in his mouth, the explosion of minty flavor refreshing him with its healing power.

He offered a handful to Paolo. "Have you tried these? They taste like the tears of Chios."

Paolo put the whole bunch into his mouth, inhaling and chewing at the same time. His eyes grew wide. "I've smelled this on the docks at Smyrna, but I've never tasted mastic. I see why it's such a valuable commodity."

Seba nodded. "Mama thinks it's a miracle that Doctor Turnbull brought her to Menorca, where the sister trees of her Greek ancestors grow." He drew air all the way to the bottom of his lungs. "That's why this island feels like home to her."

Paolo took a step toward Seba. "You're not considering staying, are you?"

"Yes. No. Oh, I don't know, Paolo. I need to think it through." Seba hesitated. "It would be good to spend the winter with my parents, but I prefer the open sea."

"That's what I'm trying to tell you, Seba. You'd be miserable here all winter, huddled in the cold while your mates are sailing. And what about me? Peter is top-notch and there is no finer sailor than Captain Alexiano, but they're not my best friend."

They walked the rest of the way in silence, and as soon as Paolo crossed the threshold of the Rementeria home, he did exactly as he had promised: he took an armful of apples and pears from the olivewood bowl on the table and two loaves of bread from a box on the sideboard, shoved them into a burlap sack, and turned back toward the front door. Artemis had pounced on a fly on the sideboard, and released it when Paolo scratched her behind the ears. "Artemis, you're welcome to sail with us as well. Remember all the nice, juicy rats on the *New Fortuna?* They'd be yours for the taking."

Artemis followed Paolo out the door, considering the bevy of rats on the orlop deck, then turned back toward Seba. He searched her wise little face for a sign. "What do you think, girl?" he whispered. "Are we to leave tonight?"

As if in response, Artemis followed Paolo down the path, her tail swishing happily from left to right. As Paolo reached the gate, however, Artemis turned and ran toward the stables, seemingly enticed by an errant field mouse. *You're no help, girl.*

Seba ambled around the back of the house and climbed the ladder to the roof. In his home village of Sessera, Seba often slept under the stars. He liked the feeling of being alone, a tiny speck of humanity under the great expanse of sky. Menorca offered that same opportunity, including the aroma of mastic trees in the distance. Scops owls hooted in the dark, and a pleasant breeze brushed across his skin. He did his best thinking on the roof.

*When Artemis ran to the stables, was that her message that I should stay and be the dutiful son? Or was that permission to leave because she'll watch over Mama and Papa? Can I endure the entire winter inside the crowded house with my parents and my new cousins?*

He considered. Camila was kind, and she *did* have a softening effect on his mother. She and Nicolas were perfect together, and Agnete was thrilled with the possibility of being an adopted grandmother to a growing family.

Fernanda was blunt and opinionated, but very smart and funny, rather like Papouli. Ignasi, though, was bitter and angry, and justifiably so: after all he'd endured at the hands of that evil tyrant, Brumbaugh, he struggled to find good in the world. But Kostas, with his patience and kindness, was helping him find his way back.

The responsible decision would be for Seba to stay and ensure his parents' safety. But what if he was meant to be on the sea, flying high, sharing adventures with his best friend and learning from one of the greatest captains ever to spin a ship's wheel? He turned these thoughts over in his mind for a long time; deciding to stay, then the next moment resolving to leave.

Seba didn't intend to fall asleep, but after a full day and night of wedding festivities, followed by the pleasant breeze and solitude under a midnight sky, he did.

#

Seba awoke to the sound of a loud crash in the stables, followed by the horses' frantic squealing. He was disoriented; he didn't know how long he'd been asleep. His eyes flicked to the eastern sky. It was still several hours until daybreak; Venus had not yet risen, but Jupiter, who rose at nightfall, was still visible.

He scrambled down the ladder, lit the oil lamp that Fernanda kept outside the kitchen door, and ran toward the stables. Fernanda was beside him in a flash, her long nightgown flapping behind her as she ran.

What they found shocked them both. An oil lamp had overturned and was beginning to burn the hay. Seba pulled a blanket from a rack on the wall and laid it over the fire, but the flames were lapping the haybales on the near wall. He tried to stomp it out with his feet, to no avail. The horses stamped and whinnied, pushing against the doors to their stalls. The heat from the flames increased, threatening to catch the building on fire.

Fernanda ran to the large barrel used to water the horses and dipped a wooden bucket. She yelled to Seba, "Grab another bucket! Hurry!"

Seba pulled a wooden bucket off the nearest bench and filled it to the brim from the barrel. He ran and tossed the contents of his bucket on the flaming hay, just as Fernanda had done. The water drenched the fire well enough to permit them to stomp out the embers.

Fernanda said, "Seba, toss another bucket on the fire while I let the horses out." Seba did as instructed, coughing and wheezing from the clouds of smoke that rose from the hay. He turned toward the rear stalls and his heart dropped. Kostas lay on the ground between the stable doors, with Zephyr nuzzling his neck and stomping her back hoof.

"Fernanda, come quick! It's my father." He dropped to his knees beside Kostas.

Fernanda dashed to Kostas's side and felt the side of his throat for a pulse.

Seba felt all the blood in his body rise up into his head. He gasped, "Is he alive?"

"Alive, but unconscious," she said. The horses continued to whinny. Fernanda turned her attention to them. "What is it, girl?"

Zephyr tapped her back hoof and raised her muzzle skyward, her body pulsing with agitation.

"Clever girl," Fernanda said. "See, she's telling us what happened. Kostas fell from the hayloft. I need to examine him for broken bones." She leaned over Kostas, murmuring, "What were you doing out here in the middle of the night?"

Seba looked up where Fernanda had pointed. In the weak light of the oil lamp, he saw several bales of hay close to the edge of the loft; the rope pulleys looped over the rafters swung forward and back. One bale hovered precariously on the lip of the loft, leaning toward the floor. It appeared to be on the brink of falling on their heads.

Zephyr grabbed Seba's shirtsleeve with her teeth, trying to pull him to standing.

"Yes, girl. I'll get it." Seba ran up the ladder to the loft and pulled the bale away from the precipice. Zephyr and Euros immediately stopped whinnying. They were more concerned about saving Kostas than escaping from the fire themselves. "Thank you, friends," Seba said softly. "What would we do without you?"

He quickly returned down the ladder and bent over his father opposite Fernanda. "I think he was trying to drop the haybales for the horses. But why so early, before it was light? And why would he attempt it alone, after a long day of celebrating the wedding?"

Fernanda delicately pressed Kostas's arms and legs, looking for fractures. "I don't know," she said. "Perhaps he couldn't sleep after all the excitement, although I don't see how. We were all exhausted. I could have slept for two days straight."

A realization dawned on Seba. "But that's exactly it," he said. "He knew you were tired, and he wanted to help. He wanted to see the look on your face when you came to the stables and found your chores already done. You know, like the *xotiká* and the *tsankáris*."

Fernanda stared at him. "I have no idea what either of those words mean. Please, get some cool water from the barrel to put on your father's head. Perhaps that will revive him."

Seba ran to the large barrel, which was almost empty after putting out the fire. He scooped some water with a wooden ladle and knelt beside his father. He dipped his fingers in the ladle and gently patted Kostas's face with the cool water. "Wake up, Papa. Let us know you're alive."

Seba squeezed his father's hand. He was elated when he felt his father squeeze back.

"Fernanda, did you see that? He gripped my hand. He heard me!"

Fernanda looked relieved, but her expression was serious. "That's a good sign, Seba. Perhaps you should keep talking. What did you say before? Something about *zo-dih-KA* and *zan-KAR-is*?"

"It's one of my father's favorite stories. It's about an old shoemaker, the tsankáris. This is how my Papouli told the tale: The tsankáris was very honest and hardworking, but nevertheless lived in poverty. He had cut out his very last piece of leather to make a pair of shoes, meaning to awake early the next morning to finish his work. After that, he didn't know what the future would bring. He said his prayers and went to bed, leaving all his cares to the divine creator. In the morning, he awoke in great wonder to find his shoes completed with the finest workmanship, a masterpiece of delicate stitching and design. That day, a customer entered his shop and offered to pay a much higher price than usual for those shoes; that's how well-made they were.

"That provided the shoemaker with enough money to purchase leather for two more pairs of shoes. Again, he cut out the forms that day and left them on his workbench to finish the next morning. He said his prayers and went to bed happy, if not confused. When he awoke, he found two more exquisitely made pairs of shoes, which, again, he sold for a handsome price. Now he had enough money to purchase leather for four pairs of shoes, which he expertly cut during the day and found mysteriously finished to perfection the next morning. This went on for some time, and the shoemaker began to earn a comfortable living.

"One evening, the cobbler and his wife decided to stay awake to discover how his leather cuttings magically became shoes each night. They were amazed to see two little xotiká—elves, you'd call them—hard at work. They were naked themselves, but they could stitch, pull, ply, rap, and tap like lightning. The shoes were finished in no time, and the xotiká cleaned up the workshop and bustled away quicker than the wink of an eye.

"Now, it's a rare and wonderful thing to have the blessings of the xotiká, and naturally the cobbler and his wife were grateful. Seeing that the xotiká had no clothes of their own, the wife thought she might sew them miniature shirts, pants, vests, and coats to show her appreciation. Her husband agreed to make them each a pair of tiny shoes. The cobbler and his wife wanted to show how grateful they were for all the little xotiká had done for them. They worked all day and left the tiny clothes and shoes on the workbench that night, hiding behind the curtain when the little creatures appeared.

"The xotiká arrived and were delighted with their gifts. They donned the clothes and shoes and danced merrily around the shop before traipsing out the door, never to be seen again. And though the xotiká never reappeared, goodness followed the cobbler and his wife from that time forward, as long as they lived."

Seba felt his father squeezing his hand tighter and tighter as he told the story, which filled Seba's chest with hope.

Fernanda was smiling now. "That's a lovely little story, and one I've never heard before. We should share it with Camila and Nicolas."

Kostas whispered, "Yes. Bless the couple."

Fernanda fell back, startled. "Kostas, hush and lie still. I need to determine the extent of your injuries. I'll ask you questions and you squeeze Seba's hand for yes. If the answer is no, don't squeeze at all. Do you understand?"

Kostas squeezed Seba's hand. Fernanda proceeded to press on Kostas's torso, shoulders, arms, hands, legs, and feet, asking if he could feel the sensations. Each time he squeezed Seba's hand. After Fernanda was finally satisfied with her patient's condition, she asked, "Do you think you can stand?"

The sky was beginning to lighten when Fernanda, Seba, and Kostas reached the house. The going was excruciatingly slow, but Seba was heartened by the fact that his father could walk at all. He winced each time he took a step, obviously in pain, but denied there was anything wrong.

Camila and Agnete were awake yet bleary-eyed, preparing bread for the day, as they did each morning before dawn, wedding or not. Nicolas was still in bed, and Ignasi sat in a kitchen chair overseeing the bread production.

Agnete ran to Kostas and put her hands on his face. "*Agape mou*! What happened?"

Seba said, "He had a fall in the stables."

Fernanda and Seba helped Kostas to his bed while Agnete clanked bottles, jars, mortar, and pestle around in the kitchen until she had prepared a balm for the pain. In a few minutes, she returned with a bowl filled with a soft, moist mixture of plant material with a strong bittersweet smell of pine and grass. Agnete swooped in and said to her husband, "Where does it hurt?"

Kostas gave his wife a wan smile. "I'm fine, *agape mou*."

Agnete kissed Kostas on the forehead. "Don't you lie to

me, Kostas Krizomatis." She called to Camila in the kitchen. "Do you have additional stores of arnica? We have plenty of comfrey and ruta, but I used the last of the arnica for Ignasi's poultice. I'll need to get more, or find a substitute. Kostas hurts all over."

Camila entered Kostas's room, followed by Ignasi. She said, "Of course, Agnete. Anything for you and Kostas. That was the last of the arnica, but we could substitute willow bark. Is this the same salve you created for Ignasi?"

Agnete slathered the poultice on Kostas's shoulders. "Yes, with the addition of comfrey for bone healing. For Ignasi, I've used ruta for relief from bruising, and arnica for swelling and pain."

Camila tapped her chin thoughtfully. "I believe I know where the wild arnica grows north of here, and there are willow trees along the road to Alaior. Remember, Ignasi? You and I collected baskets of arnica last fall. Perhaps Nicolas or Seba can forage for more today and collect a bit of willow bark as well. You can tell them where to find it." She sighed. "It's a pity Paolo won't be able to assist. He told me at the wedding that he was leaving with Doctor Turnbull today."

Seba flushed.

"In fact," Camila continued, "Paolo seemed to think you were going as well, Seba. Why are you still here?"

Seba surveyed his parents' room: his father lying helpless in his bed, brow furrowed and shoulders drawn, his mother anxiously dabbing him with a healing salve, and Camila, Fernanda, and Ignasi nearby, their faces taut with concern.

Seba fought to keep his voice even. "They won't be back until spring. I can't leave now."

Fernanda crossed her arms over her chest. "Seba, think

about what you're saying. We can care for your parents. You talk my head off with stories of the sea until I feel like I'll turn into a fish; you know it's where you belong!"

"That's enough, Fernanda!" Seba said, rather louder than he intended. "My parents need me, and I'm not going anywhere. I've made my decision."

Fernanda stared at Seba, her arms still crossed. Then she turned to Agnete as if to say: *He's your son, all right.*

# 14 BECOMING MENORCAN



*October 14, 1767*
*Mahón, Menorca*
*Afternoon*

The following weeks were a blur for Seba. Each day was spent tending to his father and Ignasi, helping Fernanda and Camila with the horses in preparation for the Festival of Our Lady of Grace, and trying not to think about the salt spray and trade winds racing across the deck of the *New Fortuna*.

It had been six weeks since the wedding, and in the event that Camila might be with child, everyone agreed that Seba would ride Zephyr in the festival. Riding Zephyr, encouraging her to test her speed, and feeling the wind in his hair as they flew over the meadows was as close as Seba could get to the freedom of being on the water.

Zephyr was also incredibly patient when Camila tried to teach Seba how to remain in the saddle during the notorious hind-legs walk. It was imperative that he not fall. It would ruin the luck in the coming year if the caixer fell from his horse while riding through town.

Fernanda said, "Seba, you will remain in that saddle or you will answer to me."

Her fist was in the air, very similar to the poses Agnete would strike when she was angry, and Seba got the point. "I'll try my best," he said.

"No, you will do better than try. You *will* remain in the seat."

Seba said, "Yes, ma'am," then clamped his hand over his mouth.

Camila burst out laughing. "It seems you're no stranger to a scolding, Seba."

Seba's face was crimson. "Stop wasting time. Let's get to work."

The sisters giggled and teased Seba, mimicking his gruff "Let's get to work" every time he slipped from the back of the saddle when Zephyr reared up on her hind legs. He refused to give them the satisfaction of a response, even after he'd fallen off at least twenty times. He picked himself off the ground, dusted off the back of his trousers, and climbed back in the saddle.

A few times Zephyr snorted when Seba slid out of the saddle and smacked the ground with a thud. "Are you laughing at me, girl?" he asked. Across the paddock, he saw that Euros had turned away, as if he couldn't bear to witness Seba's humiliation. Seba said to himself as much as to the horse, "Don't you worry. I never give up. I'll keep going until I get it right."

And on the twenty-first attempt, he did just that. Zephyr walked the entire length of the fence on her back legs with Seba in the saddle. *Success!*

"Thanks for being patient with me, girl."

Zephyr tossed her head back and pranced around the training yard, Seba thrusting his arms above his head in victory.

Seba was excited and terrified at the same time. Guiding Zephyr as she walked on her back legs around the stable yard was quite the accomplishment; doing the same thing in the town square amidst throngs of raucous celebrants, banging drums, blaring brass horns, and barking dogs was another endeavor altogether.

When he wasn't practicing for the festival, Seba spent time with his father and Ignasi. Sometimes the three would sit in the stables with the horses, talking of farm tools, oppressive governments, and Kostas's many inventions. Seba was thrilled at his father's progress. Fernanda said the fall from the loft had actually knocked Kostas's hip joint back into place, something that no physician could have done. He was still bruised and his muscles were weak, but his limp was almost gone. And as a fellow survivor of torture, he was the only person from whom Ignasi would take advice

Ignasi said, "Kostas, we were young when we lost our parents. You remind me of my father. He was always tinkering with something or another in the barn or stables."

"I believe tinkering is the reason I became a ship's engineer. I enjoy experimenting and making machines more efficient."

Seba said, "Ignasi, Fernanda tells me your father was a great hunter."

Ignasi's eyes took on a faraway look. "Yes, there was no swifter arrow on the island. He taught me everything he knew." Ignasi held out his arms. "But now that my back muscles are severed, I can't draw a bow. I miss it. That damn

Brumbaugh! If I ever have the chance—"

Euros snorted from his stall, interrupting Ignasi's words.

"I know, boy," Ignasi said, a little shamefaced. "But I can't help it. That evil despot makes me so angry, I want to break him in half with my bare hands."

Kostas pulled on his beard. "You know, when I was in Constantinople, I was introduced to a crossbow. Have you heard of it?"

"No, my father never mentioned it."

"The Ottomans called it an *arbalest*. I've never experienced such power. You don't draw it back like a bow; you crank it, as if winding a well-rope. It's very simple. The string holds itself and the bolt waits on your prey. It may be exactly the thing to return you to your hunting days."

"No, Kostas," Ignasi protested. "I'll never hunt again. I haven't the strength."

"It wasn't only your strength that made you a hunter," said Kostas. "It was your eyes and your patience. You've still got those. The crossbow can make up for the rest."

"I don't know. It might make me feel worse if it doesn't work."

Kostas would not be deterred. "Your mind is sharp, Ignasi, and I could use your assistance. Why don't we build a crossbow together? Seba, you spent many days assisting me at Sessera's shipyard. You'd be a great help on the crossbow as well. Wouldn't you two like to humor an old man?"

Ignasi smiled weakly. "After all you and Agnete have done for me these past weeks, how could I refuse? I'm grateful for both of you."

Seba thought that building a crossbow would be a welcome distraction from his daydreams about the adventures he could be having on the *New Fortuna*. "I'd like to help, too," he said. "Thanks, Papa."

Fernanda entered the stables with apples for Euros and Zephyr, who nickered affectionately. "You two have been working hard, preparing for the festival," she said. "You deserve extra treats today." The horses agreed, whinnying playfully and flicking their tails.

Kostas said, "The three of us are going to build a crossbow. What do you think?"

Fernanda finished feeding the horses before putting her arm on Ignasi's shoulder. "I think it's a wonderful idea. Brother, I believe you'll be back to hunting before winter, if Kostas's engineering skills are any indication. His ingenious new plow has cut our harvesting time in half. Why didn't we think to make a seed-planting plow before now? We could have doubled our production. Even Zephyr and Euros enjoy pulling it around the fields. Don't you, friends?"

Euros and Zephyr bobbed their heads up and down in response.

Fernanda continued, "If this new crossbow returns you to hunting, Ignasi, we'll have so much food we'll set up our own stall at the market."

#

Ignasi's recovery was frustratingly slow. The welts on his back oozed and scabbed, then oozed again, which often led him back into the dark corners of his mind. Kostas was always there, however, to support him and lighten his burden.

They talked for hours, trading stories of the injustices they'd suffered at the hands of their respective oppressors, along with Kostas's tales of the Greek heroes who succeeded against overwhelming odds. Ignasi didn't always agree with Kostas, but at least he was engaged.

Occasionally, Seba listened to their debates, such as the one they'd had the prior evening.

"Kostas, you cannot tell me that the Trojan War was worth the cost. The Greeks should never have left their shores. Countless deaths, including that of the great warrior, Achilles. The destruction of an entire city, including women and children. For what?"

"You make a good point, Ignasi; it's one our ancestors have considered for centuries."

"And the long journey back home, fraught with danger? If I remember correctly, Agamemnon was murdered upon his return."

Kostas didn't argue, but Seba couldn't help himself. "Yes, but we wouldn't have the *Odyssey* without the Trojan War! It made heroes and legends of our ancestors. They demonstrated courage, fortitude, and strength. It is part of our legacy!"

Ignasi simply nodded, as if to say this argument wasn't worth the cost either.

Seba said, "Tell me I'm wrong, Ignasi."

"I just did."

Kostas intervened. "And this is another legacy of our great ancestors, who valued thought, open discourse, and reasoned arguments. The mark of a civilized society. Like inventions to make our lives more meaningful." He smiled. "Such as a crossbow."

The crossbow became the family's all-consuming project, everyone thrilled with Ignasi's reignited interest in life. Kristobal, never one to pass up the opportunity to learn something new, offered to help them, volunteering to acquire parts to be used for the trigger and stock through his "connections" at the wharf. Seba laughed to think of Kristobal negotiating with seasoned sailors twice his age.

Several days later, Kristobal arrived with wooden parts for the crossbow he "acquired" from the savvy carpenter, Francesc Pellicer, as well as a small metal trinket box embellished with three cherubs dancing in a garden of flowers. Gall bounded beside him, gave his signature rooster crow, and plopped down in a pile of hay at Zephyr's feet.

"Good day, friends! I've come from the port with your supplies and a surprise. Nicolas has arrived from Corsica with gifts for everyone. He'll be along later, after his business in the port is concluded."

Seba said, "What's in the box?"

"Baubles, rings, and a few coins that Nicolas acquired in his travels. I believe this was a gift from an Italian sailor from Leghorn." Kristobal winked at Seba, who grinned. *Nicolas must have won the trinket box in a game of Crown and Anchor.*

Kristobal continued, "Each one of us is to choose a treasure from the box. Fernanda, why don't you go first?"

Fernanda dipped her fingers into the box and pulled out several silver chains. "Only one, you say? That's hardly charitable." She chose one long silver chain and returned the others to the ornate box.

Kostas chose a gold coin and Ignasi retrieved a brass Sant Roc medallion.

Kristobal said, "Go on, Seba, I'll choose after you."

A small gold ring with an orange gemstone gleamed from inside the box. Seba picked it up and slid it onto his smallest finger. It was snug.

Kristobal squinted at Seba's finger. "Ah, the topaz ring. Good choice, Seba. I had my sights on that as well."

Seba recalled the amber rings on Kristobal's fingers at the wedding feast and struggled to remove the ring from his finger. "It's yours. I believe it's too small for me."

"No, no-no-no. I couldn't take it from you."

Seba said, "Kristobal, I insist."

Kristobal gave a whoop of pleasure and easily slid the ring on his fourth finger. "I was hoping you'd say that. Thanks, Seba!"

Seba chose a silver coin that felt heavy in his hand. "Let's take this box to the house. Mama is going to love this tiny alabaster cross. I believe Camila will choose a silver chain to match Fernanda's."

Nicolas arrived as they sat down to a meal of baked eels, leeks, chard, and raisins, spiced with saffron and cloves. As always, he had a new story for them: his latest revolved around his overly zealous praise for a local merchant's cooking.

"I suppose I complimented the food too enthusiastically. But of course, I was hoping to make a sale. The merchant invited me to his family home for supper later that evening, and when I arrived, I was greeted by the merchant's daughter, who had already stitched my initials into her kerchief! The old dog told her I'd come to court her!"

Camila raised an eyebrow. "What did you do?"

"Well, darling, I had to think quickly. I feigned a deep-seated vow of celibacy in order to make my escape." Nicolas flashed a smile at his sweetheart. "When I returned to the ship and shared my tale, it turns out I was the fourth unintended suitor for the merchant's daughter this week!"

Ignasi laughed so hard he called out, "Stop, or you're going to reopen my scabs!"

Seba was glad to see Nicolas. But he was even happier that Ignasi could joke about his wounds.

Ignasi said, "Nicolas, perhaps you can take me with you the next time you travel there."

Nicolas chuckled. "Fancy yourself a Corsican bride, do you, brother-in-law?"

"I wouldn't mind adding to our family. I see how happy you and Camila are together."

Agnete patted Ignasi's head and hugged the happy couple. "You were married under the blessings of Sant Lluis. Give it time, my darlings, and you may be expanding our family before the next harvest."

Ignasi clapped his hands. "That would be wonderful. I look forward to becoming Uncle Ignasi."

Camila smiled demurely. "I suppose now is as good a time as any, seeing that the family is gathered together and my dear Nicolas is at home."

All eyes turned toward her expectantly. She lowered her gaze. "I've been so emotional these last few weeks, and I feel different in my body. I believe Agnete's prediction is already coming true. In fact, this morning I cleaned up the wooden cradle our father made when Fernanda was born. It provided sweet dreams for Fernanda, then me, and finally Ignasi when we were infants. I believe it's ready for the next generation."

Nicolas dropped to his knees. "Camila, do you mean it?"

Camila said, "It's still early, but my grandmother always said women know about these things."

Agnete agreed wholeheartedly. "My *yiayiá* said the same. You and Nicolas will be wonderful parents. Congratulations! God bless you both."

Seba looked around at his family. He was glad in their happiness, of course, but he couldn't help but feel restless. *I'm so stupid. They didn't need me here. Why did I stay?* "Congratulations, you two," he said, rising to his feet. "I'm going to go tell Zephyr and Euros the good news."

When Seba arrived at the stables, Zephyr was agitated.

"Do you want to go for an evening walk, girl? I need some fresh air as well. Let's go to the cliffs above the wharf."

Seba and Zephyr walked to the town and found a spot under a few oak trees near the cliff's edge. They watched the sky catch fire as the sun set in the west. They stayed there until long after the moon rose, Seba imagining he was on one of the ships below, a part of the crew preparing for a new adventure.

# 15 EVICTION

*October 15, 1767*
*Mahón, Menorca*
*Midmorning*

The next morning, Seba and Zephyr were slowly walking back along the dirt road, Seba looking forward to some thinking time on the roof with the cool breeze blowing from the west. When he passed the first stone-walled pasture leading to the house, however, he saw a commotion in the distance and a heap of chairs, tables, and other furniture that had been tossed into the yard like garbage. A wooden headboard flew out the second floor window and landed hard on the ground, where it broke into several pieces. Seba heard Fernanda's voice, arguing loudly, but he couldn't make out her words.

Seba heard a voice in his head. *I must hide Zephyr.* The thought came unbidden. Why would he think such a thing? Perhaps, he reflected, it had come from Zephyr herself.

Whatever its source, the suggestion was too powerful to resist. He dismounted, making sure they hadn't been seen.

"Go to the far pasture and stay hidden in the trees. I promise I'll find you." Zephyr trotted off toward the line of trees that marked the Rementeria Arandia property.

Seba ran to the house, adrenaline coursing through his body. As he neared the front door, his veins went to ice. A group of British soldiers were marching in and out of the house, carrying out the family's belongings and tossing them into the yard. Fernanda attempted to argue with the most senior officer, but he blatantly ignored her.

Agnete ran to Seba and squeezed his arm. Her brown eyes were swollen with tears and ringed in red, the fire all but gone from them. "Sebastian, they're taking our home!"

"What?"

Agnete pointed to Fernanda and the officer who pretended she didn't exist. "That man barged into the house with a paper in his hand and told us that our home was now owned by the British military. Oh, I don't understand! How could this happen?"

Kostas and Ignasi, leaning on each other, walked slowly from around the back of the house. Seba ran to them.

"Son, bring Ignasi a chair from the kitchen. Use the back door."

Seba was back in a flash with two wooden chairs from the kitchen, one for Ignasi and one for his father. Ignasi said, "Brumbaugh will never be satisfied until he's ruined our lives."

Seba's brain was full of fog. "What are you talking about?"

"Whatever he wants, he takes. Don't try to resist. Look at me; I'm the example of what happens when you fight back. It's no use. Brumbaugh will keep taking until there's nothing left."

Seba said, "I need to stop this."

A man in uniform passed them, carrying the clothes trunk from Seba's bedroom.

As he was about to heave it onto the pile of furniture, Seba addressed him in English. "Wait, those are my things. Why are you throwing them out?"

The soldier, surprised to hear English from a local's mouth, said, "We're commandeering this home for the good of the Royal Navy and the Crown, under the auspices of King George the Third. It is every British subject's duty to support the Crown, and as our commander, Elias Brumbaugh, is in need of a home, he has ordered us to seize this one. It's all in the documents."

"Why can't the commander build his own home? Why does he have to take ours?"

The soldier stopped and stared at Seba. "You don't understand, do you? The island hasn't supplied the resources we need to build a mansion fit for the commander. At what with the shipwrecks and the delays from England, it could take decades to build him a proper home. It's your civic duty as subjects of the realm to turn over your residence."

Seba thought that was the most cruel and stupid thing he'd ever heard. "Is the Crown providing us with another home?"

"Well, I don't know anything about that. You'll have to ask the commander."

"Elias Brumbaugh?"

"Yes. Who else?"

Seba was afraid the man was going to say that. "Can't you give us a few days to make arrangements?"

"Sorry, mate, but we must fulfill our duties or we'll be

charged with insubordination. I'm not keen on being flogged in the public square, so I do what I'm told. Best you take your things and leave. If the furniture isn't gone by sundown, we have orders to burn the lot."

Seba heard a scream from the window above, and looked up to see Camila and one of the enlisted men tugging on the wooden cradle her father had made. Camila's hair had fallen from her headscarf and covered her face, such that she looked like a wild animal. Her bedgown over her nightdress were disheveled and torn, and her shrieks pierced the air like knives.

The man's hand gripped one side of the cradle; he was trying to pull it toward the open window to throw it out, but Camila had wrapped herself around it as if it were a part of her she refused to abandon.

"Let go, you vixen! I have my orders."

"No!"

Camila had wrapped her legs around the wooden bedframe for support and refused to release the cradle. The man pulled and tugged, but the weight of the cradle and Camila's fierce determination had them held in a stalemate, neither one willing to let go.

But in the end, that's exactly what the soldier did. He removed his hands from the cradle, and Seba watched with horror as Camila fell backward through the window, still twisted around the cradle. She seemed to fall very slowly, landing in a crumpled heap in the dooryard.

The soldiers halted their labor to gawk, but only for a moment. Agnete, Fernanda, and Seba ran to Camila's side, Kostas and Ignasi following behind.

Ignasi said, "What have they done to you?"

Camila clutched her belly; her breath came shallow and shaky. "This can't be happening."

A pool of blood bloomed under Camila's skirts, and Agnete began barking orders—for cloths, hot water, and a pennyroyal tincture from the kitchen. "Sebastian, quick, go around back!"

Seba dashed again to the back door, avoiding anyone in uniform. He pulled a glass bottle of pennyroyal from the wooden shelf, a stack of clean linen cloths from the side table, and poured hot water from the hearth into a stone jar.

With his arms full, he sprinted to Camila, handing everything to his mother. She dipped the cotton cloths into the amphora of hot water, then poured the pennyroyal tisane onto a cloth.

"Camila, I need to place this poultice on your stomach."

Camila was curled up like a fire spiraling inward, writhing like a snake. "It feels like knives cutting me from the inside out," she whimpered. "Please, make it stop!"

Agnete put her hands through the tears in Camila's nightdress and placed the tisane-soaked cloth on her skin. Camila howled, drawing her knees up to her abdomen. Agnete soaked another cloth in hot water, poured the pennyroyal decoction on it, and laid it lightly on Camila's brow. As Agnete worked on one side, Fernanda knelt on the other, pressing her sister's bones to check for breaks.

"Do you have back pain? Do you feel dizzy? Are you going to be sick?"

Camila writhed and sobbed, unable to form words as she thrashed about on the ground.

Fernanda searched the area until she located two palm-sized stones; she dropped them into the amphora of hot water and removed Camila's slippers. When the stones were heated, Fernanda placed them on the bottoms of her sister's feet.

Kostas, Ignasi, and Seba watched the women work,

unable to do anything to help. They knelt around Camila and Agnete and whispered prayers for the soul of her unborn child.

*Holy Mary of divine grace, mirror of justice, seat of wisdom, mystical rose, comforter of the afflicted, morning star, health of the sick, Queen of Peace, deliver us from our present sorrow. Through Christ our Lord. Amen. Amen. Amen.*

Camila's body shook as her sharp cries turned to keening moans. The family knelt together around her as soldiers threw their belongings into the grass. They didn't know what to do or where to go.

"Where's Nicolas?" Seba asked.

Ignasi said, "He tried to reason with the men, but when they refused to listen, he saddled up Euros and galloped to his Aunt Theodora's for help. He hasn't returned."

"Cowards," Seba spat. "Elias Brumbaugh should be tried for murder."

Fernanda's eyes flashed. "I'll kill him myself."

Two soldiers carried Camila's wooden trunk out of the house and tossed it carelessly onto the grass; her dresses and skirts tumbled out like dirty laundry. A diminutive figure was silhouetted in the front doorway. Seba felt a zing of electricity race through his body. *Brumbaugh.*

Elias Brumbaugh called out orders to the soldiers as if he were commanding a ship. "Make sure you get everything out of here. I want this dirty place scrubbed from stem to stern. The wagons with my belongings will be here before midday. I expect to have everything in place in my new home by sundown. I'd like to have a good night's sleep in my new lodgings."

Seba made a fist and punched it into the open palm of his opposite hand. "This won't stand. Captain Brumbaugh!" he called in English. "I need a word with you."

Brumbaugh stopped in his tracks, surprised that he was being so addressed by a Menorcan. It had the desired effect of gaining his attention, along with the undesired effect of sparking his anger. His brow furrowed until his eyebrows joined together. "How dare you speak to me that way? Where did you learn English?"

Seba bit his tongue so hard that he tasted copper and salt. He counted to ten in his head, praying he could remain calm. Ignoring Brumbaugh's questions, he said, "This home has been in the Rementeria Arandia family for generations. They are related by marriage to Madam Jurada Theodora Alexiano. Surely other arrangements can be made."

Brumbaugh laughed derisively. "I should have you whipped for your insolence. The Royal Navy is improving the lives of everyone in Menorca. Offering up these meager lodgings is the least your family can do for the protection we provide. Your lack of appreciation is exceedingly dangerous."

"Is this truly the best choice, though?" Seba pivoted. "This home is so far from the fort, and not as big as the governor's house. I'm sure the British government can build you a home much grander than this one in town."

Brumbaugh considered the statement, but more out of pure surprise that Seba would address him that way. "I do deserve a grander home, I won't deny it," he drawled. "But I haven't the time to wait for that. The new settlement at Georgetown is still under construction. The junior officer barracks have only just been completed." His face grew hard again. "Not that I owe you an explanation. Move, you're wasting my time."

Seba dug in his heels. "But why so soon, without notice? Couldn't you give us an opportunity to find other lodgings, to pack our belongings ourselves, and to make arrangements for transport? It's only two days until the Festival of Our Lady of Grace. This is cruel and unnecessary. It's unbecoming of an officer of your status."

Brumbaugh stepped closer to Seba and pressed his forefinger into Seba's chest, his eyes narrow. "Another word from you and I'll have you thrown into the garrison prison until you die of old age. That is, unless the vermin kill you first. I suggest you turn around and assist your family in gathering their effects. They are free to go wherever they wish on this island." He smirked "Yet another example of my great munificence on behalf of His Majesty King George."

Seba wanted to grab Brumbaugh's finger and break it in half, but Kostas approached, so close that Seba could feel the warmth of his father's arm. Kostas bowed to Brumbaugh and said in Menorquín, "Pardon my son, Captain, he carries the passion of youth."

Brumbaugh removed his finger from Seba's chest and rubbed it on his trousers as if he'd accidentally stuck his finger into a chamber pot. His voice was haughty as he turned on his heel toward the house. "At least someone in this habitation has a modicum of civility."

Looking over his shoulder, Brumbaugh called out to two men carrying a large wood-framed mirror through the front door. "No, don't remove that. I like it very well, and the family has offered it to me as a gift, in thanks for my protection as Acting Commander-in-Chief and Post-Captain of the Defense Squadron and Dockyards of Port Mahón, on behalf of His Majesty's Royal Navy in Menorca." Brumbaugh gestured toward the stables. "When you've emptied the house, move to the stables. Anything found there is included in the gift from these grateful British subjects. I hear tell there are a few prized Menorquín horses here, who would do well in my service."

Seba's fingers curled into a fist. But as his arm drew back, he felt Kostas's grip on his shoulder. "Patience," whispered Kostas. "Now is not the time to fight. Think of Camila and Nicolas, and what they've lost. Now is the time for us to care for our family."

Seba dropped his hand and turned to gather up the clothes and the usable furniture. Together, he and Fernanda gingerly lifted Camila and placed her into the family's garden cart. "We're going to the Sisters of the Virgin Mary," Fernanda said. "The convent will take us in."

#

The weary family passed through the gates of Sant Roc and turned left toward the convent. The nuns took an oath of poverty, charity, and healing. They cared for the sick, be they animal or human, and like St. Francis of Assisi, they had a deep love and respect for all creatures. For the most part, the British government left them to their own devices, allowing them to exist in peace and solitude.

King George I had declared that the local inhabitants were granted religious freedom, as long as their ecclesiastical leaders were native islanders. In 1718, under the first British rule of Menorca, before the island was lost to the French in 1756, the king had approved ten articles written by the Archbishop of Canterbury regarding the activities of the "Churches and Convents of Minorca," which included the requirement:

*That it will be for the Peace and Safety of the Island to be wholly discharged from the Government of the Bishop of Majorca and of the Archbishop of Valendia, and from all manner of Dependence upon either of them; And that the Convents in like manner be discharged from all Dependence upon and Obedience to any foreign Generals or Provincials.*

As a result, the Sisters of the Virgin Mary were free to provide their services to the townspeople, caring for those who managed to successfully transverse Quarantine Island only to fall ill after entering the town of Mahón. With open arms, they welcomed the tired, the poor, and those burdened by hopelessness. At this moment, Seba and his family were all of those things.

The autumn breeze blew from the north, bringing a harbinger of the coming winter. A winter without their home. The oak and chestnut trees had begun to change color, the harvest was in full swing, and Seba couldn't help but think that everything was dying all around him.

When they reached the convent's large wooden doors, Fernanda knocked loudly. When they swung open, it was Kristobal who stood behind them. He leaned forward to greet Fernanda with a kiss on each cheek, but gasped when he peered into the cart behind her.

"Is that Camila? What happened?"

Fernanda's voice broke. "It was a nightmare, Kristobal. They've taken everything from us."

Kristobal's eyes grew wide. "What do you need?"

"Would you do us a kindness and water and feed Zephyr? She's had a difficult night, as have we all. And send word to the Madam Jurada that she and Nicolas can find us here."

Kristobal frowned. "I'm so sorry. Of course." He pointed to the large chapel inside the grounds. "Take Camila to the abbess, in the chapel. She will send for the doctress."

Fernanda said, "We can't thank you enough, Kristobal. You're a godsend."

They were met by a group of nuns at the chapel steps. Tears sprang to the eyes of the nuns as they heard Fernanda's tale. The abbess directed two young novices to transport Camila to the convent's doctress. Agnete had not let go of Camila's hand in the long the journey from their home, and Seba knew she would not leave Camila until she was satisfied that her young cousin was out of danger.

"Beloved Mary, Our Lady of mercy, hope, and compassion, has brought us to this refuge. I pray for her unfailing protection, wisdom, and guidance, now and forever. Amen, amen, amen." She walked behind the novices, cradling Camila's hand and whispering prayers to herself.

The abbess opened her arms to the others. "Welcome, brothers and sisters. Enter into our care in peace. You have suffered much. This house and these grounds are yours for as long as you need. May the peace of our Lord comfort you."

They followed the abbess to their new lodgings, in a building adjacent to the convent's outer walls. It served as housing for a few of the convent's animals, as well as those to whom the nuns offered refuge, including Kristobal and Gall. Made of stone and three stories high, their new dwelling reminded Seba of the houses in Sessera. As in his old home, the nuns' donkeys and few chickens were housed on the first floor with the tools that they used to farm the little plot of land behind their house. The floor above the animal pen held the kitchen and sleeping quarters; at the moment, the only residents were Kristobal and Gall.

Gall, as it turned out, had been born at the convent with five littermates for whom the nuns immediately found homes. As most of the townspeople had their own roosters and hens, they didn't want a vocal sheepdog. Kristobal had already taken to calling the big fluffy dog Gall on account of his dawn howls. When Kristobal's father died, the abbess said that Gall had volunteered to be his guardian.

Kristobal opened the door for them. Gall was exuberant to have guests until he saw their downcast faces. He pulled his tail between his legs and gave a howl like a wail of sympathy.

# 16 FESTIVAL OF HORSES

*October 17, 1767*
*Mahón, Menorca*
*Late Morning*

"How can I ride in the festival after everything that's happened?" Seba groaned. He was curled up on the straw mattress by the hearth, still in his nightshirt. "No one wants to celebrate. The town won't miss one rider."

Fernanda kicked him with toe of her boot. "Seba, get up. We have never missed the festival and we are not starting now. Get your uniform. Now."

"No one will miss me. Go ahead without me."

"Aren't you the cousin who told us you never give up?" Fernanda needled. "The one who swam the deadly currents of the Strait of Chios? Lord knows I've heard *that* one more than a few times. I suppose that was merely a story you tell to make yourself look good."

Seba rolled over and rubbed his eyes. "Fine. I'll go."

Camila sat in a chair by the hearth, a bandage wrapped around her midsection for support. The convent's doctress had treated and released her the prior day, advising her to rest and stay off her feet as much as possible. She said, "I know how you feel, Seba, but it would cheer me to think of you riding Zephyr through the crowd. Lord knows we could use some good luck after all we've been through."

Fernanda added, "You wouldn't want to deprive Zephyr of her day in the sun, would you?"

That was the last thing Seba wanted to do. "Of course not."

Fortunately, they'd saved the caixer uniforms when the soldiers threw their belongings into the yard. Seba wore the one that had belonged to Camila and Fernanda's father. The shirt and trousers were white, and Seba wore a black vest embroidered with tiny golden flowers, a black coat with a long tail, a gold cravat, and a black felt hat. Well-oiled black leather boots and white kid gloves completed the uniform.

Seba brushed Zephyr until her coat shined like obsidian. They'd also managed to save her saddle blanket, a treasure handed down from the girls' great-grandmother, who had embroidered it with lilacs and violets and trimmed it in white fringe. Zephyr's bridle was decorated with ribbons featuring elaborately stitched buttercups, and her headpiece was a five-pointed star embellished with lavender and gold thread.

Camila braided gold and purple ribbons through Zephyr's tail, and the leather strap around her breast was joined in the middle by a medallion that displayed a shining red heart in the center of an intricately woven St. John's cross encircled by finely-threaded scrollwork. Zephyr stamped her feet impatiently, tired of the preparation and anxious for the performance.

Nicolas and Euros had returned from Theodora Alexiano's with bad news. She had filed a complaint with the British government in London, but it would be weeks or months before a determination was made. She said there was nothing else she could do.

Fernanda and Euros, too, donned their uniforms for the festival. In contrast to Zephyr's gold and lavender adornments, Euros's saddle blanket, bridle ribbons, and headpiece were threaded with designs of red and white.

As they entered the gates of Sant Roc, Seba's hands shook. He was left-handed, which made it more difficult to communicate to the right and left with both reins linked together and his dominant hand unable to assist. Early on in his training, he had floated the idea to Fernanda of flipping his hands to grip the reins with his left and the crop with his right, ensuring that he wouldn't fall; but Fernanda had lectured him sternly about tradition, accusing him of trying to ruin the festival before it began. He had not raised the subject again.

It seemed like that conversation occurred in another lifetime, though it had only been weeks before. Indeed, every moment since they'd stepped foot on Quarantine Island seemed filled with mist and fog, ups and downs, joy and pain. It felt like an earthquake with no end.

Inside Sant Roc's gates, a horde of hundreds of revelers cheered, waving ribbons and flags, and crowded to get a glimpse of the famous Menorquín and their caixers. Seba's melancholy thoughts were swept away by the throng, replaced by a vision of Alexander the Great entering Ephesus after the battle of the Granicus.

Fernanda and Euros were in the lead. The enthusiastic mob dashed in between Euros's front legs, stretching their arms to touch his breastplate, which was an elaborately wrought St. John's cross. Euros's crucifix was identical to the one worn by Zephyr, but made from silver. It caught the light and sparkled like a diamond in the midday sun.

It was said that anyone who touched the heart of the Menorquín as it stood tall on its hind legs would have good luck in the coming year. That's why the people of Mahón were jostling and knocking into each other with outstretched arms; they were reaching for their luck.

Seba took a deep breath. "Here we go," he whispered, guiding Zephyr into the mass of festivalgoers. He tried to keep his head up; but the way the citizens ducked, dodged, arched, and coiled themselves into precarious positions for the sole purpose of touching the horses' hearts distracted him from his task. Zephyr must have felt him wobble, because she snorted loudly, spewing a misty shower of mucus on the closest revelers.

To the brave celebrants who had just tapped her heart, he called, "That was a special blessing of luck for you!"

Seba, Fernanda, Zephyr, and Euros processed through the streets of Mahón all afternoon, traveling from street to street and making sure that everyone who wanted to reach for their luck had the chance. Seba had a few close calls in which he almost landed on his backside in the middle of the crowd; but each time, Zephyr adjusted and saved him from disaster. In the late afternoon sun on this glorious October day, Seba tasted the allure of Menorca's magic.

Finally, it was time to return home. They were exhausted and famished, forced to smell the grilled meats and fish all day, but with no opportunity to stop and partake. Kostas and Agnete had filled baskets for them, and promised to meet them at the convent after sundown.

As they trotted back to the Sisters of the Virgin Mary, Fernanda brought Euros alongside Zephyr. Fernanda's face was flushed from the day's activities and the warm sun, and she pulled her hair out of the tight bun that had been coiled beneath her hat. Her wavy hair stuck out in all directions and she ran her fingers through it before returning her felt hat to her head. "Aren't you glad you participated?"

Seba leaned forward to kiss the top of Zephyr's head. "Yes," he admitted. "Thank you for forcing me out of bed. Zephyr was amazing."

"She's come to love you, Seba," said Fernanda. "I can tell."

"I've grown fond of her, too," he smiled. "Of course, she's no Matilde . . ."

Fernanda laughed, and Seba ran his hands through Zephyr's mane. Having the great horse as his constant companion had helped keep him from despair in the last few months. Not only was she as fast as the legendary Greek west wind with whom she shared a name; the Zephyros of myth was known to bring good tidings, and this equine Zephyr had done the same for him and his family.

They returned the horses to the stables in the evening, where Camila and several nuns were waiting for them with a huge basket of rosemary olive bread and a wheel of bright yellow Mahón cheese. "A small snack for the hungry caixers while you tend to your horses," Camila said. "Agnete has grilled vegetables, pickled cucumbers, and *sobrassada* waiting for you afterward."

Camila helped Seba and Fernanda brush the sweat from their horses before massaging Zephyr's and Euros's tired muscles. "Seba, you were wonderful," she said. "You and Zephyr make a great partnership."

"Thank you, but shouldn't you be resting? How are you feeling?"

Camila touched her hand to her belly. "It hurts, but not

as much as yesterday. Besides, being around Zephyr and Euros improves my condition like no other medicine I know."

"I understand. And I agree, Zephyr is a wonderful partner. She saved me from toppling backward a few times. I'm sure she prefers you as a caixer, but she tolerated me today, and I'm grateful."

As reward for a job well done, the nuns had prepared a special gruel of warm oats and applesauce for the horses. Seba made sure they had clean bedding, and the sisters covered them with several layers of soft cotton blankets.

After the horses were cared for, Seba and Fernanda returned to Kristobal's house, where they were again welcomed with fanfare, this time from Kostas, Agnete, and Ignasi.

"Sebastian and Fernanda, you were amazing! Nothing lifts the spirits like seeing these noble Menorquín shower the city with blessings. Eat, you two must be famished."

"Thank you, Mama. It was a good day."

Fernanda poured fresh coffee into two earthenware mugs and handed one to Seba. "Your son did a fine job today, Agnete, although I nearly resorted to bodily harm to get him moving."

Agnete laughed. "A fine strategy, one I've employed myself with favorable results."

Seba didn't mind the teasing; he loaded a wooden bowl with grilled eggplant, onions, squash, and peppers, sliced a wedge of cheese from the wheel, and broke one of the bread rounds in half, stuffing most of it in his mouth at one time.

"Sebastian, you were extraordinary on that horse, and so handsome in your caixer uniform! If Papouli could have seen you, his chest would have split open with pride."

Fernanda said, "You were impressive, as well, Agnete.

You weaved in and out of the swarm as if Zephyr's breastplate called you to it. When I saw you duck under Zephyr's forelegs, I couldn't believe my eyes!"

Agnete held her hand in front of her and examined it. "I touched this hand to the cross at Zephyr's breast and felt as if I had joined with the Savior. After the events of the other day, I thought of the words of Isaiah: *When you walk through the fire, you will not be burned; the flames will not consume you.* Well, we've certainly been through the fire and come through."

Camila heated coffee in the copper briki, and when it came to a boil, she reached for Agnete's clay mug. Seba said absently, "It's best to let it come to a boil twice."

Agnete smacked Seba's arm with a cotton rag. "Not that 'boiling twice' nonsense again? Camila, you make it as you wish. Now that my son has traveled the world, he thinks he knows best."

With a wink at Seba, Camila put the briki back on the fire for a second boil.

"Don't forget I saved your life this year, as well, Mama."

"I'll never forget that either, my brave and stubborn rescuer."

Camila said, "Well, I believe you're both very courageous. Agnete, your bravery today ensures your luck in the coming year."

Ignasi hobbled into the kitchen. "I hope you'll forgive me if I don't feel particularly blessed this year. These sores on my back don't seem to be healing, despite everything we've tried. It feels as if my skin is dead. And who knows what evil that pissant tyrant has planned for us next?"

Ignasi had a point. Agnete, Camila, and Fernanda had gathered every herb on the island and combined them in a hundred different ways to keep Ignasi's wounds from becoming infected; while they hadn't become worse, as such, they were not healing properly. Several weeks prior, a yellowish pus had begun to appear in the cuts. They scabbed over, but did not go away; and if Ignasi happened to bump into something or turn over in his sleep, the scabs opened and his sheets were streaked with mucus in the morning. Trying to gather all their furniture and carry it to the convent hadn't helped, either.

Seba thought for a moment. "Ignasi, Doctor Turnbull has traveled the world with various merchant ships, and mentioned that several of his friends became commissioned with the Royal Navy. Perhaps there's a military physician who has a treatment for your wounds."

Ignasi's voice was gruff. "Are you mad? They're the ones who did this to me, Seba. I don't want their help."

"It wasn't a doctor who did this to you. It was that wicked authoritarian, Elias Brumbaugh."

"They're all the same to me, Seba. Elias Brumbaugh didn't attack my sister."

"No, but his mismanagement of this island created the circumstances that allowed it to happen."

Ignasi waved his hand. "I don't want to talk politics with you, Seba. I'm not asking anyone from that garrison for help."

"I understand. But if I go, and I can find something to help you, would you agree to that?"

Ignasi sighed. "I've had enough of people telling others what to do with their lives. You do what you want; I'll not stop you."

Kostas frowned. "I will. It's too dangerous, Seba."

Camila poured a cup of coffee for Kostas. She was clearly uncomfortable with the conversation's turn, but she would do anything to help her brother.

Seba said, "Papa, you told me that when the wind and tide bring unexpected changes, the sailors must adapt. Well, I'm adapting. It's time for us to help ourselves. I'm going to find a remedy for Ignasi."

"Seba, a crowd of happy festivalgoers is not the same as a military garrison. You don't know what you'll face."

"I disagree, Papa. They have surgeons there, maybe even doctors, who treat the injured soldiers. Can you imagine how many of them get hurt doing stupid things when they're drunk? These physicians have to help. They swear an oath. Doctor Turnbull showed me."

Seba ran to his wooden chest and retrieved a small leatherbound book, a medical text, written in Greek. He turned to a page that he had marked, and read to his father:

*I swear by Apollo the physician and Asclepius and Hygieia and Panacea, and will call all the gods and goddesses to witness that I will observe and keep this oath according to my ability and judgment.*

*I will reverence my teacher in this art. Equally with my parents, I will allow them what is necessary for their support and consider their family as my own and teach them this art without reward or agreement. I will impart all my acquirement and instruction to my own children, those of my teacher, and to pupils who have taken a professional oath, but to none else.*

*With regard to healing the sick, I will devise and order for them the best diet, according to my judgment and means and I will do no damage or hurt to them. Neither will I administer a poison to anyone when asked to do so, nor will I counsel anyone to do so. Similarly I will not give to a pregnant woman any medicine with a view to destroy the child. But I will keep pure and holy both my life and my art. I will not cut for stone but will give that labor to surgeons worthy of it.*

*Into whatsoever houses I enter, my visit shall be for the*

*convenience and advantage of the sick, and I will abstain from all intentional harm, especially from abusing the bodies of man or woman, bond or free. And whatsoever I shall see or hear in the course of my profession, as well as outside my profession with regard to the lives of others, if it be what should not be published abroad, I will be silent and keep it secret to myself.*

*If I faithfully observe this oath, and break it not, may I thrive and prosper in my fortune and profession; but if I break it and forswear myself, may the opposite befall me.*

Seba closed the book and shook it at his father. "If I go to the garrison and ask for a physician, they're bound by oath to help me. And perhaps they'll have news of Doctor Turnbull and Paolo."

"I have no idea what you said, Seba," Ignasi admitted. "But your oration was inspired. I'll never step foot in that garrison myself, but you do what you please."

Kostas would not disagree with Ignasi. He bowed his head in defeat.

Seba hugged his father. "Thank you, Papa. I'll leave in the morning and I'll return before you can say *galaktoboureko*."

# 17 HOFFBREET

*October 17, 1767*
*Mahón, Menorca*
*Morning*

At first light, Seba was up and out of the house. As he opened the convent's gate, he felt a nibble on his shoulder. "Hello, Zephyr. How did you escape the stables? I'll take you back."

Zephyr snorted her displeasure and took a step forward. "No, girl. You can't come with me."

She maneuvered past Seba and through the gate, where she turned and waited.

Seba reached for her mane, but she took a step backward. He said, "I don't know what to expect at the fort. If anything happened to you, I'd never forgive myself. You saw for yourself how unhinged Elias Brumbaugh is. Besides, you need your rest after yesterday."

Zephyr stared at him through her long eyelashes. Seba

tried to scoot around behind her so he could direct her back through the gate, but she sidestepped him again. At last, he sighed. "Fine. You win." *And they call* me *stubborn.*

Zephyr snorted in approval, and Seba used the stone wall as a foothold to climb onto her back. Her whole demeanor had transformed; she seemed carefree again.

They followed the three-mile path from the convent to the fort at St. Philip's, which in Menorquín was called Castell de Sant Felip. The azure sky matched the color of Menorca's diminutive rock thrushes, who warbled to each other, their happy melodies carried upward by autumn's sweet breath. Bowered by a canopy of dark green leaves, the shy little birds happily flitted among the quince and persimmon trees that lined the well-trodden dirt road to the fort. *I hope Brumbaugh doesn't find a reason to torture you, little thrushes.*

White puffy clouds scudded briskly from west to east with the autumn winds. It was still quite warm in the sun, but the breeze cooled the sweat on Seba's forehead as soon as it formed. Zephyr trotted happily, occasionally lifting her nose to take in the pleasant smell of orchards and fresh meadow. Along the way, they passed stone-fenced pastures dotted with doe-eyed cows nibbling the clover.

Seba passed several stone-towered windmills, their white sails whipping against the spars as they cheerfully ground the barley harvested from the year's spring planting. Soon the winter barley would be sowed in the fields that had lain fallow over the summer. The millers labored day and night to supply bread to the Royal Navy, while the sheep and goats ambled through the fields eating what had fallen from the sheaves.

The ramparts of St. Philip's rose in the distance, surrounded by mounds of dirt, limestone, dusty bricks, and other construction debris. The garrison was being fortified and expanded by British soldiers, assisted by local Menorcan boys looking to make extra money for their families.

Seba pulled Zephyr to a halt. About fifty yards ahead, the road was blocked by a large wooden cart that had been overturned, one of its wooden wheels rotating like a spinning wheel that had lost its yarn. A young man with a thin build and golden skin was hurriedly gathering long-stemmed plants and squatty brown roots that had spilled onto the ground, throwing them haphazardly into several baskets strewn around the cart. He wore the loose breeches of a navy landsman, the lowest rank of enlisted recruits.

A group of British officers on horseback trotted out from the fort, their brass buttons gleaming in the sunlight. By the quantity of gold trim on their collars, cuffs, and wide lapels, Seba judged them to be high-ranking. He steered Zephyr off the path to an outcropping of scrubby pines. He dismounted and remained hidden, peering around the trees to watch.

The encounter was brief. Seba couldn't quite make out the words, but he understood that the officers did not intend to assist their fellow soldier in his distress. Instead, they tormented him, trotting their horses in a circle around the upturned cart, kicking up clouds of dust and laughing scornfully at the young man, who scrambled to keep his plants from being trampled. With a parting shout that sounded like *"Hoffbreet,"* the officers spurred their horses to a gallop, heading northward on the same path that Seba had traveled.

When the officers were well out of sight, Seba and Zephyr emerged. "Let's see if this stranger needs some help, girl."

As they approached the young man, Seba saw that he wore a thin, barely discernible mustache that matched his slim build. His hair was the color of sand, and his brown eyes were flecked with gold. His eyes met Seba's for a moment, then he reached for an overturned basket and began depositing the plants and stems into it. Seba couldn't tell if he was Menorcan or British, but something about him struck Seba as familiar.

Seba took a guess that the young man was British. He asked in English, "Do you need assistance?"

The young man, not looking up and continuing to collect his plants, replied, "You speak the King's English?"

"If you can understand me, then the answer must be yes."

The disheveled soldier finally raised his eyes and smiled wanly. "Then I answer your question with my own yes. I need to gather my aromatics."

"What is that?"

The young man held up several long coriander stems, their tops covered in circular brown seeds. "These are my gin-making ingredients. By the looks of this trampled mess, my next batch will be ragwater." The young man handed Seba a basket. "Shake the dust off the cuttings before putting them in here. My mates will hoist me up and throw me from the watchtower if their rations taste like dirt."

Seba tried to salvage the plants, brushing them off on his trousers before placing them in the basket; but most of them were soiled and weeping their innards. Half the coriander seeds were gone, smashed into the dirt or scattered into the grass. The formerly verdant plants were covered in powdery nut-colored earth. "Why didn't those officers help you? Aren't you all soldiers? And what was that they shouted at you when they galloped off?"

The young man's face flushed crimson. "Oh, you heard that?" His gaze fell to, and remained on, the rosemary cuttings and iris bulbs in his hand. "*Half-breed*, that's what they called me. How I've come to loathe that word."

Seba cocked his head. "I don't understand."

"Half-breed is my unlucky lot in life as the bastard son of a British officer and a Menorcan mother. Perhaps if my mother had lived. . . ." The young man sighed. "Believe me, I've suffered much worse than this for being of mixed blood."

Now Seba understood. His good friend, Buğra, from Smyrna, one of the kindest, most open-hearted people he knew, was Greek on his mother's side and Turkish on his father's side, straddling two worlds while never fully belonging to either one. Even Paolo had judged Buğra as "half-Greek," assuming he could never understand their true heritage.

Seba, however, had found the opposite to be true. Buğra's struggle to understand and reconcile the two disparate parts of him led him to discover more than any of his "full-blood" peers. He also had a tremendous ability to extend compassion to everyone he met, knowing firsthand the power of empathy and kindness.

"I'm sorry about your mother. What about your father? You say he's a British officer? I imagine he'll want to hear about your mistreatment and censure those officers for harassing his son." *That's what Papa would do.*

The young man's eyes pinched together, his expression shifting from shame to a combination of pity and exasperation. He exhaled slowly, as if he had been tasked with explaining the celestial movement of the planets to an earthworm.

"Er, you *do* know what a bastard is, don't you?

Now it was Seba's turn to flush with embarrassment. "Yes, but—"

"Then you understand why my father will never intervene publicly on my behalf." The young man stood tall and threw his shoulders back. "Now that you know the depths of my disgrace, you are under no obligation to assist me. Go on about your business." He waved his hand as if shooing away a pesky fly.

Seba redoubled his efforts, furiously throwing plants into the basket. "I wouldn't leave you to clean this mess by yourself. I certainly don't care who your parents are."

The young man wiped his hands on his breeches and said, "That's very kind of you. In return, would you like a nip of my special recipe?"

The young man felt around under a blanket that had fallen out of his cart. He pulled out a canvas bag and removed a corked green glass bottle. Ceremoniously pulling the cork with a loud pop, he said, "Topping batch, this one is." He offered the bottle to Seba. "After you."

Seba took the bottle and waved it under his nose. It was herbaceous, somewhat similar to mastiha. He took a small, tentative sip and was surprised that it didn't burn his throat. He handed the bottle back.

"It's good. Very smooth. You made this yourself?"

"Indeed." The young man raised one eyebrow and returned the bottle to Seba. "That was nary a dram you tippled. Go on, irrigate your breadroom."

Seba took a hearty gulp and surprised himself by managing not to cough. The spirits swirled down his throat then surged like lightning into his brain.

"I've never tasted anything like it."

"Aye, it's the most potent potable in the Mediterranean. This clear liquid is either the glue or the ruin of the Royal

Navy, depending on whom you ask. If you ask me, it's a bit of both."

Seba's eyes grew wide. "You mean that's gin?"

The young man chortled, "Oh, you're rich! I'll play along. No, it's plum juice. Picked the fruits from the trees myself."

Seba dropped the bottle back into the young man's hand like it was a hot potato. "You make that vile drink? Why?"

The young man was not offended in the least by Seba's tone. "Why, indeed! I've asked myself that very question many times. I suppose the answer is because I enjoy the work, and I'm good at it. I take Mother Nature's bounty, and together, she and I create something festive. And delicious."

He took another sip from his bottle before pushing the cork back into the top. "In the right hands, it's not poison at all. If the soldiers weren't so bored and underused, with no prospects for career advancement, they wouldn't overindulge. You said yourself it was good."

Seba frowned. "That was before I knew what it was. I've heard stories about the evils of gin."

The young man laughed so hard he almost dropped the bottle. "You're a right wag. Imagine disregarding your own senses for the stories of others. Oh, I say, you're rich!"

The young man had a point about disregarding one's own experience, but Seba couldn't deny the suffering of Camila and Ignasi. If it wasn't gin that did it, then what was it?

When they had gathered up all the plants and turned the cart right side up, the young man said, "Thank you very kindly. I see you are heading in my direction. Are you looking for work at the fort?"

"Oh, no. I'm looking for a doctor." He hesitated. "And

information about my friends."

The young man put his arm around Seba. "I may be able to return your kindness with access to information."

"What do you mean?"

"This evening the soldiers will line up outside the distillery to receive their daily gin rations. Why don't you join me? I could always use an extra hand. When the boys arrive, you can ask them whatever you like."

The sun felt brighter in that moment. Seba couldn't believe his good luck.

"Thank you. It seems as if we were meant to help each other today, doesn't it?"

"Aye, our meeting was a stroke of good luck if there ever was one."

# 18 DISTILLATION

*October 17, 1767*
*Mahón, Menorca*
*Evening*

The garrison was a city in itself, more or less the size of Mahón. The young man gave Seba a short tour, pointing out the general store, the forge, armory, the quarry, limekiln, guardrooms, stockade, carpenter's shop, water wells, kitchen, bread store, and barracks. They stopped to water Zephyr and the young man grabbed a bundle of alfalfa, which he tossed into his cart.

That evening, as Seba helped the young man rearrange the tables toward the distillery's door in preparation for the distribution of rations, Seba suddenly stopped and knocked the butt of his palm against his forehead.

"You showed me around the whole garrison today, and I just realized I never introduced myself. My apologies. I'm Sebastian Krizomatis. Everyone calls me Seba."

The young man took Seba's outstretched hand and gave it a collegial shake. "Chief Distiller Arnau Brumbaugh, at your service."

Seba froze and Zephyr snorted from behind the distillery, where she rested under the shade of an oak tree.

"What's wrong?"

"Nothing." Seba lined up the bottles of gin on the table as Arnau demonstrated, but his mind was racing. He could hear his mother's voice in his head. *The apple doesn't fall far from the tree, Sebastian.* "Your father wouldn't be Elias Brumbaugh, would he?"

Arnau Brumbaugh frowned. "Yes. And I see that look in your eye. He's not as bad as everyone says. He's arranged for my education and given me his surname, despite the fact that he never married my mother." He shrugged his shoulders. "Have you met him?"

"Not really," Seba lied. "Last year, in the public square, he ordered seventy-five lashes for Ignasi Rementeria Arandia, though the offense should have garnered ten lashes. There was no reason for such a harsh punishment. That's why I'm looking for a doctor."

Arnau's mouth pressed into a thin line. "I remember. I *also* saw the stitches in Steven's leg where some wild animal tore it to pieces. Steven said he went to the home to have the dog impounded, and instead was beaten nearly to death."

"Do you know why?"

"N-n-no," Arnau said slowly.

"Perhaps you should ask Steven if he was doing something that might have caused the wild animal to bite him."

Arnau's expression was quizzical. "I can't imagine what he could have done. He drinks more gin than anyone I know. Usually sleeping it off, he is."

Seba didn't want to discuss it. His stomach was feeling sick. "Where is your father now?"

"I haven't seen him around the garrison recently," Arnau admitted. "I believe he's scouting for a new home in Georgetown."

"I don't believe he is, actually. He confiscated a home that had been in my cousins' family for generations. Threw them out like they were common rubbish."

Arnau raised his brows. "That's news to me. They're building a proper British town south of Mahón, named for the king. Red brick facades, white sash windows, and large promenades, very rigid and symmetrical—rather like the Royal Navy. I thought my father was planning to build a home there."

"Why doesn't the British government provide homes for the officers?" Seba asked. "Isn't he the Post-Captain?"

Arnau smacked his open palm on the table. "I don't have to justify the Royal Navy's policies in Menorca, or my father, to you! Elias Brumbaugh may not be perfect, but he has given me the opportunity to do something I love, and I don't care where he lives."

Seba's face reddened. "You'd care if you'd seen how he treated my family. He's a monster."

"Take that back!" Arnau's fingers were beginning to curl into a fist. "I owe him everything, Seba. No one else would have offered me this post. If you don't like it, take your well-fed horse and get out. I've enough difficulties in my life without you and your judgments."

Seba hated Brumbaugh, but he felt as if he understood the young man before him. "I'm sorry, Arnau. I meant no disrespect to you," he said. "My family is suffering; that's why I'm here. It was wrong of me to take it out on you."

Seba held out his hand in a gesture of conciliation, and

Arnau took it.

"Apology accepted. Let's not speak of my father any further," he said. "His name causes a row wherever I go."

As the sun sank behind the warehouse, the rank and file lined up outside, calling loudly for their gin rations. They threatened all kinds of violence against Arnau and anyone within the fort's walls if they weren't serviced immediately, but Arnau ignored their vituperations: "You'll wait your turn like everyone else, or you'll get nothing!" he cried.

The line of soldiers groaned and grumbled, stomping their boots like horses before feeding time. "One more thing," Arnau shouted. "Anyone who has real information for my friend, Seba, here, will get to move ahead in line for rations. None of your bare-faced lies, mind you." He turned to Seba. "All right, go on, ask your questions. But hurry; the faster we dole out the gin, the safer we are."

Knowing how sailors loved to gossip, Seba thought it best to start with a request for sailing news. He asked everyone in line whether they had recent information regarding the *New Fortuna*. They all offered something, hoping it would get them ahead in line and out the door with their thick-glassed bottles of gin, but most of what they said was completely fabricated and easily dismissed. Others had family connections such as siblings and cousins sailing with the Navy; they sometimes sent letters via military ships on their way back to Mahón with news and supplies.

One serviceman said, "Yes, Captain Alexiano, is it? He's quite a navigator, as my brother tells it. Fought off Barbary pirates near Malta some time back."

Seba's stomach flipped. This person had actual knowledge of Captain Alexiano, which was more than anyone else thus far. He said, "Yes, that's right. Where is he?"

"Possibly Elba. My brother is the surgeon's mate on the merchant ship *Henry and Carolina*. Our father wanted us to become physicians, but we wanted to sail, so we told him we were apprenticing to surgeons in the Mediterranean." The man gave a sly grin. "It wasn't *really* a lie, now was it?"

Seba gawked at the man, unable to believe his good luck. "You're a physician?"

"Lord, no. My brother and I are physician apprentices of a sort. I help Doctor Lind here at the fort in exchange for him teaching me the medical arts, and my brother is surgeon's mate to the *Henry and Carolina's* Mister Bowling. Where's my gin?"

Seba held his hands up. "Wait one moment. I asked you about Captain Alexiano's whereabouts. Do you know?"

"My brother wrote me a letter while they were anchored in Porto Ferrajo, saying the *New Fortuna* had a run-in with privateers off the coast of Corsica. Malta all over again, the way he told it. Anyway, about a month ago, the *New Fortuna* came limping into port with her foremast split in two. According to my brother, some big fellow, one of Alexiano's crew, fired all the starboard cannons and sunk the privateers before they could get away. Then they reloaded and shot the bloody pirates right out of the water. Said they learned that tactic right here in Port Mahón."

Seba grinned. *It must have been Paolo. He wanted a fight and he got one. I'm glad they're safe.*

The man folded his arms across his chest. "I'm a busy man and I'm tired of asking. Where's my gin?"

Seba asked, "After we give you the gin, do you mind if I ask you a few medical questions?"

"Aye. Hand over the diddle drain and you can ask whatever you want."

Seba called to Arnau, "Get this man his rations!"

Arnau waved for the man to move up in line and handed him a full green bottle. "Much obliged, Ralph, much obliged."

Seba and Ralph exited the back door and leaned against the oak tree. Ralph quaffed a quarter of the bottle in one long gulp and wiped his mouth with his forearm.

Seba said, "I was on the *New Fortuna* when we outran the Barbary pirates off Malta. We were also involved in the privateer attack here in Port Mahón a few months ago." Seba pulled off his cap to show his scar. "This is my constant reminder of that battle."

Ralph leaned in and whistled low. "Whoever stitched you up did a fine job. Now get on with your questions. I've work waiting for me in the surgery."

"What do you recommend when someone has had serious lacerations that won't heal? Mind you, we've applied a host of treatments, but what do you do when the wounds are large and jagged?"

Ralph took another swig of gin and pointed to Seba's head. "Why do you ask? By my view, your cranium's well-nigh healed."

"Not for me, it's for my kinsman. He was . . ." He hesitated. "He was in a battle, of a sort. We've tried honey, aloe vera, garlic, and fresh herbs, but they haven't been effective."

The man tapped his finger on the bottle of gin. "A combatant? In that case, I'm happy to assist. My grandfather sailed with the East India Company, and he swore by turmeric for most any laceration. It's a right shame it's so hard to come by."

Seba's face fell.

Ralph said, "I've seen lacerations close themselves up in a matter of days with turmeric. Of course, the really deep ones from a cannon blast or a broad blade take a bit longer."

Seba's friend Meleia bought turmeric from the spice road merchants in Smyrna. It was not native to Anatolia or Chios, and Seba hadn't seen it anywhere on Menorca.

"Where can I find it?"

Ralph shook his head. "This island's too dry to grow turmeric, but my brother brought me some from West Africa. Doctor Lind and I boiled it down, dried it, and crushed it into a powder. We've tested it on every ailment this fort throws at us."

Seba was almost afraid to ask, but he had to try. "Can you spare any?"

"I suppose, if it's for a combatant. You look something of a war hero yourself with your scar, so I don't believe Doctor Lind would mind. By all rights the turmeric belongs to me anyway, as it was a gift from my brother." Ralph stood up. "I'll meet you back here in an hour with the turmeric powder *and* my empty gin bottle." He winked. "Perhaps we'll have a trade."

Seba helped Arnau distribute every last bottle of gin, and just as Arnau was to show him how he made his special batch, Seba's new friend Ralph brought him a brown jar filled with yellow powder, stoppered with a large disk of cork. In exchange, Seba filled the man's bottle to the top from Arnau's "private cache." Seba put the jar into his leather bag and stashed it in the corner of the distillery, and the man returned to the surgery singing a lively tune about a mermaid with a comb and a glass in her hand.

Arnau built up the fire under the copper alembic, which was the second and final phase of the gin distillation process. Arnau had filled the alembic halfway with the base spirits, which, on account of the military's relentless demand for gin, were made with whatever Arnau could get his hands on: barley, wheat, potatoes, oats, and even wine from fermented grapes.

"Seba, will you hand me that bowl of dried juniper berries?"

Seba picked up a huge wooden bowl half-filled with juniper, which had a strong herbaceous aroma. Stronger than mastiha, but not dissimilar. It was obvious that the gin Seba tasted yesterday owed its strong herbal flavor to these berries.

Seba asked, "I thought you said these berries were lost in a shipwreck off the Tuscan coast."

Arnau pointed at the alembic, indicating that Seba should empty the entire contents of the bowl into the opening. "Oh, that was a problem a few years ago, but we've solved it since then. When the British took over from the French, they drank every drop of brandy on the island. When that was gone, they were forced to drink the local wine, all the while complaining heartily that it was too weak. They wanted their gin, but no one here knew how to make it, and juniper trees aren't native to the island, so we could never supply enough juniper berries. They've been importing and planting trees for the last few years, and the production is increasing, but much of our supply comes from British and Dutch imports. We're always running low!"

Arnau gathered orange and lemon peels from another bowl and threw them into the alembic with the juniper berries, along with several large stalks of rosemary and the chopped bulbs and fronds of wild fennel that grew all over the island. He wagged his eyebrows at Seba.

"That's why I add these, to make up for the fact that we never have enough juniper. It's much better than that tasteless rot from London."

Seba nodded in agreement, although he had never tasted London gin. It was obvious that Arnau knew of what he spoke, and he hovered over his concoction like Seba's mother tended to the spice blend in her *dolmades*.

"How do you know how much to add?"

"Oh, loads of trial and error; to tell you the truth, most of the soldiers don't care as long as it's nice and strong. I rely on my own palate and those of my friends to get it right."

Seba grinned, Fernanda's admonishments long forgotten with the good news that Paolo and Doctor Turnbull were safe and he had a new salve to share with Ignasi. "I'd be happy to help you with that. What I tasted yesterday was excellent, as flavorful as the best wine, with a flash of lightning hidden inside."

Arnau passed Seba a green bottle like the ones they had distributed to the soldiers, but smaller. "Try this one. I made a new batch a few days ago, and I added cumin seeds. Like fennel, the cumin plants are everywhere around here."

Seba removed the cork and took a small sip. He tasted the warmth of the cumin. "Hm. I like cumin on its own, but I don't know if it adds anything to the overall flavor."

Arnau clapped his hands together and placed the lid on the alembic, which had a long copper tube running from its lid to another closed copper vessel with a spout at the bottom. "My thoughts exactly! You were meant for this, my friend," Arnau crowed. "I'm quite in earnest; you were born to be a gin maker. And I could use an extra set of hands. We have permission to pay our civilian workers, so I could provide you with a wage. Can you return tomorrow?"

"I believe I can," Seba said. "Thank you, Arnau. I appreciate everything you've done for me, and it's been a treat to help you around here. I have to give my family this medicine for Ignasi, but if everything goes well, I'll be back tomorrow."

Arnau smiled. "Good luck and godspeed, my friend. I wish you well with your family."

Seba and Zephyr trotted home under the light of a waning gibbous moon. The spars on the windmill took on an ethereal appearance under the moon's pearly beams, an enormous butterfly on the verge of flight. The thrushes were nestled in their branches; the only sound was the clip-clop of Zephyr's hooves on the gravel path.

Zephyr seemed relieved to be heading back. She was tired from the excitement of the garrison: the shouting of the rank and file, the construction noise, and the cacophony of hissing, clanging, and thumping from the distillery. "We had a good, day, girl, didn't we?" Seba tapped his leather bag. "I pray this is what Ignasi needs to speed his recovery." *And I might be bringing home a little money. Perhaps that will soften the blow of knowing I'll be producing the "vile drink" my family has come to despise.* "Let's hurry home."

Seba guided her to the convent's stables, where he brushed, watered, and fed her before leaving her to share the exploits of the day with her brother, Euros. By this time, Seba didn't give a second thought to his notion that the horses communicated with each other wordlessly. In solidarity, he offered them a nod and a wordless evening farewell. *Good night, Zephyr. Good night, Euros. Sweet dreams.*

Seba was surprised to find everyone still awake and talking around Kristobal's kitchen table. The room was warm and cozy, smelling of fresh-baked bread and rosemary. It wasn't home, exactly, and perhaps they'd never be allowed back to the Rementeria Arandia land, but there was a silent consensus among them: they were together and grateful for the monastery's refuge.

"I'm back from the garrison with good news." Seba held

the jar high in the air. "A physician's apprentice received this from his brother, who sails the South Atlantic Ocean as a surgeon in training. I told him I needed a salve for someone who was attacked, and he said he was happy to assist a combatant."

"That's not true," Ignasi frowned. "I'm no soldier."

Kostas leaned back in his chair. "You most certainly are, Ignasi. Perhaps not in the traditional sense, but you defended your sisters with valor, and you've been battling to regain your health for the last two months. I can't imagine a more fearless warrior."

Ignasi stood. "Thank you, Seba. You didn't have to risk doing this for me. If this salve works, I will be indebted to you for the rest of my life."

Seba winked at Fernanda. "A wise woman once told me there is no obligation to repay the kindness of family. That includes cousins."

Seba showed his mother how to make the turmeric paste, precisely as Ralph, the surgeon's mate, had shown him. Agnete slathered it on Ignasi's back, and Kostas promised to sit with Ignasi all night to ensure that he didn't accidentally turn over in his sleep.

# 19 GEORGETOWN



*Five months later*
*March 18, 1768*
*Georgetown, Menorca*
*Evening*


Paolo had been right about the Menorcan winter. Seba turned seventeen on a blustery late December day when the tramontana blew so powerfully that everyone, even Gall and the enterprising Kristobal, remained indoors. Agnete prepared Seba's favorite cake, a sweet yeasted bread filled with raisins, pistachios, and dates. That evening, as the wind howled down the chimney, Nicolas sang, Kristobal and Camila danced, and Seba played a wooden *floghera* Kristobal had liberated from the convent's chapel. Artemis sat in the corner grooming herself, looking for all the world like a queen who had commissioned the entertainers for her amusement. Gall hovered attentively beside her like a royal coxcomb.

The winter winds persisted through February, and still there was no word from Dr. Turnbull and the *New Fortuna*. They were expected back before Lent, but the tramontana had kept them, as well as many other ships, from Port Mahón.

Seba had returned to the distillery several times, but each time, he and Arnau had argued—about Elias Brumbaugh, about the soldiers stumbling about drunk in the town day and night, about other high-ranking officers who had commandeered homes from unsuspecting Menorcans who'd lived there for generations. Seba pleaded with Arnau to intervene and use his position to influence his father, to no avail.

After several testy exchanges, Seba had stopped going to the fort. The nuns had a hundred jobs for him to do around the convent anyway, and although he hated the feeling of being penned inside the stone walls all winter, he couldn't deny that his dialogs with Euros and Zephyr made it bearable.

Seba learned through Kristobal that Arnau had opened a gin shop in Georgetown, the Royal Navy's settlement south of town. It was to be for the commissioned officers who used their personal funds to purchase food and spirits more to their liking than the military's mediocre rations. As a rule, soldiers were discouraged from running businesses while employed by the Royal Navy, but Elias Brumbaugh believed the shop would restore his troops' flagging morale.

One late afternoon in mid-March, Seba worked alone in the monastery's gardens, preparing the soil for planting. Winter had loosened its grip on the island and ships were returning to the port after months of delays. Seba expected to see Dr. Turnbull any day now. In the meantime, he fantasized about besting Elias Brumbaugh in combat, like

Heracles subduing the Nemean lion in bare-handed *pankration* combat. He stomped on the shovel he was using to turn the earth, then swung it around like a staff, jabbing and thrusting it in the air. Engrossed in his imaginary battle, Seba didn't hear the footsteps behind him.

"See, Arnau, I told you he was a capable fighter."

"You're right, Paolo. Even if I can't see his opponent."

Seba whipped around and found himself facing Arnau and Paolo, conversing like old friends.

"Paolo! I'm so glad to see you, my friend." Seba held out his hand, which Paolo took before locking him in an embrace that was more like a wrestling hold. "And Arnau! What are you doing here? And how do you know Paolo?"

Arnau offered his hand and Seba took it; the grip was tentative, given all that had transpired between them. Their greeting was a cordial affair until Paolo threw his arms around both of them and squeezed them together like he was pressing cheese through a cloth.

Paolo said, "We moored at Quarantine Island last evening, but there's such a backlog in the port that they waived the quarantine period for us and directed us to disembark at Georgetown's new wharfs. This place is growing by leaps and bounds, Seba! It's good to be back."

"How did you meet Arnau?"

"You can't blame me, Seba. We had a mishap with the provisioning in Leghorn, and I haven't had a drop of retsina, ale, or barley beer for two weeks. The first thing I saw when I walked up the steps from the docks into Georgetown was a friendly spirit shop called the Juniper, with this jolly proprietor. We had a grand time trading stories, and Arnau told me about a former acquaintance who had left his employ to join a monastery. When I found out it was you, I made him bring me here." Paolo looked concerned. "You haven't traded the mariner life to become a monk, have you?"

"Of course not," Seba smiled. "It's a long story." He gave a sideways glance toward Arnau before adding, "And a sad one. I'll tell you later." Seeing Arnau's discomfort, he changed the subject. "How did you get inside here? I imagine the nuns were surprised to receive a visit from a gin shop owner and a sailor who smells like he hasn't bathed in weeks."

Paolo chuckled. "Kristobal let us in. If any of the nuns questioned us, he told us to say we were your long-lost cousins, previously believed drowned in a shipwreck." Paolo gave a low whistle. "That kid is something else, isn't he?"

"I'll say. He's got more savvy in his little finger than ten grown adults."

Several novices walked by the gardens, intrigued by the visitors. "Perhaps we should go somewhere else to talk, before we get him into trouble," Seba said.

Arnau looked pleased. "Why not come by the Juniper? I'd love for you to see the place, Seba. I have several local Menorcan workers assisting me, and I've installed the new alembic, twice the size of my old one." He turned his eyes to the ground. "And I promise I won't mention you-know-who."

Seba nodded. "I'm game. It will be good to escape these walls."

They stopped by the stables to water and feed Zephyr, Euros, and the rest of the convent's string for the evening. Arnau had brought several apples with him from the shop, left over from his new experimental recipes. They brushed the horses, gave them apples and clean blankets, and closed the stable doors, Paolo complaining all the while that he was still rocking on the sea, despite the fact that he'd been on dry land for a full twenty-four hours.

Seba had taken to climbing over the convent wall rather than going through the front gate; it reminded him of his village on Chios and allowed him to escape the attention of the novices. Arnau and Paolo were amenable to a stealthy exit, and Seba stashed a rope in the bushes so he could return without disturbing the nuns after hours.

It was a thirty-minute walk from the monastery to Georgetown, and the March winds, though still brisk, came from the west, bringing a welcome hint of spring.

The new settlement at Georgetown hummed with activity: merchant sailors who'd been redirected from Port Mahón, construction debris from all the new buildings going up, military officers strolling the wide gravel pathways surrounding the central quadrangle, and drunk patrons spilling out of all the public houses that ringed the square.

Arnau unlocked the Juniper's front door and gave Seba a quick tour, which was interrupted several times by Paolo chiming in, acting as if he were Arnau's business partner, even though they'd met only hours before.

"The Crown frowns upon us setting up private businesses outside the fort, but with the clamor for gin, having a shop in addition to the garrison's distillery has become a necessity," Arnau said. "And frankly, I quite like operating my own concern."

The space was bright and open, with high ceilings, a few tables, and a long counter that ran from the front door to the back of the shop. Patrons could order gin to take back to their quarters or relax and enjoy a tipple at the Juniper's welcoming oak bar. The large copper alembic and distilling equipment occupied the rear of the space on a newly milled pine workbench, along with neat shelves stocked with corked glass bottles and baskets of ingredients.

"It's impressive, Arnau. I'm happy for your success." Seba's words had an edge. He couldn't deny that he liked Arnau; he also couldn't deny that Arnau's opportunity was bestowed by the same tyrant who had taken everything from Seba's family.

"I'm starving," Paolo said suddenly. "Arnau, which place has the best victuals around here?"

"You can't go wrong anywhere. Oysters are plentiful, and the dish of the season is meats of all variety stewed with plums, pears, saffron, and cloves. I've supped at the Crown every day this week."

Most of the pubs in the newly-established British settlement were named for King George III, but all had different signs to distinguish them. In addition to the Crown, there was the King's Arms, with the heraldic crest of King George flanked by a golden lion on the left and a white-and-gold unicorn on the right; the King's Head, with a full-color profile portrait of the reigning monarch; and the George, bearing a white silhouette of the king riding a pale horse across a field of black.

They opted for the King's Arms, usually frequented by off-duty officers and enlisted men, but today also filled with merchants diverted from the backlogged wharfs at Mahón. They passed under the sign of the lion and unicorn and wedged themselves into a table in the back.

Arnau ordered three plates of plum-stewed duck and three pints of ale. The drinks were delivered quickly, but they had to wait for some time for their meals. They passed the time with Paolo's stories of his latest adventures securing recruits from the mountains of Gythieo, on the northwest coast of Laconia.

"Doctor Turnbull said the Greeks in the Mani Peninsula had largely been left to themselves, too far to be of consequence to Sultan Mustafa. That turned out to be bad information. The recruits came barreling down the hills on horses, with the Ottoman cavalry shooting at them—and us!—from the ground. I don't know how they made it onto the ship, but we've two hundred more Greeks for our expedition, and Doctor Turnbull has concluded his solicitations."

"You mean we're actually leaving for East Florida?" Seba was ecstatic. *Finally, my chance for freedom.*

Paolo held up his mug. "As soon as we provision the ships, we'll be on our way. Doctor Turnbull has secured six vessels in addition to the *New Fortuna*. They'll be overflowing with passengers and supplies in short order."

As Paolo lifted the mug to his mouth, a junior Royal Navy officer tumbled into him, spilling ale over the both of them, and splitting Paolo's bottom lip with the mug.

Paolo leaped out of his chair. "Watch yourself, you oaf!"

The officer had glassy eyes and the red bloom of a drunkard's nose, bulbous with large pores. Instead of apologizing, he shoved Paolo in the chest with both hands, sending him staggering into Arnau.

"Filthy colonial!" he slurred. "How dare you speak to me?"

Paolo bristled. "You're so drunk I speak the King's English better than you, you stupid brute!"

Seba's mind leapt back to the tavern brawl in Smyrna, in which Paolo might have killed a government official with his bare hands had Seba not intervened. He stepped between them; but the drunk officer had already taken a swing at Paolo, which Paolo countered before throwing a punch of his own. Another soldier picked up a wooden chair and broke it over Paolo's back, knocking both him and Seba to the ground.

Arnau yelled for everyone to stop, but it was too late. Seba scrambled to his feet and, along with Arnau, tried to pull Paolo away from the drunk officer, who now had two companions wrestling, punching, and kicking Paolo with frenzied anger. Paolo, who was big, strong, and an excellent fighter, was holding his own against the onslaught, as well as evading Arnau's and Seba's attempts to pull him from the fray.

When Paolo landed a donkey kick on the officer's chin, all hell broke loose. Even if they could have reached him in the melee, Arnau and Seba didn't have the strength to subdue an angry Paolo.

Seba yelled, "Paolo, stop! It's not worth it!"

Arnau shouted, "Stand down, Paolo!"

Paolo turned toward the sound of his friend's voice, which was a grave error, because the soldier took advantage of Paolo's distraction and kicked him in the groin. To Paolo's credit, he did not double over despite the excruciating pain; he mustered the raging force of five men, pummeling everyone and everything in his sight.

By now several British guards had come running. One grabbed the officer and shoved him aside, but Paolo didn't notice the change in adversary; he wound up and punched the guard so hard in the face that he broke the man's nose. He might have murdered the man, as Seba feared, when the sudden crack of a pistol shot brought the brawl to a standstill.

Seba turned toward the sound, and the blood in his veins turned to ice. In the pub's doorway stood Elias Brumbaugh, holding a smoking gun over his head.

"As Acting Commander-in-Chief and Post-Captain of

the Defense Squadron and Dockyards of Port Mahón, I'll not have this kind of violence in my new town! Arrest this man for assaulting my best guard." He looked down at his underling, whose nose lay at an awkward angle and whose eyes were already swelling shut. "And get Jones to the surgeon."

Several guards pinned Paolo down and snapped iron cuffs around his wrists. Brumbaugh stood over him. "It's a shame you assaulted an officer in His Majesty's Royal Navy. We could have used a fighter like you in our ranks."

Paolo made no reply. He curled his lip and spat in Brumbaugh's face.

Brumbaugh slapped Paolo hard across the cheek with the back of his hand. "Do you know the penalty for assaulting an officer here in Menorca?" he hissed.

"He jumped on me. Split my lip," Paolo retorted. "I only defended myself. What kind of outfit are you running here, letting your drunk officers wreak havoc in the public house?"

Seba froze. *Paolo, no. Shut your mouth.*

"No one challenges the authority of Elias Brumbaugh. One hundred lashes. In this square. Next Saturday."

Seba gasped. *That's a death sentence. Ignasi barely recovered from seventy-five, and he's double Paolo's size. Paolo won't survive.*

Arnau grabbed Seba's arm. "We need to leave before my father sees us, or we'll be next."

Seba nodded. As they snuck around the street corner and back to the gin shop, they heard Brumbaugh say, "Justice will prevail."

Arnau was shaking. "He's taken leave of his senses. One hundred lashes? That's barbaric."

Seba felt sick. His mind raced. Paolo could not become

Elias Brumbaugh's next victim. "I have to get back to the convent," he said. "Forgive me, Arnau."

Everyone was asleep when Seba returned home; he climbed straight to the roof to think. It was cold, but his body thrummed and crackled with nervous energy. *How can this be happening? When will it stop?*

What Seba needed, he thought, was someone with the authority to counter Brumbaugh's, someone who could halt this madness. His racing mind produced a name: Theodora Alexiano, the most powerful woman in Port Mahón. True, she hadn't been able to save the Rementeria Arandia home, but in her defense, she'd had no notice. With a week, perhaps she could save Paolo. He knew he had to try.

# 20 MADAM JURADA

*March 19, 1768*
*Mahón, Menorca*
*Morning*

As the sky began to lighten, Seba washed up, donned his best clothes, practiced his plea, and walked to the home of the Madam Jurada. It was a short distance from the convent, a large mansion that housed both her residence and her administrative offices. He entered the courtyard and knocked on the door.

A young woman answered, dressed in modest clothing and a large white apron.

He ventured a guess and spoke Greek. "*Kaliméra*. My name is Sebastian Krizomatis. I do not have an appointment, but I'd like to request an audience with Madam Jurada Theodora Alexiano. Is she available?"

The woman smiled, curtsied, and led Seba into the home's expansive foyer. He had never been inside a building filled with so much light. The floors were tiled in colorful mosaic patterns, and chairs were covered with luxurious Ottoman silks. The value of the upholstery and other fabric coverings would have paid for a fleet of merchant ships like the *New Fortuna*.

They walked through a long, well-lit corridor to the rear of the home, which overlooked the harbor. The serving-woman said, "The Madam Jurada will be taking her breakfast in a few moments. Please wait in the dining room."

The dining table was so large that it could have seated twenty people, and it featured an intricate design of black walnut inlaid with cherry and mahogany marquetry set off by an elaborate star pattern. The delicate dishes and bowls were glazed in translucent light, featuring a baroque floral design of cobalt blue clustered leaves, flowers, and diaphanous vines. The center of each piece was embellished with a trio of dancing dragonflies rendered so masterfully that they gave the impression of motion. This was similar to the china service of Dr. Turnbull's sister-in-law, Dr. Despina Marguerite du Robin. Paolo and Seba had been fortunate enough to dine with Dr. Robin after Seba had saved Paolo from a fight in Smyrna, very much like the one in the King's Arms. *I see the pattern. Paolo nearly kills someone, and then I have a meal in the finest home I've ever seen*, Seba thought sardonically. *I'd rather do without the meal.*

Theodora Alexiano entered the room and bowed graciously. She was dressed exquisitely in a purple and pink silk gown, her peppered hair piled high on her head and pinned up with gold hairpins dotted with large pearls. "Sebastian Krizomatis! I haven't seen you since the wedding. I wish you would visit me more often." She took his hands in hers and kissed him on both cheeks. "To what do I owe this pleasure?"

"I'm afraid it's not pleasure that brings me to your door."

Theodora motioned toward the table for Seba to sit. "I'm so sorry, Seba. Tell me what troubles you."

The serving woman entered the dining room carrying a tray filled with pastries, fruit, breads, and tiny blue-and-white cups, each holding an egg as if on a pedestal. She filled the table with the mouthwatering breakfast and returned to the kitchen for more.

Theodora said a blessing and Seba realized he hadn't eaten in a day.

"Madam Jurada—"

"Please, I've told you before, call me Theodora. We're family, now that Camila and Nicolas are married. Cousins."

"Yes. Do you also remember my friend Paolo, from the wedding?"

Theodora placed a woven blue-and-gold napkin in her lap and handed Seba the plate of pastries. "Yes, of course. Strapping young man. Quite an appetite, as I recall. How does he fare?"

"Very badly. That's why I've come."

A look of concern crossed Theodora's face. "Is he ill? I have a physician who resides on the premises. I'll call him at once."

"He doesn't need a physician, at least not yet." Seba swallowed and launched headlong into his petition. "Paolo's been arrested and sentenced to one hundred lashes. It's to happen next Saturday. There was a brawl at a public house in Georgetown. He didn't hurt anyone on purpose, but in the fighting, Paolo broke the nose of one of Elias Brumbaugh's guards."

Theodora's mouth was a thin line. "How horrible. Deliberate violence is more to be quenched than a fire."

"That's why I've come to you. Doctor Turnbull said you

were the most successful council member in the island's history. You're the only one who can save Paolo. We need you to intervene."

Theodora dabbed the corners of her mouth with her embroidered napkin and reached for an egg cup. She tapped the egg, removed the lid, and dipped her spoon into it.

"I'm afraid it's not that simple, Seba. My position here in Port Mahón is somewhat delicate. I am not afforded the luxury of commuting British governmental sentences, or even voicing my opinions in that regard."

"But this isn't about voicing opinions," Seba said. "You would be preventing a miscarriage of justice. And saving Paolo's life. He will not survive one hundred lashes, and you know it. No one could."

Theodora calmly ate her soft-boiled egg, which Seba found astonishing. *How can she eat after hearing this news?*

"I understand your concern, Seba, but I do not have authority over Captain Brumbaugh. As Jurada, I must maintain a working relationship with the garrison officers. Captain Brumbaugh is considered the Commander in Chief here. The current British governor of Menorca has never stepped foot on this island, despite being commissioned over two years ago."

"Would this governor have the power stop Brumbaugh?"

"He's the only one who could, if he were here. Menorca's British governors largely rule in absentia, including Governor Howard. There are rumors that Sir John Mostyn has been commissioned to replace him, but who's to say he'll be an improvement?" She looked unhappy. "Elias Brumbaugh is in control here, whether we like it or not. If I were to overstep my bounds, Brumbaugh would view it as defiance of his authority. He treats this island as his fiefdom. I know his type; I've had to manage that manner of masculine overcompensation for most of my life. If Captain Brumbaugh thought I was undermining his authority, he'd double Paolo's punishment in an instant."

Seba felt tears of frustration welling in his eyes. "But we must do something! I won't stand by and watch my best friend skinned alive because a deranged despot wants to put on a display. I won't!"

Theodora sighed. "I see you have the same Greek temper as my twin brother," she said. "But expression of anger does not serve me in my position. You must calm yourself, my friend." She slid the dragonfly china plate loaded with fruit pies in Seba's direction. "Have a pastry. It will soothe your anger. I'll make my personal physician available to Paolo to ensure he receives the best care for his wounds. It's the best I can do under the circumstances."

Seba pushed the plate away, knocking several cheese tarts onto the lace tablecloth, the fat soiling the pristine fabric. "How can you eat pastries as if nothing is wrong? One of your Greek brothers has been given a death sentence by that monster and you won't lift a finger to help!"

Theodora's eyes grew wide. "I know you're disappointed, Seba, but my hands are tied. If it were anyone other than Elias Brumbaugh, I might have been able to make a plea on Paolo's behalf. However, the Acting Post Captain, or whatever he calls himself these days, is pig-headed and too powerful." She put her hand on his. "Paolo is strong and spirited. Perhaps it won't be as bad as you think."

Seba pulled away and pushed his chair back; its legs made a sharp scraping sound against the terracotta-tiled floor. "Thank you for your time, Madam Jurada. Enjoy your breakfast. I'll see myself out."

Seba walked the streets of Mahón for several hours, wracking his brain for a way to save Paolo. When he realized he'd circled the walls of the convent for the third time, he hung his head and went inside.

Seba found his family seated around the kitchen table, the aroma of oyster stew wafting from a large iron pot on the fire. Previously, the aroma of salty oysters, chervil, and black pepper made him feel safe and secure. Now it caused his stomach to churn. Agnete ladled the thick soup into olivewood bowls stacked with pieces of crusty bread, as she had done many times over the last several months, and sprinkled flakes of Menorcan salt over each serving. She said the blessing, and Seba imagined Jesus breaking bread at the Last Supper.

When Seba refused to eat, Agnete said, "Sebastian, what's wrong? You missed supper yesterday and breakfast this morning. We've been worried sick about you."

"Let's everyone eat their meal first, Mama." *You won't have an appetite after you hear my story.*

When the dishes were cleaned and all were seated around the hearth, Seba told the whole shocking tale. It was as if all the light in the world had disappeared. Fernanda felt it too; she scooped up a few logs and tossed them on the fire. "We have to get him out. He won't survive."

Ignasi said, "I wouldn't wish this fate on my worst enemy. Except perhaps Brumbaugh himself."

Seba nodded. "I've been walking the streets of Mahón all morning, trying to work out a plan to save Paolo."

Agnete's usual fiery countenance was dimmed. She crossed herself and said, "It breaks my heart to imagine my pumpkinhead in chains. I will pray for him with every fiber of my being." She reached in her pocket and squeezed the small alabaster cross.

Camila said, "I'll go with you to the chapel, Agnete. We need to tell the sisters what's happened. They will join with us in prayer."

Seba stood and kicked over a stack of kindling by the hearth. "Prayer alone is not the answer! Didn't you tell me the Lord helps those who help themselves? I'm not going to sit by and let Elias Brumbaugh torture my best friend. Paolo was set upon by a pack of drunken bigots. They're the ones who should be flogged. And Brumbaugh himself deserves worse."

"If the punishment is set for next Saturday, that gives us seven days," Camila said. "Perhaps we can find someone to intervene before then."

Agnete put her hand on Camila's arm. "Your cousin is right, Sebastian. Give our Creator an opportunity to send us a miracle. It may come through Mary, our Lady of Good Hope, who has never failed me."

"What's wrong with you two?" Seba's voice was raised. "Have you heard anything I've said? We do not have the luxury of time! Doctor Turnbull arrived yesterday. He's resupplying the ship for the voyage to East Florida. The *New Fortuna* will set sail before Saturday, and we're not leaving without Paolo."

Agnete ignored Seba's protests. Clasping her hands over her heart, she said, "I wish Nicolas was here. He'd find a solution."

Camila brightened. "Yes, I believe he is scheduled to return this week. My brilliant husband will think of something."

"Do you really think Nicolas can do anything?" Seba said. "I just came from Theodora Alexiano's home, and she sat there eating pastries as if everything was fine! She's nothing more than a cowardly politician!"

Camila frowned. "That's unfair, Seba, and you know it."

"What I know is that if Theodora is powerless, Nicolas won't be any different. His connections are nothing compared to the Madam Jurada's, and she said her hands were tied. If they can't save Paolo, then I will."

Kostas took a deep breath. "It's too dangerous, Seba. Do you believe you can take on the entire garrison yourself? Don't be foolish. We've survived Brumbaugh's tyranny thus far, and we will continue to do so. Go with Doctor Turnbull. Pursue your dream. We will take care of Paolo, as well as we did Ignasi. That's what families do."

"How can you say that? My dream is Paolo's dream as well. How could I go anywhere knowing that I left Paolo to be tortured? Or worse? I will get him out of this trouble, and we will board the *New Fortuna* together. Whether you help me or not." With that, he stormed out of the house.

# 21 RESCUE



*March 19, 1768*
*Mahón, Menorca*
*Midday*

Several hours later, Fernanda found Seba in the stables, sharing his tale of woe with Euros and Zephyr. The horses were listening attentively, snorting and pawing at the ground. It was clear they too believed that Brumbaugh was the one who deserved a hundred lashes.

Fernanda kicked a bale of hay and the door to Euros's stall, then pushed her headscarf back. Her amber eyes flashed. "We can't let him get away with this. I want to help."

Camila entered behind her sister, followed by Gall, who was uncharacteristically quiet. "Fernanda is right," she said. "We've been talking about Paolo since you stormed out, Seba. Come back to the house so we can discuss this. Perhaps there is something we can do."

"What is there to discuss?" he cried. "No one is listening to me anyway! Can't you leave me here to my thoughts?"

Camila said, "Seba, give us a chance. You've had all night and day to process this information, and we were blissfully breaking bread when you surprised us. You can't save Paolo alone. We are stronger together."

Gall gave a quiet crow, and Zephyr and Euros whinnied simultaneously. Seba was outnumbered. "Fine," he said.

Seba reluctantly followed the sisters back to the house. Gall trailed them, as if ensuring that Seba could not change his mind and turn back. They returned to the kitchen, where Fernanda announced, "You were right, Seba. We need to take matters into our own hands. We can do it together."

Kostas said, "Tell us what you're thinking, son, and we will do our best to help."

Ignasi said, "I may not be as mobile as I once was, but I am willing and able to spare Paolo from this horrific fate."

Seba scanned their faces: Fernanda's red with anger, Camila's hopeful and expectant, Papa's thoughtful and calm, his mother's fiery and determined. He could not risk putting them in danger. Heat flamed into his cheeks. "No. None of you have been inside the garrison. It's unsafe for all of you. The risk is too high. I'll go alone."

Fernanda slammed a log into the fire. "And do what? Sebastian Krizomatis, you've lived with us for, what, seven months? Yet you dare to tell us what we can and can't risk? You believe us to be inept fools? If so, you're no better than Brumbaugh." She pulled off her headscarf and thwacked it against her leg, her oxblood-colored hair wild and unruly. "I expected more from you, cousin. Isn't hubris one of those Capricornus traits Doctor Turnbull blathered on about? You've enough hubris to fill the Mediterranean Sea."

Camila stood tall. "My sister's tongue may be sharper

than a dagger, Seba, but she and I are in accord. We all have suffered at the hands of Elias Brumbaugh, especially my brother and me. But look at us! We are not beaten. Let us help you find a way."

Gall expressed his solidarity with a great rooster-like crow.

Just then, Kristobal climbed up the ladder from the animal pen. He said, "What's all the commotion? Have I missed a family meeting?"

They took turns relaying the shocking tale of Paolo's imprisonment and impending torture. Kristobal thought for a moment, then said, "I have an idea."

He leaned forward and launched into a rambling, convoluted scheme. It was a scheme that could only be concocted by an eleven-year-old with an active imagination, replete with disguises, diversions, and explosions, and one that would require the participation of everyone in the room. Seba was only half-listening; by the time Kristobal's scenario reached its breathless climax in a full cavalry charge with hidden snipers, Seba had stopped paying attention altogether. A plan of his own making spun into existence in his mind.

Seba's plan was simple. He'd wait until nightfall. The moon had been new two days prior, and the skies would be mostly dark. The garrison prepared for battles by sea, and would not pay attention to one person scaling the western walls, especially after midnight, when most of the rank and file was soused or sleeping. He'd ascend the wall near the fort's distillery, using a rope and hook. Arnau tossed his dirty uniforms in the distillery's back corner until washing time, and Seba would don the attire of a soldier to get close to the garrison's stockade.

Arnau had shared that the keys were kept on a hook near

the jail cells, where two guards kept watch through the night, which usually meant playing Crown and Anchor or card games to stay awake.

Seba would grab two bottles of gin from the distillery and offer them to the guards in exchange for a conversation with the prisoner, bringing another bottle for himself full of water. Arnau swore that no soldier in his right mind could refuse the challenge of a drinking game. Once the guards were passed out, Seba would take the key from the hook, free Paolo, and the two of them would sneak back over the wall, arriving at the convent before sunrise. They'd pack their belongings, sneak down to the wharf, and have Kristobal row them to the *New Fortuna*, where they would hide out until all of Dr. Turnbull's ships were outfitted and ready to go.

Seba had prepared himself a cover identity, as well. If he was going to impersonate a British enlisted man to gain access to Paolo, he would channel the great entertainer, Vaios Georgelos, his Papouli. Seba would become William George, an apprentice blacksmith in St. Philip's iron forge. He prayed it would work.

The family's only responsibility was to ready the horses, keep a lookout for the fugitive pair, and have Kristobal in the skiff at daybreak to transport his human contraband across the harbor.

A few hours after sunset, Agnete kissed Seba's forehead and handed him her alabaster cross. "Godspeed, Sebastian. Bring my pumpkinhead to me so I can say goodbye."

Kostas hugged his son. "I am against this plan, but I pray that you succeed."

The sisters took turns kissing Seba on each cheek and wished him the luck of Our Lady of Grace. Kristobal, who had been irritated that Seba disregarded his scheme in favor of working alone, left even before Seba finished explaining the rescue plan. *As long as he's waiting for us on the skiff tomorrow morning, all will be well.*

The convent was a little over two miles from the garrison. Seba went the long way around Cales Fonts, which was the name of the district before the British had dubbed it Georgetown. He encountered no humans on his way southeast toward the fort, only the sounds of bleating from the pastures. He quietly crept alongside the road where he'd first met Arnau and his overturned herb cart. When he reached the western wall, he tied his grappling hook to the thick length of cordage and tossed it up onto the wall.

The iron clattered and rattled until it caught in the mortar between the stones. Seba counted to two hundred in his head, his ears alert for any indication that he'd been heard. The extended silence gave way to relief, and he began climbing hand over hand. He clambered over the top, wound the rope around the hook, and leapt into the darkness, his soft boots skidding on the ground.

Again, Seba counted in his head, making sure there were no patrols or regulars out and about for a midnight nip of gin. He tiptoed to the back of the distillery, where he hid the rope and hook in a large growth of rosemary. Seba tried the distillery's back door. It didn't budge. *Arnau has never locked this door. Why now?*

Walking around the side to the south window, he found it shuttered as usual. He tugged on the wooden shutter; latched tight. However, the wood was warped just enough for him to fit his finger in the opening and flip up the iron catch. The hinges creaked as the shutter swung open. Seba held his breath.

His boots silently slipped over the windowsill and Seba

dropped into the pitch-black distillery. With one hand on the wall, he inched toward the corner where Arnau typically threw his dirty uniforms. To his relief, he spied a pile of woolen breeches. Dressing quickly in Arnau's clothes, Seba rolled his own into a ball and shoved them under Arnau's ragpile of cotton cloths he used to strain the herbs from the gin.

He grabbed two full bottles, then filled an empty one with water and corked it. He shoved all three into his trousers, and climbed back out the window, making sure not to scrape the glass bottles against the window frame. He secured the latch, turned, and assumed the posture of a soldier as he walked across the open courtyard of Fort St. Philip. *So far, so good.*

The stockade was situated between two guardrooms which served as the barracks of those on guard duty. As he rounded the corner of the guardrooms, he encountered the night watch: two guards seated at a small card table lit by an iron lantern. The soldiers half-heartedly played a game of draughts.

"Go on, then. It's your move."

"No, mate, I jumped your piece."

"Oh, right. Hullo, I'm all out of diddle drain. Give me a tipple of yours."

"Fancy me your mother, do you? Want some pap as well?"

"We're friends, aren't we? I gave you a nip of my rations just last Thursday."

"Oi, that you did. All right, but don't take it all."

The guards running out of gin was more than Seba could have wished for. He said a silent prayer to Calliope, the muse of eloquence, for the right words.

"Someone call for diddle drain?" he said gaily. "I just so

happen to have extra rations."

The guards rose to their feet, knocking over the table and fountaining the wooden game pieces into the air.

"Who's there? Name and rank."

Seba mimicked Dr. Turnbull's accent as best he could, hoping it would be enough. "William George, smith's apprentice under command of Master Armorer Archibald Faber."

"What's that, Archie got himself an apprentice? Since when?"

Seba tried to be as vague as possible, wracking his brain to remember every story Arnau had ever told him about the fort. "A time ago, when that scoundrel Samuel Hamilton deserted."

"Oh, yes!" said the first guard. "I was sent out on the first search party. They had us scouring every house, convent, and nunnery on the island for that renegade. They haven't found him yet, eh?"

Seba shook his head, fighting to keep calm under the pressure. "I'm afraid not." He reached into his pockets and pulled out the bottles of gin. "Now, who's game for a bit of Crown and Anchor?"

The first guard leaned forward, but his colleague held him back. "I'll ne'er refuse the white ribbon, but what's this about? It's near midnight, I reckon. Unusual time for a visit from the forge."

Seba was ready. "Master Faber wants me to check the size of your prisoner here. He's forging the chains for next Saturday's lashing. After what happened with that big character last year, ripping the ropes from the stockades, he wants to get the size right." Seba held his breath; it was a transparently stupid story, but he hadn't been able to think of anything else. *This had better work.*

"I remember," said the guard. "Big fellow. Makes sense, but why in the middle of the night?"

"Master Faber said the prisoner was a mite troublesome. It might be better to get the measurements while he slept." Without waiting for the stupidity of that statement to sink in, Seba continued, "No need to hurry, though. He'll be asleep all night. Let's have a drop and a game of Crown and Anchor. Winner pockets the juniper juice." *Does this sound English enough?*

"I favor a horse of that color. Let's on it."

Seba had no idea what that meant, but the guard who had leaned in was practically drooling at the sight of the bottle in Seba's hand.

Seba plopped both bottles on the table. "Here you go, mates. These are on Master Faber. Show him your gratitude next you see him. Have you got dice?"

The guards popped the corks off their bottles and each took a long quaff. Seba wouldn't need to play any drinking games with these men; they were easier targets than he'd expected. One of the guards pulled three dice from a leather pouch. Red heart, red crown, red diamond, black spade, black anchor, and black club. Exactly as Nicolas had shown him. Seba was prepared to chalk the game board and offer to be the banker, but they never got that far.

The guards had been drinking most of the night, and after an hour of "bonus rations," as they called it, they were both soused, their heads falling forward on the table.

When Seba was sure they had drifted off, he searched the guardroom until he found the iron key hanging on a hook inside the door. A loud, grumbling snore from one of the bunks all but sent him dashing out of the guard room as the key ring scraped across the wall; but he steadied himself and waited three more breaths before creeping out of the building toward the stockade and its cells.

"Pssst. Paolo," he hissed. "Where are you?"

A groggy voice responded. "Who's there?"

"Shhhh. It's Seba. I've come to get you out of here." Seba unlocked the door. It creaked on its old hinges, rusted from too much salt water and too little maintenance. He froze.

Paolo hurried through the open door, then stopped to give Seba a bear hug. "Thank you, friend. It's horrible in th—"

"Hush! No talking until we're out of here. I have a rope by the western wall. Follow me."

Seba closed and locked the door, then replaced the key ring on the hook in the guardroom. Paolo almost let out a whistle when he saw the drunk guards with their cheeks plastered to the table, but Seba knew his old friend too well. He slapped his hand over Paolo's mouth before any sound escaped.

They stayed to the fort's outer walls, crawling as quickly as they could manage on their hands and knees, following the tracks of the domesticated dogs that patrolled the fort for rats and mice. The pace was excruciatingly slow, but the outline of the distillery and its warehouse loomed in the dim light, thirty yards away. They passed the kitchens; only the infirmary building stood between them and the western wall. Seba could taste freedom.

A voice came out of the dark: "What's that, Jack? Prowling for moles again? Baker didn't give you any supper?"

The boys froze.

"Don't be shy, boy, Doctor Lind's letting me practice my surgery, but only on my off hours, and not yet on the rank and file. Fancy a nice coney?"

Footsteps approached. "What's wrong, Jack? Got a

friend with you?"

They were caught, but the voice was familiar. Seba stood and nodded to Paolo to do the same.

"Ralph, is that you?"

"Aye. Who's there?"

Seba said, "Remember me from the distillery? You gave me a portion of turmeric paste in exchange for an extra gin ration."

"Aye. What are you doing skulking around in the middle of the night? Trying to steal from Doctor Lind's stores?"

"No, no, no. I'm taking a new prisoner to the jail. He had to relieve himself, which is why you mistook us for your dog."

Ralph came eye to eye with Seba and looked at his uniform. "When did you enlist? I've not seen you since that day in the rations line. Thought you were a civilian."

"Oh, a while back. The Navy's always looking for laborers." Seba cleared his throat with a dry cough. "We'll be going now. Good luck with your surgery."

A long silence ensued. Seba took a step toward the distillery, pulling Paolo behind him.

"The stockade is in the other direction."

"Oh, yes, right. Must have gotten mixed up in the dark."

Ralph took a step toward Paolo. "Ho, wait a moment! He's not new! This man came close to killing one of our men; Doctor Lind and I worked on the poor chap all morning. His face was a wreck. That prisoner's not to leave the jail under any circumstances. A hundred lashes he's getting, and deserves more!"

It was over. "Paolo, run!"

Seba and Paolo took off toward the distillery, Ralph screaming and calling for the guards to catch them. "Guards! Guards! Our prisoner's trying to escape!"

Seba and Paolo crossed the thirty yards in less than ten seconds, but it wasn't fast enough. Before they reached the distillery, shots were fired and a thick cloud of smoke enveloped them. The sharp sulfurous smell of burnt gunpowder singed Seba's nose. Through the haze, a line of guards emerged, flintlock muskets pointed directly at the pair of them.

# 22 THE BLACK HOLE

*March 20, 1768*
*Fort St. Philip, Menorca*
*Midday*

Down they went, down into the dark. Seba and Paolo were tossed into the garrison's special prison for the worst offenders, aptly named the "black hole." It was a festering pit below the fort's eastern walls, a rotting cave at least twelve feet underground and darker than a starless night. Its subterranean walls dripped a bilious slime that smelled of rotting fish and feces; the only furnishing was a slops bucket. A dim shadow of dark gray hovered beyond a high grate above their heads, the only indication that light existed anywhere in the world.

The black hole was so narrow that neither Seba nor Paolo could lie down without rubbing against the weeping walls of black mucus. It was as if Brumbaugh had designed the garrison's underground prison as an oversized chamber pot, and Seba—appropriately—felt like shit. A stinking cloud of fetid air hung over the boys as they startled and scooted to avoid rats, slugs, and cockroaches that scuttled across the slick floor.

"Seba, what were you thinking? My situation wasn't dire enough? You wanted to make it worse?" Paolo clapped his hands slowly, the hollow sound reverberating off the cold stone. "Well done, you succeeded."

"Please, Paolo, be quiet."

"Don't want to hear how my situation is lousier than before? Perhaps you should have thought of that before you botched my rescue."

"My apologies for trying to save your life," Seba huffed. "I need to think, and your complaining isn't helping."

"Oh, forgive me. How about the lice crawling all over us? Are those helping?"

"Shut up!" Seba's voice echoed off the stinking stone walls.

The boys had been hurled into this black hole by order of Captain Elias Brumbaugh, who'd been notified of the foiled outbreak by messenger to his home. The very home that he, Elias Brumbaugh, had stolen from the Rementeria family.

Seba said, "Why can't you control your temper? Every time we find ourselves in trouble, your rages are to blame."

"Oh, that's rich. I suppose your poorly planned escape has nothing to do with our circumstances? At least they fed me in the other prison. If they throw any victuals down to us here, I'll have to fight a dog-sized rat for them."

A rat scurried over Seba's shin, punctuating Paolo's statement. Seba kicked at the rat and a bolt of electricity ran up his leg. He had twisted his ankle landing at the bottom of the pit at an awkward angle. His body twitched involuntarily in disgust. *Is this all my fault?*

"I'm sorry. I only wanted to help." He took a long, shuddering breath. "Seventy-five lashes almost killed Ignasi, and I couldn't bear the thought of them giving you a hundred. You would have died."

Paolo's breath came out of his chest, loud and heavy. "I know, my friend. But now it's going to be worse for both of us."

"You don't know that. You did nothing but defend yourself at the King's Arms, and the rescue was my misstep. Let them punish me."

"Don't be a fool, Seba. We're *both* going to get a hundred lashes. If we're lucky." Paolo kicked the filthy bucket, sending it into the wall and filling the pit with the stench of excrement and sour urine.

Seba's hand flew to cover his nose and mouth. After a time, he said, "If we don't die of putrefaction first."

They could not tell the passage of time, but what seemed like many hours after they'd been dumped into the black hole, they heard voices above. The most terrifying belonged to Elias Brumbaugh.

"Master Drumbert, throw down the rope. These prisoners must be brought before the soldiers for trial."

Someone opened the grate, threw down a thick rope knotted at several intervals to provide footholds. Seba and Paolo climbed out of the black hole, squinting in the dim light. Two guards with bayonets stood behind Paolo and Seba, the steely points of their weapons poking into the middle of the boys' backs.

Elias Brumbaugh pointed down the passageway. "To the casemate. We'll read the charges there, with our rank and file as witnesses."

They followed him and the man called Master Drumbert

down a long hall until they came to the casemate, a large artillery room with an arched ceiling and two gunports on the outside stone wall. Two five-ton cannons sat at each gunport, dark and hulking, like pairs of ominously indifferent judges. A British flag was tacked to the wall behind the makeshift tribunal, fluttering in the draft from the open embrasures.

A high-backed wooden chair had been dragged in for Elias Brumbaugh and set atop a platform of crates. Stacks of thirty-six-pound cannonballs were positioned on one side of the room, a silent jury witnessing the farce. Opposite the iron jury, at least a dozen soldiers in uniform stood, awaiting the prisoners.

Seba scanned their faces. These were some of the same men to whom Seba had happily provided gin rations with Arnau. *I wonder what lies Brumbaugh has told them about us.* He realized that these men had not been called here to witness the judicial process; this was simply a diversion Brumbaugh had concocted for them to stave off the boredom of garrison life, something to keep them occupied so they weren't stumbling about drunk, causing chaos in Mahón.

Seba and Paolo were brought to the center of the room to stand before Brumbaugh, who, though seated, looked down on them from his perch atop the wooden crates.

Seba searched the room for a means of escape. He and Paolo might be able to fit through the gunports, but they'd likely be impaled by bayonets in the back before they crossed the thresholds. Even if they managed to abscond without being stabbed in the back, the fall from the gunports would likely result in broken bones. If they managed to land unscathed, they'd probably be picked off by pistol fire as they ran from the fort. *It's hopeless.*

Elias Brumbaugh was in full military regalia, from his bicorn silk and beaver-furred hat to his brass-buckled leather shoes. The gold-fringed epaulets on each shoulder and his seat on the high-backed chair gave him the appearance of a monarch. *He thinks he's the king.*

"Master Drumbert, read the charges."

A thin uniformed man, with a reedy voice to match, unfurled a large piece of parchment and began to read.

"Whereas, information upon oath duly given this day by one Oliver Jones, so sworn and subscribed from his hospital bed in Fort St. Philip, hereby showing that the accused hereby known as Paolo Partella has levied war against our lord King George the Third in his realm by assaulting an officer in his place and doing his office, thereby establishing himself as an enemy of the King; and

"Whereas information upon oath duly given this day by one Ralph Porter, so sworn and subscribed in the surgery of Fort St. Philip, hereby showing that the accused hereby known as Paolo Partella has committed sedition by attempting to escape lawful detention for his crimes against the Crown; and

"Whereas the aforementioned Paolo Partella, being a subject under the dominion of His Majesty King George the Third, did knowingly and unlawfully act in traitorous contravention to his duty and allegiance under the Statute made in the twenty-fifth year of the reign of King Edward the Third; now therefore,

It is hereby determined by His Majesty King George the Third's loyal servant, Acting Lieutenant Governor Elias Brumbaugh, that the aforementioned Paolo Partella has committed high treason and is charged in violation of said statute, the Treason Act."

Elias Brumbaugh said with a sneer, "Accused, what do

you have to say in your defense?"

Paolo whispered to Seba. "I didn't catch all of that. What did they say?"

"I didn't understand it all, either, but I believe we're on trial. You must defend yourself."

Paolo worked his hands together in frustration. "Where is the judge? The tribunal? In Smyrna the accuser may not also act as the judge. What's happening here?"

Seba whispered, "I'll wager Brumbaugh makes his own rules. It's my fault we're in this predicament. If you want, I'll speak for you."

"You know this scoundrel better than I do. Go ahead."

Seba stood, his voice loud and clear. "The accused is not guilty of treason. He was berated and physically assaulted by a soldier, whose colleagues joined in the unprovoked beating. The accused was in fear for his life and defended himself as anyone would have done in the same situation. As for allegations of escape, the accused is innocent. His cell was unlocked, and he believed he was free to go."

The soldier witnesses grumbled and called out obscenities. One threw an empty gin bottle at Paolo's head. Paolo ducked just in time, and the bottle hit his armed guard in the chest.

The guard called out, "Watch your aim, you idiot, or I'll use this rifle's blade on you!"

The witnesses laughed at the spectacle and the armed guard fumed, poking Paolo so hard in the back that Paolo tottered forward. A hole in the back of his shirt showed that the bayonet's point had made contact. Paolo growled and turned back toward the guard until Seba touched his arm.

Seba whispered, "Stay calm, Paolo. We're surrounded by uniforms."

Paolo's voice was hoarse. "He drew blood! If he does it

again, I won't be responsible for my actions."

Brumbaugh held up his hand and said in an imperious voice, "Settle down, men. In due time. Let's not injure the traitors until their sentences are carried out."

Elias Brumbaugh whispered into Master Drumbert's ear, and the man with the thin voice said, "The accused's position has been duly considered by Acting Justice Elias Brumbaugh. The defense is wholly without merit and is hereby rejected. Treasonous miscreant Paolo Partella is sentenced as follows: tomorrow, at precisely three hours past noon, he is to be taken to the town square where he shall be hanged by the neck, but not to death; being alive cut down, his privy members shall be severed, and his body divided into four quarters to be disposed of at the Acting Lieutenant Governor's pleasure."

Seba said, "No!"

Paolo whipped around to face Seba, the point of the guard's bayonet scraping against the same spot on his back. "They're going to hang me? What else?"

Bile crept into Seba's throat and he lost his voice.

Master Drumbert unrolled a second parchment.

"Whereas, information upon oath duly given this day by one Ralph Porter, so sworn and subscribed in the surgery of Fort St. Philip, hereby showing that the accused hereby known as Sebastian Krizomatis has counterfeited as an enemy of His Majesty King George the Third by impersonating a commissioned officer; and

"Whereas, information upon oath duly given this day by one Ralph Porter, so sworn and subscribed in the surgery of Fort Saint Philip, hereby showing that the accused hereby known as Sebastian Krizomatis has committed sedition by attempting to aid a prisoner's escape of lawful detention for his crimes against the Crown; and

Whereas, the aforementioned Sebastian Krizomatis, being a subject under the dominion of His Majesty King George the Third, did knowingly and unlawfully act in traitorous contravention to his duty and allegiance under the Statute made in the twenty-fifth year of the reign of King Edward the Third; now therefore,

"It is hereby determined by His Majesty King George the Third's loyal servant, Acting Lieutenant Governor Elias Brumbaugh, that the aforementioned Sebastian Krizomatis has committed high treason and is charged in violation of said statute, the Treason Act."

Elias Brumbaugh leaned back on his makeshift throne. "Accused, what have you to say in your defense?"

Seba seethed, not realizing how firmly his bottom lip was clenched between his teeth until he tasted blood. He spat on the stone floor.

Brumbaugh casually peeled off his calfskin gloves finger by finger, as if preparing to examine his manicure. "Speak, accused! Or has a cat got your tongue? No explanation for your treasonous acts?" Brumbaugh sniffed derisively before addressing his witnesses. "I know the type, men. They believe they can take advantage of everyone and everything in their path, but when they meet a worthy adversary, they crumble like the rubbish they are."

Seba found his voice. "This trial is a mockery. I will offer my defense to an impartial decision-maker, but as there are none present, I will say only that I am innocent of all charges against me."

Brumbaugh bristled. "Once a failure, always a failure." He murmured into Master Drumbert's ear.

The high-pitched whiny voice said, "The accused Sebastian Krizomatis, having refused to offer a defense to Acting Justice Elias Brumbaugh, is sentenced as follows for high treason: tomorrow, at precisely three hours past noon, he is to be taken to the town square where he shall be hanged by the neck but not to the point of death; being alive cut down, his privy members shall be severed, and his body divided into four quarters to be disposed of at the Acting Lieutenant Governor's pleasure."

Elias Brumbaugh nodded to the witnesses, and the rank and file removed scraps of food from their pockets. It looked as if they'd gone to the garrison's kitchen and dumped the stinking refuse into their pockets solely for this purpose. They hurled the scraps of rotting and fermented food at Seba and Paolo, who couldn't avoid being struck because of the bayonets in their backs.

"Take that, you traitors!"

"Think you're smarter than our commander, do you?"

"Not so smart now, are you?"

"Dirty turncoats!"

"Hanging's too good for you, you snakes in the grass!"

Seba tried to shield himself from the barrage of refuse, but it was too much. Through the commotion, he heard a voice.

"Oh, here you are!"

Elias Brumbaugh stood on his wooden dais. "Arnau, what are you doing here? Shouldn't you be at the distillery? It's near time to dole out the rations. Why on earth have you left your post?"

Arnau blinked rapidly, as if trying to process the scene before him. When his eyes fell on Seba and Paolo covered in rotten food scraps, his mouth fell open.

Arnau sputtered, "That's just it, sir. The rations have been distributed, but half the regiment is missing. Lieutenant Browning told me everyone was in the casemate, so I came to see if I was needed."

"No, Arnau," Brumbaugh said impatiently. "You are not needed here. I'm simply ridding this island of dirty traitors, as is my right and obligation as Acting Justice, Acting Lieutenant Governor, and Acting Commander-in-Chief and Post-Captain of the Defense Squadron and Dockyards of Port Mahón."

Arnau drew back. "Traitors?"

Brumbaugh took the opportunity to preen before his men and his illegitimate son. "Yes, Arnau. They have challenged my authority, assaulted one of my best officers, and attempted to make me a fool by escaping from the garrison's prison. What would you have me do, serve them a cake?"

The soldiers laughed derisively, but Arnau was speechless. Seba could tell he was trying to assess the situation.

"Master Drumbert, why don't you advise Arnau of the sentence to be meted out against these treasonous villains?"

The reedy voice announced the cruel and unusual punishment for the third time. "Tomorrow, at precisely three hours past noon, they are to be taken to the town square where they shall be hanged by the neck but not to the point of death; being alive cut down, their privy members shall be severed, and their bodies each divided into four quarters to be disposed of at the Acting Lieutenant Governor's pleasure."

Brumbaugh nonchalantly donned his white leather gloves. "Anything else I can do for you today, Arnau?"

Arnau stood tall, but his voice shook. "No, sir. Thank you, sir. With your permission, I'll return to my post immediately, sir."

Elias Brumbaugh said, "You are dismissed. And I suggest you hurry. These men are thirsty."

Arnau turned and raced down the passage as Elias Brumbaugh addressed the soldiers. "Thank you for your service to the Crown, men. Your participation in this garrison's impartial judicial process is noted. Before I dismiss you, I request a small courtesy: Give Arnau a fighting chance to get to the distillery before you run him down."

After a dramatic pause, Brumbaugh said, "You are dismissed as well." The soldiers took off after Arnau, blatantly ignoring Brumbaugh's directive, precisely as he wanted them to do.

Brumbaugh stepped down from the makeshift dais. "Guards, take these prisoners back to the black hole."

The guards took Seba and Paolo back down the passageway, pulled up the grate to their filthy prison, and pitched them face-first into the damp, dark cave.

Covered in animal innards, food scraps, and other kitchen refuse, Seba and Paolo smelled even worse than before. They waited until they heard the guards' footsteps retreat before venturing to speak.

Seba's throat was dry and his head pounded. "We have to escape."

Paolo hung his head. Seba had never seen him so discouraged.

"Paolo, did you hear me?"

"Yes, but I have nothing to say. It's hopeless. You tried and failed. They didn't have the decency to bring in a real judge. It's over."

"Paolo, don't say that. We'll find a way out of this. I know we will."

Paolo shifted so he faced away from Seba. "Forget it, Seba. Leave me alone."

Several hours passed in silence. Seba had never felt so

alone or desperate in his life. He swayed in and out of consciousness, but his dreams were no solace. He'd been in other difficult situations, but this was the worst. Perhaps Paolo was right. Maybe they should give up and make their peace, thanking God for the short time they had on earth.

Seba was startled out of his musings by Paolo's voice.

"Seba, stand on my shoulders."

"What?"

"My sisters came to me in a dream. They told me not to give up."

Seba was wide awake. He'd pestered Paolo to tell him about his sisters ever since Paolo had mentioned them. Paolo spoke of ghosts and tragedies, sisters and a lost family, but said the details were too distressing to share. That had been over two years ago, yet Paolo refused to elaborate.

"Tell me about your sisters."

"Not now, Seba. I promise to tell you when we get out. I always believed ghosts know more than we do, and now I'm sure of it. But first, let's climb out of here."

Seba stood on Paolo's large shoulders, and he was just tall enough to grab onto and peer through the iron bars. All around was dark and silent, and the air was slightly lighter than at the sludgy bottom of the black hole, next to the urine-soaked bucket. There were no guards stationed at the grate; they must have been positioned by the casemate. Seba would worry about them later, after he and Paolo escaped.

"Can you loosen the grate?"

"I'm trying, but it's fastened with a lock and key. I'll try to pull it from the mortar."

Seba worked on the grate for what seemed like hours, until his fingernails were raw and cracked. He traded places with Paolo, who also pulled on the grate with all his might, but Paolo's stint did not last as long.

"Have you got me, Seba? I'm two stone heavier than you, you know."

*Oh, I know.* They traded places again, and through the night they took turns standing on each other's shoulders, working at the grate. At one point, Seba felt the iron frame scrape across the stone and felt a surge of elation.

Paolo said, "Did you get it? My back is about to give out."

"Almost. I'll keep at it." Seba was making headway, sliding the iron frame up and back across the opening to pull it away from the stone, until his hand slipped from the frame and he fell tumbling to the black hole's foul floor, Paolo dropping beside him in a heap.

Seba scraped his chin against the wall as he landed, and when he placed his hand on his lower jaw, his fingers came away wet. It might have been either his blood or the wall's slime; he wasn't sure which was worse. They sat looking at each other, dejected.

Paolo said, "I twisted my back. Give me a few moments to rest it. Then we'll try again."

Seba welcomed the opportunity to catch his breath, but was worried that their time was running out. He couldn't tell how many hours had passed or how long they had before they'd be led to the gallows.

Exhausted, disoriented, and defeated, Seba and Paolo fell into a fitful sleep.

# 23 LAST RITES

*March 21, 1768*
*Fort St. Philip, Menorca*
*Early Morning*


The next morning, the guards' footsteps woke Seba and Paolo from their unsettled sleep.

Seba hopped to his feet. "Someone's coming."

Paolo whispered, "Death."

Seba nodded sadly. "We had some good times, didn't we, friend?"

"Yes. And good food. Remember Meleia's smoked fish with cumin-spiced carrots?"

"That was my favorite."

"She was your first love, wasn't she?" Paolo said gently. "When you exploded her sand coffee all over the tavern, I thought she was going to wring your neck. But she warmed to you eventually."

Seba remembered that day like it was yesterday. Meleia

had been busy at the Aigókeros, putting food and drinks on the tables, clearing them, talking to the patrons, and running in and out of the kitchen. She'd tripped on a stool someone had kicked over when rising to leave, and the copper *cezves* in the sand threatened to boil over. Having watched his mother make coffee every day of his young life, Seba had sprung into action to assist, but ended up sending the copper pots toppling over like flaming dominoes. Meleia's henna-tinted curls, her skirt, blouse, and apron, as well as the area behind the bar were covered in sand and boiled coffee foam.

Paolo interrupted Seba's thoughts. "You're still in love with her, aren't you?"

Seba's throat was thick. "No. Yes. Oh, I don't know. Anyway, it doesn't matter. She didn't love me."

"I'm not so sure. I saw how she looked at you. I think she loved you, but was not willing to give up her life in Smyrna." Paolo gave a gloomy sigh. "Given our current circumstances, it was a good decision."

Seba's shoulders slumped. "Let's not talk of Meleia."

"Oh, it makes you sad? Everything about this disgusting black hole makes me sad, Seba. I try to imagine East Florida as Doctor Turnbull described it. Blue water. Bright sunshine. Thousands of mullet running along the shore. Fruit trees as far as the eye can see."

Seba closed his eyes, but the darkness was the same whether they were closed or open. He recalled Dr. Turnbull's description of his 20,000 acres along the Indian River, teeming with fish, forests, farms, and fortune.

"I so wanted to see the New World."

"Think of the adventures we would have had," Seba said. "Best friends on a grand journey."

"I knew we'd be lifelong friends when you mistook me

for Jesus," Paolo teased. Then his voice grew heavy again. "I didn't know how short a lifelong friendship could be."

"We could have made our fortunes, found our loves, and grown our families together. Just think of all those little Sebas and Paolos running around East Florida."

Paolo's voice caught. "Seba, we're never going to taste food again."

"I know. I told you my favorite meal. What was *your* favorite dish at the Aigókeros?"

"Everything Meleia made was delicious, but the stuffed grape leaves and lamb kebab were the best. Remember when you, Buğra, and I went fishing in Smyrna's harbor, and Meleia grilled our barbouni for supper? Best fish I ever ate."

Seba fought back tears of regret. "I pray my parents don't know what's happened. It would ruin them to see us hanged. What a failure I am."

A metal key clanked into the lock on the grate, and it opened with a metallic screech. The same thick knotted rope dropped down through the opening.

"Traitors!" came a harsh voice. "There are two flintlock pistols aimed at your heads. Climb the rope and put any idea of escape out of your heads."

"What's going on?" Seba called.

"The nuns have arrived to give your last rites. But should you try to break free, we have no qualms about sending you to God right now."

They looked at each other; then Paolo scrambled up the rope, followed by Seba. The pistols were immediately shoved into their backs and they were led through the same stone passageway as the day before, which sloped upward toward the familiar arch-ceilinged casemate.

The room was no longer a tribunal; it was now dressed

as a chapel. An altar held a simple wooden cross flanked by two beeswax candles, a round of bread on a brass plate, and a small matching chalice adorned with a solitary ruby. A ceremonial censer exhaled tendrils of lavender and myrrh toward the vaulted ceiling. The dark cannons that had loomed forebodingly now stood like weary guardians keeping vigil. In front of the altar sat two wooden benches that served as pews.

Four nuns somberly prepared the casemate, their coifs and veils drawn so close around their heads that their faces were obscured. One was as tall as Paolo, with a black mantle that stopped several inches above a familiar pair of iron-buckled brown leather boots. Seba's heart leaped into his throat. *Fernanda?*

Seba inched closer to Paolo and bumped Paolo's foot with his heel, then tried to gesture toward Fernanda without raising the guards' attention.

Paolo looked questioningly at Seba; Seba's eyes darted back and forth from Paolo's face to the nun's boots, his eyebrows wagging. Finally, recognition dawned on Paolo's face. His eyes grew wide as he rocked back on his heels.

The nun glanced up at them, bowed her head, and quickly looked away.

Each of the tall nun's companions were approximately the same petite size, a full ten inches shorter than Seba. The folds of their robes easily reached the floor, covering their feet as they swished against the stone. The nuns were silent as they went about their business, preparing the sacraments. Seba stared intently at each of them. The nun readying the bread and wine made the sign of the cross about ten times in the space of a minute. *Mama?! What were you thinking? Coming into this garrison, impersonating a nun? You're going to get yourself killed.*

The third nun retrieved four white cloths from a basket, along with four thick pillar candles. As she moved to place a cloth and a candle on each cannon, he noticed that the woolen belt tied at her waist was affixed with a silver brooch shaped like a cluster of leaves that spiraled out from the center, dotted with emerald and sapphire grapes. *Camila?*

The fourth nun retrieved the censer and slowly circled the room, expertly swinging the container of incense from its brass chain and whispering blessings for the space. A glint of light sparkled off the nun's hand and Seba gasped. On the nun's fourth finger was a topaz gemstone set in a gold band. *Kristobal!*

Seeing Fernanda, Camila, and his mother had given Seba a mixed feeling of hope and fear for their safety. Kristobal's presence, however, was cause for elation. The boy who'd run this town since he was six years old might actually be able to save them.

The tall nun put her hands on her hips as Seba had seen her do a thousand times when she was angry. She stomped her leather boot impatiently and shooed the guards into the corner with the large wooden cross around her neck.

"Why isn't she speaking?" murmured one guard. "She take the vow of silence? Some of them do. The brothers, I mean."

"I dunno. Never learned the King's English, maybe." The other one stretched and yawned. "Who cares? I've been standing all day, so if she wants me to sit on a stack of cannonballs over here, I'll oblige her."

"Best do as that tall one says, I suppose. She seems quite hostile, am I right?"

They went on like that for several minutes, talking about Fernanda as if she weren't twenty feet away from them.

Fernanda pretended she didn't understand them, but her nostrils flared in indignation and her eyes narrowed as she went about her work. She gripped the wooden cross around her neck so hard that her knuckles turned white. If the situation hadn't been so dire, Seba would have laughed.

Camila motioned for Seba and Paolo to sit on the improvised wooden pews. It felt like paradise to rest on a surface free from black slime and cockroaches. They stank like a well-fertilized pasture; Kristobal swung the censer around Seba and Paolo as if he were trying to bathe them with incense.

One of the guards said, "Good luck washing the stink off those savages, Sister."

Agnete, who was at the altar table, wheeled around and gave the guards that "five feet of fury" look Seba knew so well. She hissed at the guards, "Shhhh!"

Under his breath, the guard muttered, "I think this little one might be meaner than the tall one."

His mate agreed. "Wouldn't want to get on her bad side."

*You have no idea*, Seba thought.

Kristobal bent down between Seba and Paolo to swing the censer around their feet and whispered, "*Quan s'alcen els vents de l'est i de l'oest, beu a cales fonts de salvació.*" *When the east and west winds rise, drink from the font of salvation.*

Kristobal shuffled toward the altar before Seba or Paolo could question him.

The quartet of "nuns" moved with solemn grace, their black habits rustling softly as they commenced the litany of prayers and sacraments to anoint the dying. The counterfeit was flawless; living with the Sisters of the Virgin Mary had taught them everything they needed to know.

The traditional mass seemed to go on forever, Seba and

Paolo searching every word for a clue or secret message. Finally, they reached the liturgy of the Eucharist, presented the gifts, offered prayers of thanksgiving and transfiguration, and Fernanda broke the bread in two. She motioned for Seba to kneel. She said a prayer and placed a large morsel of bread in Seba's mouth before raising the chalice to his lips and motioning for him to partake. As their fingers touched, she slipped a tiny pocket knife into his hands, which he hastily tucked into his trousers.

*"El cos i la sang de Crist. Els daimons negres pujaran per trencar les cadenes de l'esclavitud."* The body and blood of Christ. *Black daimons shall ascend to break the chains of bondage.*

Seba offered the traditional response with a surge of optimism. *"Que sigui aixi."* Let it be so. Camila brought the body and blood of Christ to Paolo, who also received a cryptic message with the Eucharist.

*"El cos i la sang de Crist. Fes la teva encaixada de mans lleugera."* The body and blood of Christ. *Make your handshake light.* Paolo quickly stuffed something into his pocket before giving the response. *Perhaps it's a key to the grate.*

A guard interrupted Seba's thoughts. "That's enough, Sisters. Nothing more can be done for these filthy villains. And more importantly, it's time for dinner and I don't intend to miss the puddings."

To conclude the mass, Agnete said a prayer from the book of Isaiah which Seba knew well. It was all about freedom from slavery, a topic that consumed much of their lives under Ottoman rule on Chios, and his mother's favorite verse. It was not part of the mass, but she seemed to want to end their meeting with a strong message.

*"Is not this the fast that I choose: to loose the bonds of wickedness, to undo the thongs of the yoke, to let the oppressed go free, and to break every yoke? Is it not to share your bread with*

*the hungry, and bring the homeless poor into your house; when
you see the naked, to cover him, and not to hide yourself from your
own flesh? Then shall your light break forth like the dawn, and
your healing shall spring up speedily; your righteousness shall go
before you, the glory of the Lord shall be your rear guard. Then
you shall call, and the Lord will answer; you shall cry, and he will
say, Here I am."*

When the service was over, the "nuns" gathered the
candles, cloths, and cross and filed out of the casemate, their
black habits rustling softly down the long corridor. The
guards led Seba and Paolo back to the black hole.

"See you at the gallows. Enjoy the last three hours of
your lives."

Seba and Paolo waited for the sound of the guards'
retreating footsteps. When they were sure they were alone,
Seba said, "Did you recognize everyone?"

Paolo's voice was upbeat. "Well, the one who shushed
the guards was your mother. I've seen that withering look a
hundred times. And I almost laughed out loud at those
guards griping about Fernanda; she looked like a bull about
to charge."

Seba chuckled. "I guess they thought she didn't speak
English, but I've been teaching her what I know from
Doctor Turnbull and Arnau, and Nicolas is fluent in English
as well. Can you imagine what kind of combatant she'd
make? No one in the armed forces could hold a candle to
her."

Paolo held up an object, indistinguishable from his hand
in the black hole's deep darkness. "It was Camila who
passed me this knife."

Seba felt the tiniest flutter of optimism. "And a
message?"

"Yes. 'Make your handshake light.' I don't understand

what it means."

Seba was thoughtful. "My father told me something once; he heard it in the slave camp in Constantinople. Give the hangman a light handshake when he's measuring you for the rope, and you may survive."

Paolo's voice trembled. "We're going to be rescued."

Seba shook his head. "I don't see how they can. The hanging is in broad daylight in Georgetown's open plaza, probably with hundreds of people all around. Besides, even if the hangman chooses a rope that's too light, he'll soon realize his mistake and we'll be back where we started."

Paolo stood tall, his twisted back forgotten. "Perhaps they've planned something else. Did Fernanda give you a message?"

"Yes, but it doesn't make sense. 'Black daimons shall ascend to break the chains of bondage,' whatever that means."

Paolo ventured a guess. "It's interesting that she slipped the Greek word "daimon" into the message. My sisters always said our daimons were our guardian angels. So our black guardian angels will save us. Perhaps they're talking about themselves dressed as nuns."

"Fernanda gave me a knife as well, but no clue as to when to use it."

"Perhaps it's a three-part message, and Kristobal gave us the last fragment. He said 'When the east and west winds rise, drink from the font of salvation.' Perhaps it means that water will be involved in our rescue. I'll make my handshake light, break free from the noose, you'll cut yourself down, and they'll cause a disturbance with barrels of water."

Seba's optimism faded as he imagined his family on the quadrangle, surrounded by soldiers with weapons. "No.

It's too dangerous for them. If we're to be saved, it will be by our own hands. We can use these knives to fight the guards when they come to retrieve us. That way, we endanger no one but ourselves."

Paolo shook his head. "You attempted to rescue me alone, and look where that got us. Don't get any ideas. Have faith in the plan."

"What plan?" Seba cried. "We don't understand these cryptic messages and they didn't tell us what to do with the knives. That's not a plan, that's them giving us the means to help ourselves."

Paolo was undeterred. "It's evidence of a plan."

Seba looked doubtful. "No, it's evidence that they managed to sneak us two knives."

"You think so little of your own family?"

"The opposite. I'm thinking only of them. You weren't here when Ignasi was scourged and the sisters were tossed from their family home like common refuse. Brumbaugh's ruffians caused Camila to lose her baby. None of them have stepped foot in Georgetown. They don't know the streets or terrain, and half the town is still under construction. A rescue in broad daylight there, under the nose of the Royal Navy? It would be suicide."

"Seba, it's not like you to give up. You're underestimating your family. Their misfortunes have made them stronger." Paolo folded his arms against his chest. "You're blinded by your own pride."

Seba slapped his hand on his leg. "Pride? What do I have to be proud about? All my failures? It was me who got us thrown into this hole. Perhaps it's time we faced our fate with our eyes wide open."

"That's the same as giving up."

Seba stiffened. "Paolo, don't you understand? If they try

to help us, they will die as well. Do you think Brumbaugh will show them mercy?" Seba squeezed his temples and groaned. "If anything happened to them, I'd never forgive myself. It's bad enough I've ruined my family's legacy. No, they're not coming. They mustn't."

Paolo pounded his fist on the wall behind him. "You are so stubborn! Why can't you accept that they are capable of helping us?"

"Because I know them. You're making them out to be the heroes of our Greek stories, but they're not. They're mere mortals, and on Menorca, Brumbaugh is a god. I can't entertain the thought of anything happening to them. I won't."

Paolo picked up a pebble from the slimy floor and threw it against the opposite wall. "You're wrong, Seba. When human beings band together, they make miracles. I'll go to my grave believing in hope."

"You'll soon have the opportunity to test that theory." In the darkness, Seba held the knife in front of him like a torch. "And if I go to my grave today, I'm taking Brumbaugh with me."

# 24 BLACK DAIMONS

*March 21, 1768*
*Fort St. Philip, Menorca*
*Afternoon*

At 2:45 pm, the knotted rope was tossed into the black hole for the third and final time. When Seba and Paolo emerged from the darkness, they brushed off the bugs and filth that hung on them like a curse. If the guards had entertained any thought of checking the boys' pockets for weapons, the putrid smell that clung to their bodies immediately put them off it.

Seba and Paolo were shackled around the ankles with iron cuffs and forced to walk behind a cart for the one-mile distance between Fort St. Philip and the public plaza at Georgetown. The afternoon sun beat down on them from high in the west, and the smell of sweat and anxiety added to the black hole's lingering stench. Seba couldn't help but think of Jesus's walk through the streets of Jerusalem to

Calvary, people throwing refuse and rocks at him along the way. Camila and Fernanda called it the *Via Dolorosa*. For all the masses he attended as a child in Sessera, he had never before put himself in Christ's shoes. *Please help me, Jesus.*

Townspeople emerged from their doors to gawk at them, and the crowd grew as they neared the walls of Georgetown. Inside Georgetown's gates, which, like many of its streets, were still under construction, they met the hangman. He was accompanied by a spindly-legged youth weighed down by ropes of various lengths and thicknesses slung over his shoulder. The hangman eyed the boys up and down, then held out a hand to Seba. He shook the hangman's hand and watched as Paolo did the same.

The hangman made a show of wiping his hands on his trousers before instructing the guards to remove the shackles. "No need for the irons. Nowhere to run now," he said. He and his apprentice left to prepare the gallows.

"Sizing you traitors up, he was," said one of the guards with a leer. "Doesn't want to pull your heads clean off — that'd be a right mess."

As they shuffled toward the gallows, Seba tapped the knife at his pocket. *You're the only thing standing between me and death.*

They passed along several gravel-and-dirt streets until they reached Georgetown's public square. The gallows was a tall wooden platform eight feet off the ground. Two posts and a crossbeam were mounted to the platform's center planks. Two ropes were tied around the crossbeam, one for Seba and one for Paolo. Beneath each rope was a wooden stool, on which the condemned would stand. Seba gulped and resisted the urge to feel his neck, imagining the moment when the hangman kicked the stool out from under his feet. He shook his head to dispel the vision.

A rough-hewn set of stairs led from the ground to the gallows platform. On the left corner of the quadrangle was Arnau's gin shop, the Juniper. Arnau had given Seba and Paolo a tour of the place only two days' prior; it felt like another lifetime. Directly opposite the Juniper, across the plaza, was the King's Arms, the tavern where Paolo's troubles had begun. Somehow, a hanging between these two worlds seemed fitting.

Brumbaugh was already on the platform with his whiny mustachioed sidekick, barking instructions to the hangman before calling out to the crowd.

"Loyal subjects of His Majesty King George the Third, gather around. Today we witness the execution of justice." Brumbaugh wore his full regalia: the embroidered coat boasting the gold-fringed epaulettes, the starched cotton breeches, white silk stockings, and black leather boots with the gleaming brass buckles. He had donned the same bicorn hat and kid gloves from the day before, looking every portion the supreme leader he claimed to be.

Seba and Paolo trudged up the wooden steps to the platform as Brumbaugh spewed lies and self-serving propaganda.

"These two traitors—foreign agitators, I remind you— sought to dismantle the peace and order this garrison has worked so tirelessly to preserve. They plotted in shadows, mocking all semblance of order, and conspired to disrupt His Majesty's peaceful realm. You may recognize them as neighbors, but don't be fooled. Snakes often wear familiar skins."

Brumbaugh turned to the nasally Master Drumbert, whose lips read the sentence from beneath his perfectly groomed mustache.

"Hear ye, hear ye! For high crimes knowingly and

unlawfully committed against His Majesty, King George the Third, under his domain as duly established in law, including assault and battery of an unarmed soldier of the realm, counterfeiting as commissioned officer of His Majesty's Royal Navy, and various and sundry other acts of sedition against the Crown, the traitors to the realm known as Paolo Partella and Sebastian Krizomatis are hereby condemned to be hanged, drawn, and quartered in accordance with the duly enacted provisions of the Statute made in the twenty-fifth year of the reign of King Edward the Third."

A collective gasp swept through the crowd.

Paolo fought as the hangman's assistant forced him to stand on the wooden stool while the hangman placed the noose over Paolo's head. A sharp kick in the gut from the hangman's boot put a stop to Paolo's defiance. Paolo's shoulders slumped and he fought for breath.

Seba stood on his wooden stool and the hangman looped the noose around Seba's neck. His heart hammered in his chest; he blinked away the sweat that dripped from his forehead.

Seba scanned around the plaza. The doors to Arnau's gin shop were shuttered, but soldiers and merchants filled the various public houses around the green's wide promenade.

In the back of the green space, furthest from the gallows and closest to the harbor, he saw a swarm of figures dressed in black. Nuns' habits. With horses. *What are the Sisters doing here?*

It was as if the entire enclave of the Sisters of the Virgin Mary, some of whom had never stepped foot outside the convent's walls, had gathered on the gravel path directly opposite the gallows. The one hundred nuns must have traveled the mile from the monastery to Georgetown's central square. An army of black angels.

Seba's mind raced back to Fernanda's message in the casemate. *Els daimons negres pujaran per trencar les cadenes de l'esclavitud. Black daimons will ascend to break the chains of bondage.*

As Seba peered more closely, he noticed a number of the nuns seated upon their Menorquín horses, the jet-black cavalls blending seamlessly with the sisters' ebony robes. He couldn't pick out any faces from among the nuns; they were too far away. However, one particular nun sat taller than the others in the saddle, and there was a speck of brown beneath her robe. Seba would have sworn it was a brown leather boot peeking out from beneath the long black mantle.

Seba squinted in the afternoon sun. *She's riding Euros. The east wind.*

His heart skipped a beat. *What did Kristobal say about the east wind?* Seba searched his memory; his mind had gone blank in his panic. Then he remembered: *When the east and west winds rise, drink from the font of salvation. That means Euros and Zephyr will lead us to freedom! But how?*

Elias Brumbaugh strutted up and down the wooden platform, preening. The afternoon sun glinted off his gold embroidered cuffs, and his powdered periwig bounced like an agitated frog. He was enjoying the spectacle with no intention of rushing the matter.

"These traitors have mocked the rule of law and threatened the very existence of our civil society. You may grieve their fate, but ask yourselves: Would you trade the safety of your children for the lies of a traitor?"

Brumbaugh's words made Seba seethe. *He makes our homes unsafe. He's the traitor.*

Struggling to keep his toes touching the wooden stool,

Seba stole a glance at Paolo, who looked as if he could rip the crossbeam off its supports and strangle Brumbaugh with his bare hands.

"Know this, loyal subjects," Brumbaugh continued. "British law shall not be denied. Justice will prevail. May no man forget who wields the power here!"

Brumbaugh fluttered his arms as if conjuring magic, and the hangman and his apprentice simultaneously kicked the wooden stools out from under Seba's and Paolo's feet.

Paolo fell directly to the wooden platform with a thunk; his rope had snapped clean in half. He'd made his handshake light.

That was all Seba knew of Paolo for the moment, because he couldn't breathe. When the apprentice kicked Seba's stool out from under him, Seba's hands flew to his throat, his legs pumping wildly in the air as if he were trying to swim. His eyes bulged as he probed the crowd for Fernanda. In his mind he yelled to her. *Fernanda, now!*

Euros reared up on his back legs as Fernanda lifted her wooden cross high in the air; it was the same necklace she'd used to shoo away the guards only hours before. The symbol of protection had metamorphosed into the black angels' battle flag. The nuns spurred their horses into a stampede, raising a cloud of brown dust. People ducked under the horses, stumbled over each other, alternately screaming and cheering.

The hanging was forgotten. The spectacle of the nuns on horseback was a special blessing for those lucky enough to be present. The sisters' black robes billowed up on the cloud of dust as if lifted by a multitude of saints and seraphim; the townsfolk would not forsake this opportunity for benediction. They ran toward the horses, stretching their arms toward the Menorquín for luck, shouting and clapping, and calling for Our Lady of Grace to bestow her sacred gifts on them.

CRACK-CRACK-CRACK! BOOM!

A deafening explosion split the sky, and thick black smoke poured from the space previously occupied by Arnau's gin shop, now reduced to a pile of rubble. The black brume extended into the open space and mixed with the stampede's brown dust, stinging Seba's eyes and turning the afternoon to night.

One hand still resisting the rope around his neck, Seba reached into his pocket with his other hand and retrieved the knife. As pandemonium broke out around him, he sawed at the rope with all his might. Black spots danced before his eyes, but he would not give up; he hacked at the noose with all of his being.

Seba managed to tear through a few strands of the rope and catch a breath of air, but breathing was difficult. While he struggled to remain conscious, he noticed Paolo trading punches with both the hangman and his apprentice; weak and starving though he was. Paolo's rage had given him strength enough to gain the upper hand.

Seba called out in a rasp, "Paolo, the stool!"

Paolo dodged a blow from the hangman, kicked the wooden stool toward Seba, and said, "We need to get out of here!" Seba barely reached the wooden stool with the toe of one foot; it released the pressure from the rope enough for him to fill his lungs.

Brumbaugh bellowed orders at the soldiers to storm the gallows and shoot the prisoners, but the guards couldn't maneuver through the throng of people, horses, and soot-filled fog. In any case, most of the soldiers who had been within shouting distance were gone; the sight of the Juniper on fire struck fear into their hearts like nothing else could have done. They shouted for the fire brigade and fled like a swarm of bees toward the fire, grabbing anything that would carry water along the way. To them, life without gin was a fate worse than death.

Behind Paolo, Brumbaugh reached for his cutlass. If Fernanda had heard Seba with her mind, perhaps Paolo would, too. *Paolo, watch out!*

Paolo turned toward Brumbaugh; but before Brumbaugh could unsheathe his cutlass, Artemis's familiar screech pierced the air like the deadly wail of a harpy. She slashed Brumbaugh's face from temple to jaw; he yowled in pain as blood poured from the gash. Cursing, he wiped his eyes with a gilded silk sleeve. As quickly as she'd appeared, though, Artemis was gone.

Seba balanced precariously on the stool, straining to pull it closer. Brumbaugh lunged for him, this time successfully drawing his cutlass. Brumbaugh's sword slashed Seba's shin, shooting a line like fire through his leg, and reared back to swing again. Fear coursed through Seba's body. *No!*

WHOOSH! Something flew over Seba's head, splitting the rope in two. Brumbaugh's sword passed over his head as Seba's tailbone hit the platform hard. The force of Brumbaugh's forward movement propelled him past Seba, and he toppled over the stool.

Seba yanked at the remaining piece of rope around his neck, but it was too tight. He didn't know what had pierced the rope, and he couldn't extricate himself, but he didn't have time to try. He scrambled to his feet, kicked Brumbaugh squarely in the nose, and catapulted the wooden stool at the hangman's head. The stool's corner caught the hangman above the ear, knocking him unconscious and trapping his apprentice under him as he fell.

"Paolo, this way!"

Before Seba could move, he was violently jerked backward. Brumbaugh's white gloves, now red with blood, gripped the portion of rope that still hung from Seba's neck. Brumbaugh yanked the rope right and left, trying to knock Seba down, but Seba twisted the rope around his neck until he was facing Brumbaugh.

The sight of the port-captain struck terror into Seba's heart. Brumbaugh's lips were pulled back, and he bared his teeth like a wild animal. Blood soaked his eyes and the gash Artemis had given him poured like a fountain.

"I will not let you terrorize me or my family any longer," Seba said, his throat sore and raw.

Brumbaugh spat blood. "Brave words for a traitor."

"Your perversion of authority stops here. With me."

Brumbaugh gave a guttural roar and wrenched the rope so hard that Seba plunged off the side of the platform to the ground eight feet below.

Seba's head hit the hard-packed dirt with a whack, and stars swam before his eyes. Brumbaugh vaulted off the platform and planted his feet wide apart over Seba's body. The port-captain's bicorn hat was gone, and his periwig hung askew. Brumbaugh used both hands to press the point of his cutlass to Seba's chest. Seba was out of tricks.

"Do you think your selfish little display changes anything?" Brumbaugh sneered. "You will die for your insolence."

Seba spat into Brumbaugh's face. "You're the one who's selfish. You care only for yourself, thinking nothing of the people around you. You're a tyrant."

"My power provides safety for every subject of the Crown!"

A shadow passed behind Brumbaugh and Seba knew

what to do. He would not make the same mistake as Brumbaugh.

"Safety? Ha!" Seba scoffed. "Stealing family homes for yourself? Allowing your drunken soldiers to attack innocent citizens? Maiming those who stand up for what's right? That's not safety, that's terror!"

"Order must be kept!"

Paolo appeared behind Brumbaugh's back, wielding the gallows stool over his head.

"Order?" Seba laughed wildly. "Look around you now! Your men would rather save their gin than do your bidding. You're pathetic."

Brumbaugh drew his arms back to thrust the cutlass into Seba's heart. "You'll die with those words on your lips!"

Seba puffed out his chest. "Not today."

Paolo swung the stool across Brumbaugh's head with such force that he knocked the cutlass from Brumbaugh's hand. Brumbaugh's periwig flew across the plaza and he crumpled to the ground, prone and unconscious.

Paolo pulled Seba to standing and removed the noose from Seba's neck. Euros and Zephyr emerged from the black smoke, galloping toward them with their familiar riders on their backs.

Camila tossed two black nuns' robes to the boys, who quickly pulled them on over their heads. Fernanda stuck out her arm and pulled Paolo onto Euros's back. In a flash, they disappeared through the smoke and the mayhem.

"Seba, hurry!" Camila called.

Seba used the stool to mount Zephyr, who bobbed her head up and down with agitation. Atop their beautiful friend named for the west wind, Camila and Seba sprinted toward Cales Fonts. Every soldier, to a man, was fighting the Juniper's fire, joined by the merchants who had left the pubs and taverns to lend a hand. Several nuns guided their horses on their back legs through the throng and the smoke, showering the crowd with blessings. It was the perfect diversion for their escape.

"Camila, which way? I can't see anything in this haze."

"I don't know. We're supposed to have a guide!"

"Aahhroooo!" A rooster, or rather, a dog named for a rooster, crowed in the distance.

Zephyr took off in the direction of Gall's howl, and they found themselves off the plaza and onto the unfinished dirt roads of Georgetown's east end. Smoke billowed from Arnau's shop behind them; the nuns' stampede continued to swirl brown dust, and Camila and Zephyr lost their bearings. Fernanda and Paolo had been ahead of them but were now out of sight.

Camila called out, "Gall! Where are you?"

As if in response to Camila's voice, Artemis appeared from behind a pile of dirt and pounced on top of a stack of red bricks, her emerald eyes glowing in the haze. Gall appeared behind her, howling like the tramontana. Artemis took off down the dirt road, and although they could barely make out her silver coat through the sooty fog, Gall's enormous mass was their lighthouse.

"Zephyr, follow them!"

Artemis led them down one empty street, turning left onto another, turning right, then left again until they reached Georgetown's southeastern wall. The smoke was now behind them; Seba inhaled deeply. Before them, abandoned near a ten-foot gap in Georgetown's unfinished outer wall lay wheelbarrows, shovels, trowels, and stacks of cut stones. Camila guided Zephyr through the opening and Seba gave a whoop of delight. *"Opa!" We did it!*

# 25 CALES FONTS

*March 21, 1768*
*Cales Fonts, Menorca*
*Afternoon*

Beyond the wall, on the palisades high atop Cales Fonts's natural springs, stood a thick grove of mastiha trees. Seba drank in the minty pine aroma, cleansing the soot and dust from his lungs. Zephyr followed Gall and Artemis deep into the woods until they reached a small clearing. One hundred vertical feet below them, down the tree-lined hill, the small port of Cales Fonts spread out toward the large harbor. Boats dotted the cove, and Quarantine Island was visible to the left. A few larger ships were anchored in the harbor beyond the cove, awaiting packet boats and supplies. But for the faint smell of smoke behind them, it seemed a typical Monday afternoon in Georgetown's fledgling port.

Seba's family awaited him in the clearing. Agnete and Kristobal still wore their nun's habits from the artillery room's mass, and Gall chased Artemis around a large wooden vegetable cart. Paolo and Fernanda had dismounted and were patting each other's backs, literally and figuratively, for a job well done.

"I knew we'd be rescued, Fernanda. My sisters came to me in a dream and told me so."

"Oh, it was your sisters who told you, eh? Not me with a knife and a message several hours ago?"

Paolo threw his arms around Fernanda. "Yes, it was both! I told Seba you would bring us a miracle, and that's exactly what happened!"

Fernanda laughed. "Did you even use that knife I gave you?"

Paolo pulled the knife from his pocket. "Ha! I forgot I even had this." He grinned. "Pity. It might have come in handy."

Fernanda held out her palm. "I'll take that back now. You managed very well without it, anyway. Knocked that tyrant Brumbaugh unconscious with his own hangman's stool. I couldn't be happier unless I'd done it myself."

Agnete threw her arms around Seba's neck, squeezing him so tightly that his breath caught in his throat. "My darling Sebastian, I was so worried for you! Praise to the Almighty that you survived. We worked into the night on Kristobal's rescue plan. Everyone helped."

Seba took his mother's hands in his and kissed them. "You were amazing, Mama. We were saved by an army of black angels. How did you do it?"

"Your father and Ignasi believed that we needed to inform you of Kristobal's plan and give you the means to defend yourselves on the platform. The abbess agreed that it was our best chance to rescue you. The only way we could help you was to pass a message to you during the mass of the condemned. I've never had this much excitement in all my life."

"Papa and Ignasi were part of this plan?"

Agnete put her hands on her hips. "Of course, Sebastian. Kristobal's plan was pure genius, and everyone played a part. Praise be to the Creator for your father's wits, Ignasi's resolve, Kristobal's creativity, and your cousins' courage. Not to mention the saints and angels."

"What broke my rope? I heard a sound, and the next I knew I was on the ground. I thought it was my guardian angel."

Kristobal said, "In a way, it was. Remember the crossbow design your father and Ignasi have been tinkering with? They could hit a target dead center at forty yards, and the distance from the center of the plaza to the closest building was thirty yards. Kostas knew Ignasi could split the rope from the roof of the King's Head, so Nicolas entered the public house with the ruse of selling them his best Corsican wine. And you know Nicolas; he got them all talking and laughing such that Ignasi was able to sneak right by, climb the stairs to the roof, and shoot your noose clean through on the first attempt."

Seba gasped. "What about Papa?"

Camila smiled sweetly as she ran her fingers through Zephyr's mane. "Seba, everyone is well. Your father, Nicolas, and Ignasi will be here shortly. They wanted to say goodbye to you and Paolo before you leave."

"How *are* we going to leave?"

Fernanda put her hands on Seba's shoulders. "Nicolas has taken care of everything. We're to meet them in this clearing. They'll be here momentarily."

The waiting nearly killed Seba, but it was probably less than twenty minutes. Nicolas entered the open space among the trees, followed by Kostas and Ignasi, each riding a donkey.

Camila ran to Nicolas and kissed him. "My love, we did it!"

Nicolas's smile spread from ear to ear. "I told you there was more courage in your thumb than I've got in my whole body, my darling. I'm so proud of you."

Kostas dismounted and Seba ran to him. "Papa, you and Ignasi saved my life with a bow and arrow! Like Heracles defeated the man-eating Stymphalian birds! How did you know it would work?"

"It was Ignasi's skills as an archer that made it possible. We don't have the strength we once had, but we have our minds and our wills. They've served us well."

Ignasi dismounted and his donkey trotted happily in a circle, relieved to cast off its large rider. Weary as he looked, Ignasi's face radiated a lightness that Seba had never observed in the whole time they'd lived together.

Ignasi shook his head. "Who would have guessed, Seba? We showed the tyrants today, didn't we?"

"You shot my rope from thirty yards away?"

Ignasi beamed like a schoolboy. "I did. Thanks to both of our fathers—yours for the design and mine for teaching me to aim. I wish my father could have seen us today. He would be so proud."

Seba squinted away the emotion welling behind his eyelids.

"Seba, Paolo," Nicolas called. "Time to say your goodbyes. We need to get you down to the water and get these honorary nuns back to the convent. Arnau's diversion will only last so long."

Seba said, "*Arnau's* diversion?"

Nicolas nodded. "If it hadn't been for Arnau, we

wouldn't have known of your plight. He arrived breathless at the convent last night, ranting that his father was trying to murder you for challenging his authority. He said he watched with his own eyes a pathetic excuse for a trial and knew in that moment he could never work for his father again. He came to us, pleading to find a way to rescue you and Paolo. We all talked well into the night, revising Kristobal's original escape plan. Arnau was most eager to help. He believed he was partly responsible for Paolo's arrest."

Paolo said, "He gave us a tour of his shop that evening. I suppose if we hadn't been in Georgetown that night, we wouldn't have been embroiled in the fight."

Nicolas nodded. "Arnau showed Kostas how to create the explosion with the alembics in the gin shop, and he's waiting on Kristobal's skiff to transport you and Seba to the *New Fortuna*."

Seba was incredulous. "Arnau agreed to destroy his own business? His father will skin him alive."

"No, he won't," Kristobal said. "Because Arnau is going with you."

Seba was startled. "Wait. If Arnau, Paolo, and I are leaving, who will protect you? Haven't you all put yourselves in great danger? What if Brumbaugh and his ruffians come for you?"

Kristobal winked at Seba and flashed his topaz ring like a performer; it was a disconcerting sight, as Kristobal was still dressed as a nun. "Haven't I told you a thousand times that I've been running this town since I was six years old?"

"Yes, but this is Brumbaugh. You didn't see his face. He's sure to seek revenge, and we won't be here to defend you."

"Don't you worry about us, Seba." Kristobal tossed a few coins in the air with one hand and caught them with the other. "It would take too long to spell it all out; ask Arnau to explain it to you."

Paolo clapped him on the back. "Accept the miracle, Seba. Let's get moving. Our fortunes await."

Seba buried his face in Zephyr's mane and stretched his arms around her neck. She lowered her head until their foreheads were touching, her breath warm and steady against his chest. "I may have learned more from you than anyone, girl. How to move with confidence and grace, how to trust, and how to stand tall while helping others reach for their luck."

Then a thought entered his mind, and he knew it came from her: *How to be free.*

*Yes, girl, you taught me how to be free. I'll never forget you. When the west wind blows, I'll know it's you. Farewell, Zephyr.*

Artemis, too, was ready for her goodbye. She curled in and out between Seba's legs until he picked her up. "You're Mama's cat now, aren't you, girl? Or has that big baby Gall stolen you from me?"

A low, soft purr emanated from Artemis's chest, pulsing through Seba's arms and into his heart.

"I understand. Protect them and keep them safe. I'm going across the sea and I don't know what awaits me there, but I feel better knowing that my family has you to watch over them. I'll miss you."

Not wanting to be left out, Gall began jumping around in front of Seba and his feline crush. Artemis swatted at the big lunk, then leaped gracefully into Agnete's arms. Gall stood on his hind legs and plopped his forelegs on Seba's shoulders, licking Seba's face until it burned like sandpaper.

"Yes, boy, I'll miss you, too. You have a job as well. Help Artemis look after our family. All of them. Paolo and I are counting on you."

"Aaaahhhhrrrroooooo!"

After a round of hugging, tears, promises to write from the New World, and Agnete making the sign of the cross about a hundred times, Seba and Paolo were finally ready to go.

Agnete said, "Now, my brave boys, get in this vegetable cart."

Seba and Paolo removed their nuns' habits and Camila put them in Euros's saddlebag. Kostas handed Seba an oiled leather satchel wrapped with a thick cord. Inside were a pouch bulging with seeds, a small bag filled with the tears of Chios, several silver and gold coins, and Kristobal's topaz ring. Nicolas gave Paolo a small casket filled with breads and pastries, compliments of Madam Theodora Alexiano. It was very heavy, tightly constructed, and smeared along its seams with linseed oil and beeswax.

Paolo said, "It's a hundred feet to the bottom of this cliff. How are we supposed to get to the water?"

Kristobal said, "Stay down and we'll cover you with burlap sacks. There's a cart-track through the mastiha trees down to the wharf. Be warned, it cuts back and forth across the incline, so you'll likely be knocked around. Whatever you do, don't let go of the cart until you reach the harbor. When the wheels hit the pier, you'll launch into the water. Stay under water beneath the burlap as long as you can; it will appear as if a vendor lost control of his vegetable cart."

Seba asked, "How far out is Arnau?"

"You'll have to swim underwater for at least eighty yards to where Arnau is waiting with the skiff. When you're underwater, swim as far away from the cart as you can, as fast as you can. The harbor workers will be more concerned with retrieving a nice wooden cart than looking for swimmers."

Paolo said, "That's a shame you have to give up your cart, Kristobal."

"Already taken care of, Paolo. Kostas and Ignasi promised to build me a bigger one." Kristobal grinned. "With a false bottom."

The entire family buried Seba and Paolo in a nest of burlap and they all placed their hands on the back of the cart. On the count of three, they shoved the cart with all their might. The wooden wheels moved slowly downhill, then picked up speed until the cart was careening down the rutted path like a boulder in a landslide.

# 26 HEADING WEST

*March 21, 1768*
*Port Mahón Harbor, Menorca*
*Early Evening*

The cart carrying Seba and Paolo careered one hundred vertical feet down the hill, zigging and zagging across the gravelly path toward Cales Fonts. The short ride was so rough that Seba had to clench his teeth together to keep from biting his tongue. He and Paolo gripped the edges of the wagon as the wheels clattered below them, threatening to fly off their wooden axles.

SPLASH! The wagon wheeled onto the dock at Cales Fonts and launched into the sea like a cannonball. The cart flipped over, tossing Seba and Paolo into the harbor's cold water; the force of the collision was like slamming into a wall of ice. The burlap sacks floated around them for a moment, before taking on water and dragging Seba and Paolo under the surface.

Seba didn't dare raise his head above the waterline. His leather pouch was slung over his shoulder, and he kicked his feet and stroked his arms as hard as he could. He could feel Paolo kicking beside him; at one point, the waterproofed wooden casket knocked Seba in the head. Seba opened his eyes underwater as Paolo caught the casket with one hand and used the other to propel himself forward, his legs thrusting him through the water like a dolphin.

When Seba believed that his lungs could no longer go without a breath, he stopped to tread water and peeked only his nose above the surface. He caught a glimpse of Kristobal's skiff rowing in a circle in the middle of the harbor. Water rushed into his nose and he coughed, having to pull his entire head up and into the sky, which was a dusky purple. He saw Paolo some yards to his right, the casket of pastries bobbing alongside like a cork in a tub.

"Paolo, over there!" Seba gestured with his head toward the skiff, which was now no more than twenty yards to their left. Dockworkers were shouting, "Runaway cart!" and Seba prayed their attention extended no further than retrieving the cart. He couldn't tell if anyone had spotted them; he didn't want to think about that. Taking a deep breath, he plunged back under the water and swam with all his might toward the boat.

After what felt like an hour, but was likely only a few minutes, Seba pulled himself alongside the rowboat, keeping it as a barrier between him and anyone on the dock who might be watching. He'd lost sight of Paolo and the floating box of pastries.

Seba coughed, "Arnau!"

Arnau was all smiles. "You made it, mate! I practically chewed my fingers off with worry these last several hours.

The wharfies over there think me a right Tom o' Bedlam, rowing around in circles. I wish I'd remembered my fishing net. Get in!"

Arnau helped Seba into the skiff and handed him a set of oars. "Paolo's over there. Let's go!"

They rowed to the bobbing casket, which Seba tapped with his oar. Paolo's head popped up from the water.

"Paolo, quick!" Seba grabbed the casket and tossed it into the boat. It took both Arnau and Seba to pull Paolo into the skiff, where he landed with a water-soaked thump. They didn't have another set of oars, so Seba and Paolo each took one oar as the three of them rowed around the north point of Cales Fonts. The shouts of the dockworkers had subsided; they'd found the cart and were likely fishing around for its contents. Little did they know that the cart's contents were on their way to Quarantine Island.

The sleek outline of the *New Fortuna* came into view, bringing tears to Seba's eyes. "I can't believe we made it."

Paolo appeared misty-eyed as well. "I've never been so happy to leave a port in all my life."

Arnau said, "We're not there yet, mates. Could you put your backs into the rowing first?"

Paolo and Seba doubled their efforts, Paolo complaining, "I'd like to see your rowing muscle if you'd been in a black hole for two days with no food and barely escaped being publicly hanged."

Arnau said, "Then why don't you conserve your energy and stop blathering?"

Seba laughed. "Are you well, Arnau? You seem a mite out of sorts."

"As well as I can be after blowing up my dream. Give me a day or two, I'll sort myself out."

Paolo said, "That explosion was spectacular. So much

smoke and soot, and the soldiers raced straight for the Juniper to douse the fire. It was perfect!"

Arnau said, "I showed Kostas how to heat up the alembics so they'd explode, but I didn't have a chance to see the fireworks. Had to get this skiff over to Cales Fonts. I heard the explosion; it rattled the warehouses over here. From the sounds of it, Kostas did a superb job."

Seba asked, "Arnau, what made you decide to do that?"

"After I saw what they did to you, my friends, there was no doubt in my mind. All my life I've listened to my father spouting off about law and order, rules and discipline, obligation and honor. The grave responsibility of well-executed authority." He grimaced. "The old liar didn't mean a word of it. He only wanted power for himself. I should have listened to you the first day we met, Seba, but I suppose I had to learn this lesson on my own."

Paolo said, "What did you do when you left that farce of a trial they gave us?"

"I had to serve the evening rations, so I couldn't leave my post until after dark. I went straight to the convent and told your family everything. Then Nicolas and I went to his aunt's home and pleaded with her for assistance."

Seba scoffed. "I'm certain that did no good. I tried as well, but it amounted to nothing. She said her hands were tied."

Arnau's eyes bored into him. "That's not true, Seba! I only heard the story in bits and pieces from Nicolas and the Madam Jurada, but the gist of it is that when we arrived, she was prepared to hear our plea. Your words moved her, she said so herself. After you left her home, you know, the day before that sham trial in the casemate, she contacted the office of the British Governor. Apparently, Governor Howard had been replaced, but no one thought to inform her. A new Governor, John Mostyn, was appointed several weeks ago, and had just disembarked from Quarantine Island the day you met with her."

Seba asked, "What of it? She refused to lift a finger to help me when I needed her most."

"The Madam Jurada had made an appointment to meet Menorca's new governor this morning, and when she heard what Nicolas and I reported about your trial and the blatant miscarriage of justice, she promised to tell the new governor everything about what my father has done to the people of Menorca."

"Seba!" Paolo crowed. "That means your family will now be safe from that tyrant."

"I wish that were true."

Arnau said, "If you'll listen, my barnacle-headed friend, I'll tell you what happened in that meeting this morning."

Seba sat straighter on the skiff's bench, too excited to be offended by the insult. "How do you know what happened?"

"Because Nicolas attended the meeting before he helped save your hides today, and he told me. While Kostas was busy blowing up my shop and your family was rescuing you, Nicolas assisted me in retrieving Kristobal's skiff and rowing it over to Cales Fonts."

They approached Quarantine Island, and the boys maneuvered the skiff toward the pier, leaving it for Kristobal to reclaim the following day. They embarked on Quarantine Island one last time and waited for the *New Fortuna*'s packet boat.

Paolo said, "Arnau, what did Nicolas say?"

Arnau was enjoying keeping the boys in suspense. "Well, Governor Mostyn had apparently received several complaints about my father even before he arrived in Port

Mahón. When Theodora Alexiano told him about the trial, he was *livid*. If your family hadn't rescued you, it's very likely that the new governor would have done so. He and the Madam Jurada were planning to visit Georgetown this very afternoon. Nicolas begged off, claiming a prior engagement, and we all know what that was. In addition, Madam Jurada made sure that Nicolas delivered you a box of her best desserts, which I see you have with you, and which I am sure you will share with your newest shipmate."

Seba smiled. *She lifted a finger after all.*

Paolo said, "Arnau, I believe a nice pudin de requeson will cheer you up after losing your shop."

The packet boat arrived with none other than Captain Alexiano at the helm and Peter and a young Menorcan man at the oars. Peter looked as if he'd taken Dr. Turnbull's advice; his shoulders and arms were significantly more muscular than they had been the last time Seba saw him. Nicolas had told the captain and Peter everything, and they both wanted to be the first to welcome back their favorite deckhands. The third man in the boat was a mystery.

The captain climbed out of the packet boat onto Quarantine Island's dock. He embraced Seba with a bear hug. "Seba, it's good to see you. I see you've kept my twin sister busy. I've always teased her for choosing the boring life of a politician. Who would have known she enjoys excitement as much as I do?"

"I believe she does, sir. But I've had enough land-based excitement to last me a long time. I'll leave your sister to it."

Next, the captain wrapped his arms around Paolo. "I leave you in port for one day and you get yourself thrown into the most putrid prison in the Mediterranean. What am I to do with you, Paolo?"

"It wasn't my fault, Captain."

The captain laughed, his bushy eyebrows hopping up and down. "You always say that."

Paolo said, "I'm a new man, Captain. I'll be happy to swab the deck and coil the ropes all day long, and I won't even mind if we avoid pirates for the whole journey to the New World."

The captain clapped Paolo on the back. "A few days in the black hole can do that do you, my friend."

The mystery man came alongside the captain. "If you're looking for a new position, the captain says I can take on an assistant." He held out his hand. "Francesc Pellicer, ship's carpenter. But only for this voyage; I've signed on to work for Doctor Turnbull. In fact, he's contracted with me to build his new home in East Florida. He's told me so many stories about you two that the captain allowed me to tag along with him and Peter."

Paolo shook Francesc's hand and turned to Seba. "What do you think, Seba? Do I look like a carpenter?"

"Why not? You certainly like to pound things with your fists."

Peter had followed the captain and Francesc onto the dock. He laughed and gave Seba a strong handshake.

Seba said, "I think Peter might give you some competition in swinging a heavy hammer. You've been practicing Doctor Turnbull's *kallistheneia*, haven't you, Peter?"

Peter grinned. "Yes. The next time Paolo starts a fight, I'll be right there with him."

"You'll be waiting a long time, Peter," Paolo swore. "I have reformed."

Patiently watching the reunion, Arnau stood by with his hands in his trouser pockets. The captain turned and offered his weatherbeaten hand to Arnau. "Alexander Alexiano, captain of the *New Fortuna*. My nephew tells me Fortune has smiled on me by adding a gin-maker extraordinaire to my complement of sailors. The cook can't wait to meet you. If you're anything like these two and young Francesc here, I'll have the best crew that ever sailed the Seven Seas."

Arnau beamed. "Thank you, sir. Arnau Andreu at your service."

Seba's eyes widened. "Andreu?"

Arnau threw his shoulders back. "If we're going to the New World to make our fortunes, I've decided that I'd prefer to make my legacy with the name of my mother: Elionor Andreu." Arnau swiped his palms together, as if dusting them off. "I've had enough of *Brumbaugh* to last me a lifetime."

"You and me both," Paolo grinned.

Peter chuckled. "I have a feeling the berth deck will be full of Menorcan storytelling this evening, am I right?"

Paolo held up his casket full of food. "Stories and Theodora's sweets. What could be better?"

They all climbed into the packet boat; within fifteen minutes, Peter and Francesc had expertly maneuvered it alongside the *New Fortuna*. Dr. Turnbull was waiting for them on the main deck, dressed in his silks and his gray periwig, so full of excitement that the heels of his brass-buckled shoes scarcely touched the deck boards. The captain, Seba, Paolo, Peter, Francesc, and Arnau gathered around the portly doctor, whose face glowed with enthusiasm and anticipation as he turned in a circle, addressing each of them.

"Welcome, welcome, my friends. Seba, I've missed you. Oh, the stories I have to tell you of our travels in the Levant! And Paolo, I hear tell from the captain that you've brought puddings from Theodora. What a splendid send-off!"

Without waiting for a response, he continued, "And do you see how Peter has grown his muscles under my tutelage? I shall have to write a medical essay on the miracles of *kallistheneia*. Am I correct that we have a new crew member? A gin-maker, no less? Between you and Francesc here, whom I entreated to join our venture earlier this week, I'll have the best plantation in East Florida. Oh, how the Fates have smiled on my business endeavors. I haven't been this happy since my wedding day, when I married my—"

They all chimed in. "—beloved Maria Gracia."

They fell about themselves laughing, until the captain said, "We'll have plenty of time to celebrate when we exit Mahón. The winds haven't been this favorable since we left Leghorn, and I want to get under sail as soon as possible. All hands to your positions! We're bound for Gibraltar, and then to the wide Atlantic Ocean!"

As the sails caught the evening wind, and Menorca faded behind him, Seba stood at the ship's prow watching the harbor fan out to the vast Balearic Sea. At last, the opportunity to fulfill his legacy was at hand, and his family was safe under the care of the Madam Jurada and the new governor. More importantly, they were all where they wanted to be, with the family they'd found and the friends who'd adopted them. The ocean called. The dolphins awaited. Opportunity summoned him on the western wind. *Zephyros*.

He felt a familiar hand on his shoulder. "Our grand adventure begins."

Seba's eyes shone. "Thank you for everything, Doctor Turnbull. I don't know what my family would have done without you."

A smile played across the Scotsman's lips. "*The web of our life is a mingled yarn, good and ill together*," he said.

Seba lifted an eyebrow. "That sounds like a quote from your favorite English playwright," he said. "What was his name? Shackley?"

"Shakespeare," Turnbull smiled. "And you're entirely correct. He was quite the philosopher; I believe he has much to say about our future, which is up to us to create. Neither of us knows what lies ahead. Noble are those whose hearts lead them to sail uncharted waters."

# AUTHOR'S NOTE

This is the continuation of a fictional story I began in 2022 when my friend, Tony, told me about an ancestor from Chios who escaped the Ottoman Empire and eventually settled his family in America. With his permission, I included his family legend in a fictional story that intersects with a slice of life closer to home – the vibrant community of Menorcans who arrived in New Smyrna with Dr. Andrew Turnbull in 1768 and settled in Saint Augustine a decade later.

This book, set in Menorca in 1767-1768, draws from the historical records regarding Dr. Turnbull, including reams of the physician's correspondence discovered and made available to the public by Dr. Daniel L. Schafer, Professor Emeritus of History at the University of North Florida. Dr. Schafer allowed me to interview him in 2021, and I am deeply grateful for his generosity. To say that he is a treasure would be an understatement.

I am also indebted to the late professor David Whamond Donaldson, whose three volume doctoral thesis entitled "Britain and Menorca in the Eighteenth Century" was a source of detailed information about daily life in Port Mahón. It was through Professor Donaldson's work that I learned that British officers stole family homes from local Menorcans, female citizens committed suicide after being violated by the garrison's soldiers, public floggings were common, gin was more valuable than silver or gold, and conflicts between Menorcan judicial officers and the British government were common.

I traveled to Menorca in 2023, staying a few blocks from the cliffs overlooking the harbor and walking the town as Seba would have done two hundred and fifty years earlier. I owe a debt of gratitude to Jessie, Veronique, and Diana, who were the most gracious and kind-hearted hosts anyone could ask for.

When I arrived in Menorca, I didn't know about the *arbres de llentiscle*, or mastic trees. I racked my brain trying to find something that would tie Seba's Greek heritage to the tiny Spanish island a thousand miles away, but after several weeks in Menorca, I'd found nothing. One day, Diana lent me her bicycle, and I rode to a remote nature park north of town, past stone-walled pastures and working farms that became the inspiration for the Rementeria Arandia home. As I pedaled up and down the hills, I thought I smelled the tears of Chios.

Was I so obsessed with finding a connection that I conjured one in my head? The scent persisted. When I reached the grounds of the nature preserve, I asked a park ranger about it. She led me to a large grouping of trees with the same deep green leaves and gnarled limbs of Chios's skinos trees. The only difference was the display of tiny red berries clustered on every branch, which she said were edible. I picked a few berries and popped them in my mouth, each bite releasing the magical flavor of mastiha. When I finally stopped crying tears of joy, I pedaled back to my lodgings and began writing.

A few days later, La Fortuna smiled again with Menorca's culinary offerings. The Museu de Menorca was hosting a temporary exhibit called "The Flavor of Menorca," featuring the history of the island's gastronomy, including traditional foods that date back centuries (with recipes!), servingware, cooking utensils, bakeware, and amphorae for water, wine, and oil. I strolled past farm equipment and walls filled with paintings and photographs, and sampled food prepared in harmony with the seasons. Just in case you were wondering, the answer is yes, mayonnaise (la mahonesa) was invented in Menorca and is named for the town of Mahón. For more on that, I refer you to chef, physician by training, writer, and researcher Pep Pelfort, founder of Menorca's Centro de Estudios Gastronómicos.

Menorcan gin, thanks to the British occupation, is a cultural heritage product still produced on the island from a well-guarded secret recipe; the unique spirit is a favorite of locals and tourists alike. The same goes for Mahón cheese and Menorcan salt, both of which can thank the briny tramontana winds for their extraordinary flavor.

The Museu de Menorca exhibit also highlighted a cookbook written around 1731-1734 by the Franciscan Friar Roger, a Mahónese monk who eventually became the head cook at Saint Francis's monastery in Ciutadella. Many of the dishes eaten by Sebastian's family and friends are adaptations of Brother Roger's recipes.

Speaking of adaptations, this book is a work of fiction that draws inspiration from historical events and locations, but is not intended to be a literal or factual representation of the past. The story and characters are products of imagination, woven through a fascinating period of history for the purposes of entertainment. If you'd like to know more about Menorca in the eighteenth century, I enthusiastically direct you to the historical research of Dr. Donaldson and Dr. Schafer as well as Friar Roger's delightful cookbook.

# ABOUT THE AUTHOR

K. Pearson Bradley is an American writer of historical fiction. *Mists of Menorca* is the third book in her Merchant Tides series, a five-book series inspired by the stories of her paternal grandfather, who sailed the world with the U.S. Merchant Marine. The author also writes motivational nonfiction under the name Kim Bradley. For information on her books, as well as book signing events and other updates, visit www.kpearsonbradley.com.

# BOOKS BY THE AUTHOR

## FICTION

*Tears of Chios* (Merchant Tides Series Book 1)

*Scions of Smyrna* (Merchant Tides Series Book 2)

*Mists of Menorca* (Merchant Tides Series Book 3)

## NON-FICTION

*Shakespeare's Guide to Living the Good Life: Life Lessons for Comedy, Tragedy, and Everything in Between*

www.ingramcontent.com/pod-product-compliance
Lightning Source LLC
Chambersburg PA
CBHW071405300726
48976CB00006B/1996